Red Clark of the Arrowhead

Center Point
Large Print

Also by Gordon Young and available from
Center Point Large Print:

Fighting Blood
Red Clark o' Tulluco
Red Clark Rides Alone

Red Clark of
the Arrowhead

GORDON YOUNG

CENTER POINT LARGE PRINT
THORNDIKE, MAINE

This Center Point Large Print edition
is published in the year 2018 by arrangement with
Golden West Literary Agency.

First US edition: Doubleday
First UK edition: Methuen

The text of this Large Print edition is unabridged.
In other aspects, this book may vary
from the original edition.
Printed in the United States of America
on permanent paper.
Set in 16-point Times New Roman type.

ISBN: 978-1-68324-930-6 (hardcover)
ISBN: 978-1-68324-934-4 (paperback)

Library of Congress Cataloging-in-Publication Data

Names: Young, Gordon, 1886-1948, author.
Title: Red Clark of the Arrowhead / Gordon Young.
Description: Center Point Large Print edition. | Thorndike, Maine :
    Center Point Large Print, 2018
Identifiers: LCCN 2018026385| ISBN 9781683249306
    (hardcover : alk. paper) | ISBN 9781683249344 (pbk. : alk. paper)
Subjects: LCSH: Large type books. | GSAFD: Western stories.
Classification: LCC PS3547.O4756 R434 2018 | DDC 813/.54—dc23
LC record available at https://lccn.loc.gov/2018026385

To
SYDNEY A. SANDERS
In Gratitude and Admiration

Red Clark of
the Arrowhead

CHAPTER ONE

The cowboy lay forward in the saddle with elbow on the horn and watched the Timtons being put out of their house, off their land.

A deputy sheriff, brought along to enforce the foreclosure and prevent trouble, squatted in the shade and seemed trying to pretend that he had nothing to do with it. Deputy Marr knew that lean red-headed cowpuncher and didn't like him; knew, too, Red's feelings about having a sheriff help throw folks out of their homes on the bankers say-so. In years gone by, and not so many at that, Deputy Marr had for a little while worn a star under Red's father, a grim hard-eyed sheriff who ran the county honest and didn't let law interfere with justice. Marr hadn't lasted long. He didn't have in him what it took to ride for the old sheriff. Things had changed quite a lot in Tulluco since his death.

The Timtons had a sort of dirt-roofed cabin joined to a kind of dugout in the hillside. They were carrying out such household goods as the Johnsons, father and son, didn't want to claim under the chattel mortgage.

A fellow from down south of Tulluco who in a shy way was a bit sweet on Timton's oldest girl had borrowed a wagon and team. Timton and the fellow came staggering out with an old iron kitchen stove.

Young Johnson, a fellow of thirty or more with a broad face, sunken cheeks and sharp nose that looked like it had been pinched too much before it hardened, walked up and looked the stove over as if half-minded to say something.

Timton snarled, "Maybe as how you want it?" He was a tall hungry looking fellow, some shiftless.

Mrs. Timton called anxiously through the door, "Now you Tim, shet up! We can't he'p ourselves!" The hot Arizona sun, dry winds and much work had wilted her. She was thin and dark and must have been pretty once. Some folks said she wasn't any better than she ought to be. The Timtons didn't have a very good name.

Old Johnson was standing at the door. It was a hot day and he was sweating, with black broad brimmed hat pushed to the back of his head and a wadded bandana in his fist. He, too, was a little uneasy under the calm stare of the red-headed cowpuncher. Old Johnson rumbled in unctuous approval, "That there is right, Mrs. Timton. We are being generous to let you have your household goods. Lawful, you know, ever' stick an' chip belongs to us."

Red lifted his head a little, his eyes fixed on Old Johnson. Red hadn't seen him for a couple of years and thought he looked more than ever like a big toad that had learned to walk on its hind legs: had much the same wide mouth, big belly, flat forehead and sharp-tipped nose. Johnson glanced uneasily toward the cowboy and looked away. He did not like Red. Had not liked Red's father.

Red straightened up, hooked a knee about the horn and rolled a cigarette. He scratched the match on the leg of his pants, which looked like a pair of overalls with the bib and shoulder straps cut off. Except for his boots there was no finery about him, but there was the rawhide toughness of a range-bred boy and a blue-eyed glint in his look that was steady as the glimmer of polished iron. He wore two guns, long heavy .45s, with the holster ends tied to his legs. They were the old single action Colts with which his father for twenty years had enforced his notions of what was right in Tulluco. And anybody who knew the kid knew that he could, and would, use them if his fur was rubbed the wrong way.

A couple of dirty young uns, about ten to thirteen, both girls, came out looking scairt and moving quiet. They carried some little bundles and appeared to think somebody might snatch the things away. They half sidled up to the wagon and with nervous backward staring offered them to their dad. Timton poked the bundles into the wagon.

Red leaned forward in the saddle, spoke slow and distinct with his glance drifting from Deputy

11

Marr to young Johnson, and coming to rest on Old Johnson who mopped the back of his neck vigorously with the wadded bandana:

"Me now, I sort of allus felt sorry for myself that I wasn't rich, had me a bank and some cows, with folks owing me money. But now I see what all you got to do for to be rich, like scaring kids and makin' their folks hit the grit, well, I'm quite some pleased to ride for wages, sleep good o' night, eat my beans and—"

Young Johnson's cold pale face got a little red. He spoke up, mad. "Nobody's askin' for your opinion!"

Red grinned and went on, slow and persistent as a bottle fly's buzz. "I'm generous thataway. Freehanded-like. When I get me an opinion I just scatter it same as money. And me, I don't see how the hell you can sleep good after throwing these folks out—"

"They oughtn't have borrored if they—" That was Old Johnson, all swelled up and hot. He wasn't a tall man but was thick of shoulders, sort of spindling in the legs like a man that eats well and sets a lot. Since Sheriff Clark's death he strutted some more than formerly.

"Don't argy with him, Dad," said Young Johnson, who was the wisest, coldest and meanest of the two. His first name was Clinton.

"Oughtn't have borrored, hm?" Red asked, then went on, mild and casual: "I don't know, of course, but I bet me you bankers sort o' coaxed this man here to take a little loan for to buy himself some cows an spread out—"

"That thar is exactly what!" said Timton, sullen and indignant, glaring at the Johnsons.

Red said, "Um-hm," with much the satisfied expression of a stud player turning over an ace.

"Here!" Old Johnson blurted, losing his temper, nearly blowing up. "What call you got to stand around here insultin' folks! None o' your business to be here! This here now is my land! Get off it!" He waved a hand and glared as if expecting Red to turn tail and mosey.

Red grinned some more. He said, "Feller, I'm ridin' for Miz Dobbs. This range ain't fenced and her cows wander far. Part o' my business is to inspect what's goin' on on the unfenced range of our neighbors. An' my suspicion is that such neighbors as kick folks who owe 'em money out from under a roof need watchin' clost!"

Young Johnson said, "How dare you talk like—"

Old Johnson bellowed, "You ain't goin' to be ridin' for Mrs. Dobbs long! I'll tell her how you talked an'—"

Red stopped grinning but he didn't look mad, just sober, and said cool and sassy:

"I hear tell you got a mortgage on Miz Dobbs' Arrowhead, too. That right?"

"None o' your damn business!" Old Johnson

shouted, waggling his fist, making ends of the bandana fly.

"Well, sir," Red went on, "beef is down and times is bad. Cowmen are so mighty short of money that I wouldn't put it beyond you for to hope you could kick even her out of her house. They is some folks in this country as say you play all sorts of tricks for to get hold of ranches. So let me tell you something, feller! If ever you run any kind of a shindy—*you,*" his look shifted from Old Johnson's face to Young Johnson whom he knew as the more unscrupulous of the two, "I'll kill you! Both you!"

Red added a nod to drive the words in, then as if explaining a little, "She's been purt-near like a maw to me. Grandmaw anyhow."

Both Johnsons stood for a moment or two in dazed gaping, and their faces moved until eyes met in a kind of anxious questioning, each of the other, as if wondering how certain secrets had been guessed. Then Old Johnson came to life as if a bee had got in the seat of his britches. He wheeled about and shouted, "Marr! Marr, you hear this fellow threaten my life! And Clint's life! As Deputy Sheriff—"

Deputy Marr looked blank and said, "Hhn?" kind of like he was waking out of a doze. He pretended he had a splinter or something in a finger, and picked at it. He knew Red didn't wear those heavy guns for an ornament.

14

Timton and the fellow who was helping him, Mrs. Timton and the two little Timton young uns, just stared, solemn, uneasy, and pleased. None of them knew Red, but they knew who he was, and it was mighty refreshing to have the Johnsons talked to thataway.

Deputy Marr stayed squatted and began to roll a cigarette. He had his head tipped forward so the brim cut off all view as if, ostrich-like, what he didn't see wasn't his concern.

A voice in the doorway said, "Thank God they's somebody has got the spunk to talk back to you!"

Red looked and saw a girl glaring at Old Johnson. She was about seventeen and, in a slightly coarse but vivid way, pretty. Her voice was sharp, her eyes black. There was a gypsy-something about her, even to the sort of burned gold color of her face. Red didn't know anything about the Timtons, hadn't even known this girl was on earth. He felt a little funny, like he had been caught showing off.

Sara Timton went on talking to Old Johnson. "We ain't even got coffee and bacon! We got about a half sack of flour. My folks don't know where they're goin' even. Just heading for the mines. Me, I'm all right. I can take care of myself. But these chilern and maw. You want paw's little dab of land and the water. He was a fool for to borrow the money, but you

15

were a dirty swindler to coax him into taking it!"

Young Johnson eyed her as if about to say something spiteful but that red-head on horseback made him uneasy, so he took out his knife, picked up a stick and began to whittle. His voice had a hurt, regretful tone: "Dad, it just goes to show! The more you do for folks, the more ungrateful they are. Here we are lettin' 'em take all this household stuff and still they—"

Sara Timton put her hands on her hips, stepped from the doorway, went close to him: "And if Mrs. Hepple wasn't too high-toned for to use such stuff as is good enough for us, I reckon you'd send it over to her as a present, hm?"

Young Johnson swallowed a time or two and pressed his thin mouth tight. Some color flared into his cheeks but he wouldn't look up. Old Johnson coughed awkwardly and cleared his throat.

It was talk of the countryside that both Johnsons were in love with the second Mrs. Hepple. She was a fine looking rather flashy woman who had come into the country many years before as a widow-lady with a couple of children; both boys. There had been a great scandal in the cow country when old Hepple, a big rancher, had got rid of his wife and son and married her. As a widow, Mrs. Hepple's name had been Bush. The older of her boys was now a sort of kingpin gambler there in Tulluco and was still called Bush, Joe Bush.

16

Old Hepple had been a rip-roaring cowman and fighter in his day, but for quite a while now had been half paralyzed and folks said Mrs. Hepple went gallivanting around a lot more than was right for a respectable woman. Her carryings-on with the Johnsons, father and son, made a lot of talk.

Sara Timton walked over to Red. He straightened up, unhooked his knee, put his foot in the stirrup. She threw back her head. Her hair was thick and curly. She didn't smile but was earnest. "When you come to town you must come to the Best Bet and see me. I am going to work there."

Red felt shy and awkward. He could stand up to any man, bad men, and not bat an eye; but the stare of a pretty girl made him feel a little funny. He said, "Me and Jim of the Best Bet is old friends. I allus do my loafin' there. All us Dobbs punchers do."

"You tell them Sara will be glad to see any friend of yours, won't you?" The last two words were softly coaxing.

"Sure." Red was casual and not very sincere.

She asked sort of cautious-like, "Do you know Joe Bush?"

Red grinned a little. "Me, I was born in Tulluco. Know ever'body—or used to."

"Oh, then you know 'Gene Close?" Her tone suggested that she rather liked 'Gene Close.

17

"Him and Windy Jones? Sure. I've crawled in between their blankets many a time. We rode together a lot onct."

Sara said, "They are nice boys," and Red said, "You bet. I got to be goin'. 'Bye."

She stood looking at him. He rode at a slow trot, was slim and straight in the saddle. She went back into the house.

Red rode about two hundred feet, reined up, leaned over and peered at the ground. He turned in the saddle and called, "Hey, Timton. They is something I want to show you!"

Timton went with shambling hurried walk, peered at the ground, then looked questioningly at Red.

"Say, Timton, is that so, what she said about you all not having grub?"

"That's about the size of it. We are aimin' to go down to Monohela an' maybe do some good at mining a little."

Red opened his palm. Something fell with twinkling glitter. "Old Jeb Grimes he called my pat hand last night. Usual, Jeb is a smart feller. You can just sorta figger Jeb is makin' you a little present for to fill them young uns bellies. S'long an' luck!"

Red was off at a lope before Timton could say anything. He stooped and picked a ten gold dollar piece from the dust. He looked after Red, looked at the coin. He rubbed the sweat off his forehead with swipe of forearm and took a deep breath. He didn't have much liking for the Dobbs' Arrowhead outfit, especially not for old Jeb Grimes who was a dangerous man and from time to time had ridden in on the Timtons to nose about and see if they were eating Dobbs' beef.

Timton was not a bad fellow but he wasn't much good. Now he felt pretty choked up and warm inside. He gripped the coin hard and thrust it deep down into his empty pants pocket before he let go, then turned around and went shuffling back up to the house.

2

The little old famous cowtown of Tulluco sat on the road that led to Monohela. There was quite some mining boom on down in Monohela, so the coming and going of people to and from the mines surged through the old cowtown.

The road to Monohela skirted the range of the Hepple outfit. Lots of miners and shiftless folks, and some camp butchers, were said to be helping themselves to Hepple cows; which didn't fill the Dobbs punchers with any grief, though the feud was supposed to have died out. Bitter memories of it lingered in both cow outfits.

The feud had begun long long years before when Dingley Hepple, then a young cowman, and an even younger and newly married cowman

19

named John Dobbs argued over a double-branded calf that didn't happen to be ear-marked. The Hepple brand was H P on the right shoulder; the Dobbs, an arrowhead on the left hip. Double branding could have happened by accident only if a running iron puncher was hasty and careless, didn't look his stray calf over carefully before throwing and burning it. But it was more likely that some maverick chaser, not liking either the Hepple or Dobbs outfit, did it as a joke just to see what would happen.

Hepple was a fighter and so was Dobbs. They shot each other, not seriously. Their cowboys took up the shooting and it was carried along the range.

Now Dobbs was dead and Hepple was old and partly paralyzed.

In the beginning the Dobbses had a partner, Red's father, later sheriff of Tulluco. An honest stern man. Old Hepple had respected him, even trusted his justice as sheriff.

In Sheriff Clark's day Tulluco had been a well ordered town. There might be a lot of noise, laughter, and fun; and, after the fall roundups, much drinking and a wasteful scattering of wages. A few migratory girls seemed to know when the roundups were going to be over and drifted in to dance with the boys. The big cowmen of the country, if it had been a good year and beef was on the rise, gave barbecues, held horse races, put up purses for roping and riding. The honest hardworking boys could make all the noise they wanted, cut capers and raise hell. The lank grim hard-eyed sheriff was considerate and thoughtful toward folks that earned their wages honest; but he was hell on outlaws, rustlers, tinhorns.

Since his death and the coming of the gold excitement things had changed. There was lots of rustling. The stage was held up now and then. Murders were not uncommon. Tulluco was over run with blackleg gamblers and Joe Bush, Mrs. Hepple's son, seemed to have most to say about how things were run.

3

Red rode with spurs a-jingle at a trot into the town. He had been away from Tulluco for a couple of years, only lately returned; and though he had ridden in a time or two the past two weeks, he still stretched his neck in gawky interest at the changes that had come over the old place. The Best Bet, for instance, had added a second story of flimsy unpainted pine, and the downstairs had been enlarged to a barn-like place. It was no longer merely a saloon. It was also a dance hall and gambling house.

The dust in the street was near to ankle deep on his horse. Other horses, and wagons and horses, were kicking up dust. It rolled like smoke and drifted about. Red waggled his head regretful. He didn't like the way the country was filling up.

He went on down the street to the Stage Company office which was next door to the Golden Palace Hotel, an old two story frame with wide porch in front and an upper story where high-toned people, usually with ladies, sat sometimes in the evening looking down on the town and out 'cross the country that took on a kind of misty deep purplish color in the bright starlight.

As he swung off, a negro that the cowboys had dubbed Lucky on account of what he could do at craps, jumped over the hotel veranda. Lucky was more or less a fixture at the hotel. He grinned, "Howdy, Mistuh Red!"

" 'Lo. You gettin' fat, Lucky. How you been doin' at craps lately?"

Lucky's grin went away. He shook his head. "Mah science it is all plumb busticated, Mistuh Red. These heah gambluhs in this heah town— wu-ouf!"

"They must be pretty damn crooked if they can skin you!"

"They is fo' sho. They was a killin' agin last night. A miner felluh he objestacted an'—"

Red grunted. "Yeah, I reckon. An' got shot."

"No suh. Joe Bush he throwed a knife into 'im."

22

Red lifted an eyebrow. To him there was something unclean and treacherous about using a knife. He made mild sounds of disgust, then with jerk of thumb over his shoulder, "You want to trot my horse down to the barn?"

"Sho' do, Mistuh Red. An' you ought fo' to see how them gambluhs don't like fo' Old Jeb to stand around eyin' 'em."

" 'Taint soothin' at anytime for to have Old Jeb eying you," Red agreed.

Lucky rode off and Red went into the Stage Company office. A small dried up man with spectacles sitting half way down his nose said in a squeaky voice, "Oh, hello, you. Lookin' fer Jeb? He's in back thar. Be keerful he don't bite."

Red opened the door into a little back room. Jeb Grimes sat with hands folded on his lap and his feet on a table. He could stay motionless longer than anybody Red ever heard about.

Nearly everybody thought there was some Indian in Jeb Grimes, but nobody with a cautious regard for well-being said so. He was old but his hair was black, dead black. His face was nearly black and deeply lined. He was straight as a soldier. Jeb had been in the country a long time and worked for the Dobbses all that time, but nobody knew much about where he had come from. He was at times talkative with friends; at other times for days, weeks, you could scarcely

23

get a word out of him. He had the name and look of a killer—and was. Odds simply didn't mean a thing in the world to him. He carried a revolver, but there was usually a rifle within arm's reach and he used it for a hand gun.

" 'Lo, son." When Grimes talked his words bubbled with throaty softness.

Red squatted on the corner of a table, flung his hat at a chair. "Pretty gosh-blamed soft for a wore-out old cowhand! Settin' around town here a-waitin' for Miz George to come home. I wisht I was old and purt-near useless, so I could loaf."

Jeb grinned slow and amused. Most folks treated him with such a heap of respect that maybe he liked being talked to impudent and sassy by a boy he thought the world and all of.

Among themselves, and by many old-timers, Mrs. Dobbs was called "Miz George" by her boys, some of whom were older than even she. Mrs. Dobbs was due home from a trip. Nobody knew just what day, so Jeb was staying in town to wait and bring her out to the ranch when she came.

"You'll grow old an' useless plenty soon." Jeb spoke soft and slow as he stared at the dust-covered window, as if a little regretful about his own age.

Red laughed at him. "Shucks. You ought to let

some purty girl make a fool of you. I hear tell that makes old shypokes frisky an' joyful."

Old Jeb waggled a hand, a long slim hand. He knew Red was just trying to stir him up and make him snort a little; and he refused to stir. Just smiled and eyed Red. Jeb had slit eyes, narrowed from long years of peering into the distance.

"I reckon," said Red, swinging a leg and eying the boot toe, "I been a sorta fool this mornin'. I'm out ten dollars an' told a lie. In a way of speakin', you owe it back to me. How about payin' your honest debts?"

Jeb stared, inquiring. "How it come?"

"Well, by happen-so on the way to town I rode south, like you said I ort once in a while. I pulled up at that fellow Timton's for to water my horse and maybe smell some fried steak. Them Johnsons was there evictin' 'em."

"Good riddance," said Jeb.

"Yeah? Well me, I don't like nesters much better 'n I like a sheepherder's smell. But 'tween the Timtons an' them Johnsons for neighbors—I bet where one 'ud maybe steal a cow for the fryin' pan, the others 'ud steal a herd for the packin' house!"

"Them Timtons are an onery lot. Them Johnsons are mean, cold, an' some crafty at business—like Apaches on the warpath. Me, I'm more scairt of hyderphoby skunks 'n I ever was of Injuns. I've shot plenty of both an' know

25

whereof I make my remarks." Jeb's voice had the sound of water flowing over pebbles.

"It's joyful for to know they is something that can scare you. Me, being scairt so frequent, I thought maybe as how I lacked some manhood. Well, it sorta riled me to see them kids bein' yanked out from under a roof. I expressed some opinions, free, gratis, and fluid. Old Johnson he up and said as how he was going to see to it that Miz George fired me. Where'pon, as you can imagine, I tucked my tail between my legs and felt bad."

"I 'magine," Jeb muttered, half a-smile.

"Then I called that Timton off to one side and give him ten dollars—"

Jeb spoke in a way that isn't printable.

"I said," Red went on, gleeful and shameless, "as how I won it last night off you at poker!" Jeb, being nearly unbeatable at poker, at least among friends, snorted. "I told him he could just sorta feel it was a little something from you. So how about payin' me back, hm?"

"You was just showin' off in front o' that Sara girl. 'Gene Close is sweet on her. 'Gene'll tie yore skelp to his belt if you go makin' eyes at her."

From the way she spoke I guessed he was. She asked did I know him."

"Him an' Windy ain't the good kids they ust for to be," said Jeb, meditative.

Red grunted, skeptical. Jeb was a suspicious fellow. He had a lot of tolerance for Red's foolishness, but appeared to think other young fellows ought to act sober and settled down.

4

The stage came in. Mrs. Dobbs was not among the passengers and the driver was somebody Red didn't know.

Jeb sat down on the bench in front of the Stage Company office, rolled a thin cigarette. "We'll set till the rush is over at the Bonanzer, then go eat." Jeb did not like to be jostled by crowds.

Red sat beside him and wished for a drink, but he could not speak of it. Whisky was bad medicine for Jeb. He might go for a couple of years and not touch a drop, but when he did start drinking sensible people hightailed for tall timber. His voice stayed low but he went looking for trouble, and he didn't care how many people joined in to make it for him. He had promised Mrs. Dobbs that he wouldn't take another drink as long as he was riding for her. So Red did without his drink rather than go off alone or speak of it.

While they were sitting there two people came riding fast up the street on fine slim-legged horses. It was Mrs. Hepple and that younger boy of hers that folks called Pinky, though the name made him mad.

Red never could get over his admiring amazement at the way Mrs. Hepple sat a side-saddle. Most women rode astride, and those that did not had nothing of Mrs. Hepple's ease and grace. Red had once climbed a side-saddle just to see how it felt. It felt like he was about to fall off as if he were out of place and unsure. So he figured that Mrs. Hepple must be purt-near a better rider than any man.

She was a handsome woman with a bold dark face, bright eyes, and always wore some red about her. She carried herself a little haughty in public, yet unbent quick and pleasant when spoke to. It had hurt her name to have Old Hepple get rid of his wife and young son to marry her, and now her reputation, never the best, was bad-spoiled. She was too much with the Johnsons. Her oldest boy was a blackleg gambler. Young Pinky was not any good, either.

Red never had liked her but had always been respectful. His dad, the sheriff, had strapped him good for making slurring remarks about Hepples when he could scarcely more than talk. From babyhood Red had been a Dobbs' "man" because Mrs. Dobbs made such a fuss over him and had him out to the ranch a lot.

In not liking Mrs. Hepple Red saw, or told himself that he did, a certain watchful mean look deep back in her eyes. When she was irritated her face changed much as if she took off a mask.

There were a lot of not nice stories vaguely told of her. Everybody knew that the first Mrs. Hepple had been a lady.

It seemed queer to cow folks, at a time when beef was down and rustlers riding almost like raiders, that Mrs. Hepple appeared to have plenty of money.

Pinky was a handsome boy, up pretty close to Red's age but no more like Red than a piece of colored calico is like rawhide. He was proud of his looks and nursed them with all sorts of fancy fixin's. A bad-spoiled kid with a vicious streak that showed in a cat-like temper. Off hand, people would think he was one of the nicest fellows anywhere. He had easy manners and a smile. Red didn't have much of a downright dislike of Pinky, but just simply had no use for him. As a kid Pinky was an awful little liar, but his maw would stand up for him like a she-bear for a cub.

Now as they came riding up to the Golden Palace, Pinky looked about from side to side as if to make sure people were admiring him and his maw. He was near as proud of her as of himself. His look fell on Red, and he called, "Oh, hello there, Red!" just as pleasant and eager as if Red were a good friend.

Mrs. Hepple got off at the block hotel people had fixed there mostly for her since she came often and kept a room. She unfastened the black riding skirt, let it fall and stepped out. She looked toward Red and said, "Well, well!" Then she stepped down from the block which was only a few feet from where Red and Jeb were sitting and put out her hand.

Red stood up, pawed at his hat, grinned nervously. "Howdy, Miz Hepple." He thought she had lost some of her good looks since he last saw her. Pinky crowded in and shook hands. She asked, "When did you get back? You have been gone a long time."

"Oh a couple weeks ago. I was gone most near two years, yes'm."

"Want to ride for me, Red?" She had a rich even if slightly hoarse voice and knew how to make it sound coaxing, almost like she wanted you to let her cuddle you.

"Of course he does, Maw," said Pinky, looking Red over as if even with approval of his plain dress.

"I'm sure mighty obliged, Miz Hepple." Red felt awkward and seemed a little short of breath. "But y'see, I've a'ready gone to work on the Arrowhead. Just come to town for mail."

Pinky grinned much as if he was thinking, "Why you poor chump, go riding for that second rate outfit when you might straddle an H P horse!"

Mrs. Hepple's manner changed as if some ice water had been splashed on her. She smiled by just tightening the muscles around her mouth and lifted her eyebrows. "Oh, I see. Well, good luck." She turned away, cool and again haughty. "Oh, I see!" Pinky said, too, sneering a little. Pinky's spurs—he wore jinglebobs—rattled and tinkled alongside of her as they went up the steps to the hotel veranda.

Red clapped on his hat and heaved a big breath. He turned to speak to Jeb but held his words and blinked a little. Jeb was all huddled down with his hat pulled low. Anybody who knew him, no matter how well, wouldn't have recognized him in that posture because Jeb was always rigidly erect and his eyes met everybody's with a sort of challenge.

Red blurted, "Gosh a'mighty, you got cramps or somethin'?"

Jeb lifted his head a little and the look that went from under the hat brim toward Mrs. Hepple's back made Red know there was something pretty mysterious between them.

Red said, "Whatever the hell is the matter, Jeb?"

Jeb got up with the cautious air of being ready to turn if Mrs. Hepple looked about. "Come 'long, son. Let's eat." They walked along the street.

On the Emporium corner, Jeb stopped. He said, slow and hard-eyed: "Son, you will do me some favor just to forget and not ever to speak about it.

31

I been near caught a time or two before. It's one reason I don't like comin' to town. Some day, mebbe, you'll find out. But I hope not! Now let's go 'cross here to the Best Bet an' you can have yore drink. Then we'll eat."

CHAPTER TWO

Two months later.

It was so early in the morning that the Best Bet, open day and night, was almost deserted. The Mexican roustabout, having taken a whispered message from the bartender up stairs to where the girls slept, came back, languidly sprinkled water and began sweeping up damp sawdust with a push broom. Now and then somebody came in for a hurried drink and went on his way.

Red, at a table near the bar, played solitaire.

Jim, the bartender, a fat placid man, sleek of hair with a bulging mustache that had been dyed black, leaned on the bar reading a month old Denver *Republican*. For years and years Jim had come out from Denver every fall to tend bar at the Best Bet. The townsmen had grown to accept him as a citizen, he came so regularly and was a gentleman. Now he owned an interest in the Best Bet.

Over the bartender's head behind the bar was a placard:

Notice:
Anybody wearing guns indoors will be arrested.
Sheriff Nims.

It was a fresh placard, not yet fly specked.

Jim said, "I see they is even a piece in the paper here about how cowmen are sufferin' from rustlers down in our neck of the woods."

Red, eying his cards, grumbled, "An' no wonder! They have made it agin the law for to shoot rustlers an' horse thieves, like onct." Red added, pleased: "But that don't mean they ain't a little shootin' done to 'em, now an' then."

Sara Timton came sauntering in the back way. It was not yet quite nine o'clock. She looked sleepy but had fixed herself up nice in a gypsy costume.

Sara said, "Oh, hello, Red," just as if the Mexican hadn't told her he was down stairs.

He said, " 'Lo," and eyed her for a moment or two, thinking how much prettier she looked than when he had first seen her. She was painted some and powdered, looked a little thin in the face, had on lots of cheap jewelry and the flouncy colored skirts were attractive.

Sara pulled back a chair and sat down. "What you doing in town so early?"

Red yawned. "Me and Miz George was up nearly all night with a mess of collie pups bein' born. Then Miz George said, 'It's too near morning to go to bed. We'll have some breakfast, then you can light out for the mail.' The which was done."

"I didn't roll in until about four this morning

myself," said Sara, but Red was uninterested and went on with his game. She lay forward on her arm, her dark eyes fluttering between the cards and his face. Red switched a king for a queen, and Sara said, "Oh, shame on you! And folks think you are an honest boy, Red!"

" 'Tain't dishonest not to deceive nobody. Particular, not yourself."

She studied his face for a long time, then, "Red, were you ever mixed up in the Hepple and Dobbs range war?"

"They ain't been no range war for a long time. Just some hard feelin's."

"Think trouble will start again, maybe?"

Red said, "Pah!"

"There is talk, you know."

"They is always talk about somethin' or other that's nobody's business."

"Why don't you think there may be some more trouble?" Her voice was insistent as a fly's buzz.

He thoughtfully cheated as he spoke: "It ain't a cow outfit no more. Old Dingley, being crippled thataway, ain't snortin' around for trouble like onct. And Pinky wouldn't look so handsome if he got all smoked up."

"Supposin' Pinky heard you talk like that, Red?"

"He's got ears. If he'll bring 'em clost he can hear."

35

Sara watched him, then, "But there's Joe Bush. He's a Hepple." Her voice was low, cautious-like. "And," she added with low-toned bitterness, "he's in close with the Johnsons." Her voice dropped still lower, increased in bitterness: "They'll ruin Mrs. Dobbs if they can. Just like they did my paw!"

"They try it, an' the cattle cars to hell'll be packed with bad-hurt *hombres*," said Red off-hand, not much concerned.

Sara meditated, her look steadily on his face. "Mrs. Hepple is pretty, don't you think?"

Red grunted, noncommittal.

"Was the first Mrs. Hepple pretty?" She seemed determined to pry talk out of him.

"Oh, I was too much of a kid to know who was pretty and who wasn't five or six years ago."

Jim lay on his elbows at the bar, listening. He spoke up casually. "Been longer than that, Red. She come from nice folks back east and went home. With that boy of hers." Jim shifted his chewed cigar from one side of his mouth to the other, looked hard at Sara and seemed a little amused and mildly sorry for her.

"You haven't answered my question, Red. Do you think Mrs. Hepple is pretty?"

"Aw shucks. All the thinking I do about a woman's looks is Miz George's. Has she got her war paint on or ain't she? If so, me an' the dogs sneak out behind the corral and set quiet."

Sara struck him with languid slap. "Oh you—afraid of a woman!"

"I don't know anything it's wiser to be more afraid of. Particular if that woman is Miz George on the warpath." He pushed away the cards, lay back in the chair, let his spurred heels overhang the seat of the chair in front of him. "The Lord shore got his shuffle mixed when he made Miz George a woman."

"What's wrong with women?" Sara asked. She was weary but smiled.

"Lots. They got no business out-tirin' us men. Having more grit and being smarter. Women ought to be just purty, easy scairt, cook good, and make us men think we're some punkins. That right, Jim?"

The bartender spoke lazily. "Sure. But what ought to be, ain't—with women."

Red leaned far back against the chair, tilted his head, eyed the placard. "Whatever you reckon bit Bill Nims for to make him stick up a thing like that?"

"Law and order, son," said Jim, sarcastic. Sara made a derisive sound.

"I've knowed Bill Nims," Red went on with his eye on the notice, "since I was a little shaver. He used to ride out sometimes with my dad. I never suspicioned he was a damn fool."

"In a lot of cowtowns, I hear tell," said Jim,

"they used to be orders to take off your guns when you went into places."

"Supposing he tried to take your guns off you, Red?"

Red squinted at her drowsily. "I'm peac'ble. But I don't read well. That's all. He's wearing my dad's star. I was brought up to do whatever the man as was wearing that star told me to do." Red yawned, fitted his hat to make an easier resting place for his head against the back of the chair, shut his eyes.

Sara lay forward with chin on forearm, staring at him. He was blue-eyed, young, lanky, brown as old leather with freckle patches showing under the tan. He had rather a long nose and wide, quick-smiling mouth. She now knew all about him that could be overheard from townsmen or cajoled out of the cowboys that liked to see her pretty face attentive when they talked. He had roamed far, been through a lot of smoke in range wars and tough cow towns, and was now back in Tulluco County as a sort of pet cowboy of Mrs. Georgiana Crittenden Dobbs of the Arrowhead.

2

Red was really dozing. Sara watched him. She sighed and got up. In a tired slow way she crossed to the bar, slumped down on her elbows, put her hands in her hair.

"Whisky, Jim."

He gave her a quick look. She had changed a lot since first coming to the Best Bet, learned fast, and was downright pretty in that gypsy-get-up, with bright colors, flouncy skirts, dangling earrings and brassy jewelry. She had a temper, too.

Her eyes lifted to the *Notice*. "Jim, is it true the sheriff has throwed in with gamblers?" Jim grunted vaguely and his look advised her to shut up. "I reckon," she went on, staring at the *Notice*, "he takes his orders from that old toad of a Banker Johnson. God, how I hate him!"

Jim, mild and paternal, suggested, "If you want to linger in this town don't talk so damn much."

"All right. All right," she said petulantly. "You don't need to make a sermon. Give me whisky."

He folded the newspaper, struck a match, sucked on his chewed cigar. He took it out of his mouth, trying to see why it wouldn't light, and tried again. It did not light. He tossed the match away, bit the cigar in two, put one piece on the shelf behind him and slowly began to chew.

"What you need, Sara, is not whisky—it's a spankin'!"

"What I need, Jim," she admitted bitterly, "is a horse-whipping for being such a fool! But I can't help it. You ought've heard the way he lit into them Johnsons!"

Jim nodded. "I've heard 'im. An' seen 'im." He looked across at Red, snoozing with head back and feet on the chair before him.

A shadow fell inside the doorway. A tall man, young and pale, with mustache so waxed it looked artificial, stood there. He had black eyes with a sheeny glitter in them, and wore a blue velvet vest, polished boots and long-tailed black coat. A new silky wide-brimmed black hat was pushed up on his sleek black head. He had on a black tie and white hard shirt. He was Joe Bush, kingpin gambler of Tulluco.

He looked at Sara, then at Red, again at the girl. His grin was a sneer. "Didn't I tell you what I'd do if you ever done it again? You, gettin' up this time of morning for to—"

"Whisky!" she said, sharp of voice and rapped her knuckles on the bar.

Jim said, "Mornin', Mr. Bush," and was not answered. He put out a bottle and glass.

Sara, keeping her eyes on Bush's face, filled the glass to overflowing, pushed the bottle away, let her fingers rest about the glass.

Jim noted the look in her eyes and gave Mr. Bush a glance that was like a warning, but the gambler took no notice. Then Jim, by way of having something to do, soused a beer glass in a bucket of cold water and began wiping.

Bush showed even white teeth. His grin was very like his mother's when she smiled with muscular twitch of lips. He said, sneering and angered:

"I won't have you all wore out and sleepy at night! You get back to bed or—"

"I'm no damn man's slave!" There was a snarl-like curl to Sara's lip.

"No sass or I'll—" Bush stepped close with hand lifted.

Sara pitched the whisky, glass and all, at his face with such force that her aim wasn't good. The glass missed. Whisky splattered him about the neck and white shirt front.

He said, "Goddamn your soul, I'll show you—" and jumped at her.

In the past two months Jim had seen enough to know her for a wildcat in petticoats, so his jaw dropped and he almost let the glass slip as he saw Sara not even try to dodge but huddle her face in her hands and cringe. Bush hit her. She groaned, fell as if struck by a club and lay still.

Red's spurred boots hit the floor. What he said was the worst he knew to call a man and there was plenty of it.

Joe Bush turned with hand belt high. His pale face was ghastly white and looked as strained as if half starved. The black glitter of his eyes in so pale a face made him look grotesque. He lifted his left hand in a placating gesture, said quickly, "Now, just a minute, Red, and I'll—"

The next instant Bush's right hand flashed. A

heavy bowie went blade-first and shadow-swift so very near to Red that had he not been standing slightly sideways it would have struck deep and close to his heart.

Red's gun, fired from the hip, roared over the low-slung holster.

Joe Bush's grotesque face had a look of almost silly surprise in the instant that he teetered before he fell, face down, one hand under him, the other out in an awkward twist on the floor.

There was the sound of clattering feet in the rear as the roustabout threw away his long handled broom and ran from a back door.

Jim put down the beer glass, flung the damp cloth over a shoulder, leaned across the bar and stared at Sara. She got up slowly, pushed at her rumpled skirts. Her eyes watched Red, shifted, caught the bartender's look. Her mouth tightened.

Red peered at the gambler. "When they get that tricky they need watching clost—even after they're dead."

Jim said, "Damn!" in a soft voice. "An' him Mrs. Hepple's boy! You—" he seemed with half furtive shift of glance to be accusing Sara "—have shore played hell!"

Sara flung up her arm, pointed at the *Notice*. "Bah! Where'd Red be now if he'd paid any attention to that fool law!"

"Y'know," Red mused with meditative cock of head, "I never sorta believed tales about knife-throwers being dang'rous. Reckon they is a lot of things I don't believe, I orta. He worked it slick!"

Red prodded out the empty shell, poked in another, put the gun in its holster, with rattling scrape of long-shanked spurs went across the room after the knife.

Jim leaned far over the bar and, with confidential low tone near Sara's ear, said: "*You* are the one that worked it slick!"

"Me?"

"*You!*"

Sara shrugged a shoulder, pushed at her loose wavy hair, dipped into the skirt pocket and brought out tobacco and papers. "You tell Red and I'll kill you!"

3

People from near by, up and down the street, had heard the shot and rushed to the open doorway, saw a body down and all quiet under the thin haze of smoke that drifted high overhead.

The owner of the Bonanza from across the street, a small pot-bellied man, was the first in: "What happened, Jim?" Simpson, owner of the Emporium, which was also the postoffice, was right at his heels. One look and he said, "Red's done it again!" An old-timer stooped, took a look at Joe Bush's face, and muttered, "They'll be hell to pay!"

Close behind them came Mamie, the Bonanza

waitress. She was red-headed, not a pretty red, with a hard face somewhat bleached by steam and soapy dishwater. Mamie had grown up in Tulluco and called folks by their first names or any other names that seemed suitable.

Young Johnson, so-called though he wasn't so very young, came hurrying with pinched nose poked out and eyes a little owl-like. A voice that sounded pleased to give bad news, called at him: "Red Clark shot yore friend Joe Bush!" Young Johnson stopped as if he had stumped his toe, caught his balance, suddenly looked scairt. Somebody mumbled, "Miz Hepple'll have a fit"; and young Johnson, with out-thrust of neck and jerky movement of head until he could get a look through the crowd at Red, said between clenched teeth, "He's goin' to wish to God he'd never come back to this country!"

There was babble of questions, confusion of comment. Jim, the barkeep, set out glasses and bottles, businesslike. He spoke calm: Joe Bush (he said) struck Sara. Red, he was dozin' in a chair, woke up, give Bush a cussin'. Bush, soft as pie, put up a hand and said . . .

Sara's face set sullenly under their stares.

A bushy-faced freighter and his swamper surged in, shouldered through, looked at Bush, at Sara, cussed in approval. The way they talked irritated young Johnson. He said, loud and shrill, "The law won't stand for killings any more!"

44

The bushy-faced freighter yelled right in Johnson's face, "The law has been standin' plenty for gamblers shootin' miners that don't like to be cheated! I got me a gun right here to loan if you want to argy with the kid about it!"

Johnson backed away from the ugly freighter as if he didn't like so much bad breath in his face. Then somebody, far back toward the door, yelled, "The law stands for crooked bankers kickin' chilern out from under a roof!" Sara had spread her story to help make people hate the Johnsons.

Johnson started backing for the door, but shouted defiantly, "He killed Joe Bush an' he's got to be arrested!" He went out of the door with jeering words knocking about his ears.

"But," said somebody ominously, "Joe Bush, he's got friends."

"So's Red!" Sara snapped.

Mamie glared at Sara and sniffed. The virtuous Mamie had no use for dance hall girls. They wore bright ribbands, short dresses which was scandalous, silk stockings, often red, lots of jewelry. They painted, smoked, had an easy life of it, just dancing, singing, drinking. "Friends!" Mamie squawked. "Why, some of us knowed Red since he was knee-high to a grasshopper!"

Among those who came was Dr. Barstow, bareheaded, partly bald, wearing galluses over an unbuttoned and not clean shirt. He had a gray mustache, whisky-bloated face, mild eyes and carried a pill bag. He crouched by Bush's body. "Help me turn him over."

When the body was turned over they saw that a derringer was under Bush. He had thrown the knife and drawn the gun with incredible swiftness.

"Why, he isn't dead, quite!" the doctor announced.

Dr. Barstow, even if a broken shiftless fellow, had the physician's zest in trying to save the life of a badly wounded man. He sent out to borrow the shaft of a buggy down at the livery stable and got some boards from packing cases at the Emporium, had blankets fetched from the Golden Palace where Bush lived, and made a stretcher. Men carried the gambler down to the hotel.

Sara went out the back way, pausing at the rear door to see if Red looked after her. But Red didn't. He stood with his back to the bar, resting on his elbow. Somebody slipped two bits into the music box, wound it up, and the thing began chiming Yankee Doodle. Red was spoken to but answered with grunts.

He didn't like talking. He was thinking. Red tried to think honestly. So he had shot another man, had he? There were folks that he pretty much respected who had warned him that he had the instincts of a killer. Mrs. Dobbs, for instance, certainly wasn't squeamish. She had somehow learned pretty much about all Red had been through during the past two years up in Lelargo and Tahzo. She told him that he had done more shooting than seemed reasonable in a downright honest boy. She said he could shoot better than an honest man ought, the which made him sassy and much too ready to have trouble. He had a heap of respect for Mrs. Dobbs.

4

Sheriff Nims came in with some men following him. One of them was Deputy Marr who now had his hat brim high up like a man that means business.

The sheriff said, "Howdy, boys," and the men said, "Howdy, Sheriff!"

Nims was a big man, round of face, round of body, roughly dressed, robust, good-natured. His wife's folks owned a big cow outfit. He had wanted mighty hard to be sheriff and his folks spent a lot of money. There couldn't be a much more important job than sheriff for the title of town marshal, county assessor and tax collector went with it. Nobody was over him but the supervisors, and old Banker Johnson was chief supervisor.

Sheriff Nims pushed up his hat and strode along back to where Red stood with an elbow on the bar behind him, watching the sheriff come.

"Well, Red, so you played hell, huh?" The

sheriff's voice was a little loud, regretful, not unfriendly.

Red said nothing. He looked at the big solid silver star on the sheriff's vest as if the dull glitter fascinated him.

"I just rode in from my ranch—" He called it "my ranch" but everybody knew it belonged to his wife, who was a mighty fine woman. "—an' heard you shot Joe Bush. Miz Hepple's goin' to be mighty cut up."

"I reckon."

"Can't you read?" The sheriff tossed up his hand, pointing.

Red moved his head, eyed the *Notice* as if he had never seen it before and couldn't read very fast. He looked at the sheriff and said slowly:

"When you make gamblers and suchlike walk 'round in their shirt tails, I reckon then maybe they won't break your laws. Under them long-tailed coats they can hide a scatter gun."

"But a boy that's had your upbringing, Red, oughtn't to break no laws! If your dad's name had been signed to that there notice, would you be wearin' them guns?"

"Nor gamblers wouldn't be packin' knives—an' pocket guns, neither!"

Sheriff Nims' big tanned face colored a little, nevertheless he spoke deep-voiced and paternal:

"But if somebody else breaks laws, that ain't no excuse for you to do it. If you hadn't been wearin' them guns you wouldn't have had no quarrel with Joe Bush and—"

"If I hadn't been wearin' nothing but my toe nails, I'd've cussed him like I done. He hit a woman!"

"Oh, pshaw now," said the sheriff. "Her kind are ust to beatin's off and on. Turn around and belly up. Let's have a drink." He clapped down a twenty dollar gold piece. A sweeping gesture invited everybody to the bar. "That notice," he explained in a pardoning tone, loud enough to be overheard, "was put up since you come in for the mail last week. So naturally I reckon you didn't see it."

Red took a deep breath and eyed him, not answering. Red couldn't tell whether he sort of liked Nims for making it easy for him, or disliked him for not doing more, as a sheriff ought.

Men along the line were lifting glasses. "Here's how!" . . . "Health, Sheriff!" . . . "All the way, Sheriff!"

He acknowledged it all with a flourish and tossed whisky at his mouth, took off his hat, drew a bandana from the crown, wiped his forehead, face, and back of his bull neck. "How's things to the ranch, Red?"

"Fine, I guess."

"Any trouble with rustlers out your way?"

"Oh, I reckon maybe some squatters back in the hills eat veal onct in a while."

The sheriff looked at his watch. "Stage past due. Late again." He put the thick turnip-sized watch away. "Now, Red, next time you ride in just leave your guns at, say, the Emporium. I sorta have to not make exceptions. An' Red, I'm hopin' like hell," said the sheriff, dropping his voice to a low rumble, "Joe Bush don't die. If he don't, I reckon nothing much'll be said about it— legal, that is. But he's got friends. An' there's his maw. Anyhow, I won't rush things. S'long, Red."

The sheriff waved his hand and strode out with Deputy Marr, who looked disappointed, following.

Red leaned back against the bar with a stolid, perplexed, and cautiously thoughtful expression. Other men were leaving or talking briskly. Another barkeep had come on duty to help. Jim was down toward Red's end.

Red asked, low-voiced, "Jim, what's he mean by 'if Joe Bush don't die?' Why'd anybody think I shot 'im? What's this country comin' to?"

Jim spoke softly. "You been away quite some time, Red, and not back long. Things is changed. Lots of funny monkeydoodling these days."

Red stood solemnly perplexed.

"An' by the way, Red. You've noticed, ain't you, Sara is always here ever' Thursday morning when you come in for the mail?"

"Well?"

"Why you think she is?"

50

"I never thought."

"Other days she don't show up till about seven or after, night-time."

"You mean on account of me?"

"Do your own figgerin'," said Jim.

"I don't spend no money on her."

"That's what Joe Bush knowed, too! Made him mad. He's hired her for to loaf around the faro game he's got here. He wanted her to be his girl." Jim daintily fingered the tight curls of his big black mustache, nodded.

Red eyed a knothole overhead very much as if about to throw something at it, hard.

"And listen, Red. Joe Bush has got friends. He was sort of boss over the rig ups all over town. Whether he dies or don't, you leave your guns at the Emporium and you'll be killed. Maybe so if you don't!"

Jim moved away, wiping the bar as he went.

CHAPTER THREE

The stage went by the Best Bet at jangling trot and with cloudy swirl of dust.

Red caught a hazy glimpse of the six-horse Concord's driver, old Rim Cramer, whose hands were stiffened claw-like by so many years of holding reins. He was quite likely, if he took a dislike to any of the passengers, to put his team through a pace that rocked the stage along the edge of a drop-off in a way that set strong men to swearing and the less strong to praying.

Once the Stage Company fired him for scaring the peewadding out of one of its Eastern stockholders. Thereupon Mrs. Dobbs said emphatic that if they didn't put Rim Cramer back on his run that she would give him a herd of broncs and her old stage coach and let him run an opposition line; that she liked the way Rim Cramer drove; and the idea of an eastern chuckle-wit telling folks out west who they could have for a stage driver and who they couldn't didn't set well in her craw. When Mrs. Dobbs rared back on her hind legs and started snortin', most folks set up and give some heed.

Red ran at a jog trot, with other people jog trotting, all for no reason except to catch a glimpse of the passengers down near the corner where the stage stopped before the Company office. Today it was packed with travel-stiff and dust-covered people.

One was known as "Judge" Harris, a little dried up sharp-faced lawyer who always dressed like he had come out of a band box and looked as a puff of wind could blow him away. With him was a lightly veiled young woman. She was his niece that he had just fetched from Denver. The veil was not heavy enough to conceal her pretty face.

There was a young Eastern fellow who asked some fidgety questions and was shown the livery barn off down the street. He started for it in a big hurry.

Among others that got out of the stage was a big man in a dark suit of store clothes but who had a range-bred look about him. His eyes were narrow, his face bony, his legs bowed. Not a young man, not old, with a sort of cautiously watchful air.

Red sized him up, noticing things. There was a lumpy spot on each hip. His coat tail wasn't long enough to cover a proper six-gun holster and he didn't look like a fellow that would wear short-nosed guns. Red guessed the lining had been cut from the hip pockets and the holsters rammed down inside the pants. That would make setting down uncomfortable but at least give a fellow the sort of guns he was used to. The man had cold quick blue eyes with a sort of glisten in their look.

Red met the stranger's look with a mild stare. The fellow stared back, hard, smiled with one side of his mouth, stepped closer, said, "Howdy."

"Howdy."

The man drew tobacco and papers and began to roll a cigarette. "Long in this neck of the woods?" asked the man, sizing Red up.

"Um-some. Know ever chuck-wagon camp."

The fellow grinned, twisted the cigarette, reached for a match. Red looked at the man's hands. They were brown as his face, not calloused, not rope-burned. The cigarette he had rolled was very slender.

"My name it is Buck." He turned toward the Golden Palace, looking after Harris and the niece. "That was the purtiest girl I ever seen in my life. But she does look a little peaked." Buck slurred all of his "r"s softly.

From the sound of his voice he was likely from Texas; and, from the shape of the cigarette, near the Border. On close view, not likely to be good leather. Something pretty mean deep down under the cold glitter of his eyes. Big devil, with a chest like the side of steer. Red would have bet a dollar that he was on the dodge, else was a killer. Maybe both. Red didn't care. A few times the last couple of years he himself for a little while had been on the dodge. If Joe Bush died he might be again, right soon.

2

Red went over to where Rim Cramer sat on a bench waiting for the Company agent to get through with some business. At the sight of Red, Cramer's grin set wrinkles astir on his old weather-beaten face. " 'Lo, kid. How's Miz George?"

Cramer belonged to the inside circle of Dobbses, so Red was frank:

"Havin' conniptions fits, one after t'other. And like you know, when she's on a rampage, a parcel of Apaches sound gentle and soothin'."

"What all is troublin' of her, son?"

"Things is bad. Rustlers—my good gosh! And Rim, they is even some sheep been moved into Cocheno Valley!"

Cramer whistled, then, earnest: "Why the hell ain't they been moved out?"

"Don't fret. They're going. But 'tain't just sheep. Feed all over is getting thin. Outfits from down Monohela way, to get away from miners, is runnin' cows up toward our range." Red spoke low, glanced aside. "The Hepples, I hear tell, is plannin' to horn in!"

Cramer shook his head, skeptical. His oaths were lurid. "Why they dassn't! She licked hell outa them Hepples onct an' has still got the same men as done it ridin' for her!"

"Yeah, but for forty a month the Hepples can

get plenty of bad hombres as never heard of Jeb Grimes an' them like 'em."

Cramer lifted his hat and scratched his head. "I shore am sorry for Miz George."

"Her favorite colt broke its legs in a dog hole. Old George Robertson has got rheumatics again. That granddaughter from the East keeps her riled. I'm only just sorta mentionin' trifles, so to speak—but they send her on the warpath!"

"What else, Red?"

"Well, she's worrit some, a little, over that mortgage the which is purt-near due."

"Why won't them Johnsons renew it?"

"Why? 'Cause they'd like to own the Arrowhead themselves."

"Hell's blazes, 'tain't that bad? Is it, Red?"

"Me," said Red softly, "I got a suspicion the Johnsons are doin' what they can to make it that bad. Looky, Rim. Thick as Miz Hepple an' them Johnsons are—would she start making trouble for the Arrowhead 'less them bankers nudged her into it?"

"But she ain't started yit, Red?"

"Nope. An' the Devil is purty liable to have him a couple of bankers to toast if she does start. You eatin'?"

"I gotta argy with the agent first. You looked into the doin's of that Cross-Box outfit yet, like I told you?"

"I'm keeping it in mind for an off day. I'd hate

like hell for to catch Windy Jones and 'Gene doin' what they orn't. But I do hear tell," said Red, regretful, "they run around some with young Pinky Hepple."

Cramer went in to have his usual ups and down with the small dried up agents whose spectacles sat half way down on his nose. When Cramer came shambling out his eyes were fixed on Red in a queer look.

"Hn! So you up an' plugged Joe Bush this mornin'? Why didn't you tell me?"

"He throwed a knife."

"Miz Hepple'll skin you alive!" Cramer tugged at his hat. "An' I bet that fool law about takin' off yore guns ain't nothin' but the gamblers pullin' the wool over Nims' eyes so they'll be the only ones to wear weepons under them long-tailed coats. Bill Nims ain't a bad feller, I reckon. But he's scairt stiff he'll maybe hurt somebody's feelin' an' lose him a vote next 'lection. I'm glad to see you ain't payin' no attention to that fool law."

" 'Twouldn't be such a fool of a law if ever'body obeyed her."

They went into the Bonanza and found seats. Red put his hat on the floor. Cramer tipped his to the back of his head. Mamie flew around like a whirlwind wearing petticoats. As she scattered dishes before them, almost as if dealing cards, she said rapidly, " 'Lo, Rim Cramer! Have a good

run? It's apple pie today. The pig's doin' fine."
She swirled away with a kind of back-handed pat
on Red's shoulder to apologize for not having
time to speak to him.

Cramer, thinking it a great waste to throw
restaurant scraps to the dogs, had fetched in a
baby pig from somewhere along the line, built a
pen out back and presented it to Mamie.

Red was cleaning up a double cut of apple pie
when Lucky poked his shining face through the
door, looked about. He came in. "Mistuh Red,
Jedge Harris he wants fo' you to come oveh to
Palus."

3

The Golden Palace had been built years before
by a smooth-tongued stranger who persuaded the
cattlemen that they ought to have a proper place
to stop in when they came to town. It was badly
run down, in need of paint, repairs, furnishings.
It was now in the hands of outsiders who maintained a pinchbeck pretense of style, had table
cloths and served napkins. You got the same
napkin three times a day for a week; the same
table cloth, too, if you didn't spill enough coffee
and catsup to make it go to the washtub. Since
the hotel was full-up anyhow, the management
didn't see need in wasting money to make it more
attractive.

Harris lived there, had his office there.

The hotel looked a little deserted when Red went in. Most people were in the dining room. Red went up the stairs, strode along the hall, tapped on Mr. Harris's door. A thin harsh but low-pitched voice said, "Come in, Red."

Red opened the door. "How'd you know 'twas me?"

"How many men with six inch spurs and dollar-sized rowels am I expecting?"

Red flapped his hat at his leg and grinned.

Harris, in a neat way, looked very much as if he had been sewn in green hide and left out in the sun till the hide shrunk in hard wrinkles to fit his small body. His face was thin, sharp, his eyes birdlike in darting quickness, his hands small as a woman's.

"Shut the door and sit down, Red."

Harris got up from the table, came close, looked at Red with hawk-like peering. There was a whipcracker snap of voice:

"Why'd you shoot Joe Bush?"

"He throwed a knife."

"Why?"

"I give him a man-sized cussin'."

"Why?"

"He hit a woman."

"Why?"

"She sassed 'im and throwed whisky in his face."

"Who is she?"

59

"Sara Timton there at the Best Bet."

"A vicious cold-blooded dirty little devil! And you know it!"

"Maybe so," Red admitted.

"You young idiot!"

"I reckon."

"Red, don't you know she hoped you'd shoot if he hit her? She made him hit her!"

"Aw shucks. Why'd she wanta do that?"

"Don't ask me to explain the workings down inside the mind of a woman like Sara. She comes of a no-good family. Maybe she wanted the excitement. Maybe she had a big loan from Joe Bush and figured an easy way not to pay it back. Women such as she like the fame of having men killed on their account. Nice story for this country! The son of Sheriff Clark kills a gambler in a quarrel over a dance-hall girl!"

Red, awkwardly humble, said, "You make it look so I don't feel so very damn proud of myself."

"How'll you feel to be put on trial?"

"When 'twas self defense?" Red asked in utter amazement.

"From now on, Red," said Harris in a slow thin voice, faintly ironical as if somehow even he didn't quite approve, "the justification for homicide in this great commonweath of Tulluco County is to be determined in court."

"That you lawyers' doin's?"

"It," said Harris, still ironical, "is the doings of the Anglo-Saxon race from the days of the witenagemot and manifest in judical procedure from the acceptance of the Magna Carta."

"Um-hm, I reckon. It's plain as a hair brand after you've shaved a cow's rump. You trying to tell me I'll be arrested and have a trial by some of what you call my peers?"

" 'Peers' be damned," said Harris bitterly. "It'll mean, Red, before a pack of gamblers. Or their sympathizers. You know I'm not in active practice. I'm out here for my health. I'm not mixed up in the damn politics. But don't worry. If it comes to a pinch, I'll do what I can for you."

"I ain't frettin—yet."

Harris smiled, gazed at him with downright liking, lifted the bag of tobacco and papers from Red's shirt pocket and began to roll a cigarette. "How'd you happen to come back to Tulluco? You were superintendent or something for a big outfit up in Tahzo, weren't you?"

"Nope. Just range boss for one of Dunham's outfits. And so all out of place telling men older than me, that knowed more about cows, what to do that I wasn't happy. So I come home."

"The Arrowhead must be pretty much like home to you." Harris lit the cigarette, replaced the sack and papers in Red's pocket.

"I growed up sorta feeling Miz George was kin folks. But I never wanted to ride for her. It was too clost to home and my dad could hear if I raised hell. Of course, in them days I was young—"

The lawyer's birdlike eyes played over Red's young face and he smiled.

"You don't need to grin, Judge. I drawed man-sized wages when I was fourteen an' earned 'em."

"I know you did."

"Well, now that I've growed up and quit drinkin'—much. An' don't play no poker only onct in a while. And have got too fat and lazy to like cleanin' my guns, so think twict before I use 'em. And am otherwise a changed feller—some; well, now I don't feel so skittish about livin' among nice folks as knowed me when I wore diapers. After my maw died, I wasn't hardly weaned an' Miz George she just sorta played like I b'longed to her."

Harris sat on the corner of a table, breathed smoke at the glowing end of the cigarette, then looked up, spoke frankly:

"But you always were a little wild, Red."

"I try to raise hell, allus, for them that make trouble for the outfit I work for." Red stood up, slapped at his leg with his hat, then flipped the hat on, pulled at his belt, shook himself. "Was you wantin' anything else of me, Judge?"

A smile brightened Harris's sharp face. "Yes, you young rascal. For one thing, I want you to know I'll do anything I can at any time to help you, so if—"

"Loan me twenty dollars?"

"Twenty dollars?"

"I need it in some business."

Harris drew a buckskin pouch, opened it. "One enough?"

"Thanks." Red pocketed the piece. "Got to be. S'long." He turned to the door.

"Hey, wait a minute," said Harris, amused. "I want you to take word to Mrs. Dobbs that my niece is here. She told me to let her know so she could have Dora come out—" He turned to the door of an adjoining room, opened it. " Dora?"

A sweet voice answered, "Yes, Uncle." The slender, willowy, dark girl came in, smiled, said easily, putting out her hand, "So you are the Mister Red Uncle told me of?"

Red pawed at his hat, pulling it off. He shook her hand gingerly, dropped it. "How do? Pleased for to meet you. I gotta be goin'!" She was like a picture-book girl. He could have stood and stared at her, but jerked himself away with, "Well, s'long."

Out he went, shutting the door with a vigorous swing.

Dora was a sweet faced pretty girl. She shrugged her shoulders, spoked in an amused, resigned way. "I seem to have frightened him!"

Harris laughed. "Rattled him, yes. Frightened?

I doubt if it can be done. That boy had better look sharp or he'll be an outlaw yet. The doctor says Bush hasn't a chance. If so—well, there's likely to be the devil to pay. Red won't admit it and gets mad if you hint at it, but he has the makings of a killer in him."

He put an arm about the girl, squeezed. Her parents were dead. She was in his care now. "You'll like it out at the ranch. Mrs. Dobbs is a charming old lady even if one side of her tongue is pretty rough. And there's the granddaughter, recently from the East . . ."

4

Red went down to the Stage Company barn, got his horse and rode to the Emporium.

A clerk went behind a rack of pigeon holes marked *Post Office* for a bulging leather bag in which the mail for the Dobbs ranch had been put. Red hefted it.

"My holy gosh! I come for mail, not freight!"

He opened the pouch, dumped the mail on the floor, stooped, having a look. There were a half dozen letters which he examined carefully, and much surprised found one in a scrawling pencil addressed to *Red Clark, Arrerhed Ranch, Tuluco*. There were two or three stock magazines, a few newspapers, and eight thick mail order catalogues.

"When one fellow writes for a cat'logue," Red

grumbled, "it puts the others in mind to write, too. Here," he told the clerk, "poke these away till a wagon comes. My horse ain't a pack mule."

He opened his letter and read: *Dere sir, you done me a faver. So me Im tellin you Jim Cross of the box cross outfit has throwed in with the Hepuls an is monkein with yore alls bran. Sept for what you done fer me they cud run off all arrehed cows. T. Timton. I mean I wudnt care.*

Red swore under his breath, crushed the letter and envelop, rammed them deep into his pocket. He didn't feel good and went on saying things to himself as he slapped the ranch mail into the pouch. He carried it to his saddle, tied it on, and was starting in a hurry across the street when the clerk, with a catalogue in hand, came out of the door and called,

"Hey you, Red!"

"Now what?"

"This here on is addressed to Mrs. Dobbs herself. I thought you didn't notice."

"That's diff'rent." Red came back. "But you ain't no business man. Here me, I'm doin' what I can to keep folks from mail-orderin' what like as not you've got to sell and you—"

The busy clerk hurried in doors. Red stood with the catalogue in hand and, not wanting to stop and untie the pouch, also not wanting to carry the thing, he tore off the wrapper, opened his shirt and stuck it down inside his waist, flattening

65

it out to reduce the bulk and working it around back to be more out of the way.

He hurried across the street and into the Best Bet. The barkeep Jim was still on duty, but two other men were now behind the bar to help take care of the rush. Red signalled to Jim and went on down to the end of the bar. He saw the look of the flashy gamblers. They stared as if trying to scare somebody.

It was bad for gamblers' prestige to have their kingpin shot by a cowboy, particularly as Joe Bush, having a lot of family influence to back him, had fixed things slick for them in the town.

Jim set out a bottle and two glasses. "On me."

Red planked down the gold piece, spoke low-voiced:

"Give this here to Sara like it was yourn and tell her to vamose, cut stick, git! Go on down to Monohela or any old place."

Jim gave the coin a light flip of forefinger, pushing it back. "No use, kid." He stroked his heavy mustache. "She'd blow it for drinks. Anyhow, why?"

"I don't want her hangin' around when I come to town. I figger maybe she's a sort of joner."

"Um-m-m," said Jim, meditative.

Three gamblers walked by behind Red. They had the tense strained air of fellows who are trying not to appear a little uneasy. Jim eyed them steadily until they had gone on down to a crap table where they stopped, whispered together, glanced back.

"Watch out," said Jim, with warning.

Red said, "Sure, I'm watchin'." Then he asked, low and earnest, "You don't think, do you, Jim, she could've put up a sort of job on me?"

Jim shrugged a fat shoulder. "She's a woman."

"So I'm beginnin' to suspicion. What you reckon she had against Joe Bush?"

Jim glanced to the right and left, leaned over, wiping the bar. "I make my guess she figgered him and the Johnsons are in cahoots in the gamblin' rake-off. They're sorta running the town and sheriff. She'd burn down a house to singe them Johnsons' eyebrows. Then too she didn't like the way Joe Bush he pestered her to be his girl."

A fellow was bumping a dollar on the bar, impatient to be served. Jim moved along up. Red put an elbow on the bar, fingered his chin, brooding.

Without the slightest warning a shot was fired squarely and point blank into Red's back. One of the three gamblers had walked up as if merely passing by and simply jerked out a gun.

Red staggered, lurched sideways and whirled. There was the roar of a heavy gun as he shot from over the holster. The fellow was hit squarely in the heart and simply toppled forward like a dummy that has lost its balance.

An outcry broke loose. Jumbled oaths and panic sounds, almost hysterical. Somebody yelled with blurting squawk, furious and afraid, "Kill the . . ." It was one of the two other gamblers by the crap table. His lips were drawn back over the teeth of his wide-open mouth as if about to rush forward and bite. He swung up a short-nosed gun with wild sudden jerk; shot. The other gambler, as if trying to keep up with a signal that had come unexpected, fired too.

Red leaned forward, a gun in each hand, and opened fire. His face had a stripped, naked look. All other expressions than utter intensity were gone. He shot fast. His heavy guns boomed with a jarring kick that pitched the muzzles up in his hand. Bullets slapped at him. A bottle flew apart on the shelf behind the bar and whisky gushed. Spurts of dust came from the white adobe wall as lead flattened there. Some men went down as flat on the floor as if they had been hit; others crouched under tables. The doorway was jammed by the surge of men that had bolted in a huddle. They shoved, squirmed, squawked, trying to get through. Bullets flew wild as bees from an overturned hive. Gamblers here and there had pulled their short pocket guns to join in.

Red could shoot almost equally well with either hand. In a close mixup he was likely to blaze with both guns at once. He knocked over the two gamblers by the crap table that way; then, because of bystanders, he fired at others with a half second's pause in aim.

Within a half minute from the first treacherous shot, pointblank in the back, the guns were stilled. Red, grim and tense, peered through smoke, ready for more—almost hopeful for more. But the fight was over. There wasn't a face at the doorway but from up and down the street a pack was gathering on the run.

Red reached to a near-by table and put down a gun. With a solemnly slow movement he twisted his arm around to feel of his back. His staring anxious look changed to an expression of funny surprise. His mouth, open in a doubtful gasp, laughed.

Jim called through smoke haze, "My god, you gone crazy!"

"The joke it is on me!"

"Joke!" Jim gasped and reached for a bottle of whisky.

"I knowed I was hit in the back. I felt the thud. I says to myself, 'Red, old son, they got you!' So I thought while I could wiggle I'd make it a fight. Now I was purt-near ready to lay down and feel sick, a little. But when I reached around to feel some life blood pourin' out, I felt Miz George's cat'logue! Thank God them things are fat. Now I 'spose outa grat'tude I'll have to order my pants by mail."

Jim poured himself a big drink of whisky and

wiped his face with the damp bar towel. He shook his head two or three times as if there just weren't words suitable for now.

Red, with wary lift of eyes at people who were beginning to stir, prodded out shells, reloading. Men were getting up from under the tables. Before the eyes of the crowd that was huddling near outside the door, still hesitating a little to come into the smoke, these fellows who had been under tables tried to appear that they had stood up all the time and been interested spectators.

Two gamblers were dead, a third was huddled under the crap table, moaning with hands to belly. Another that had got out of the door had a busted shoulder.

In the jumble and hum of words, a voice called, "Where's the sheriff?" Another, louder, "Here's Marr!" And Deputy Marr was, not eagerly, pushed to the front. He said, "Now Red, you can't do things like t-this and not expect to-to—"

Red looked at him, dropped an arm and his hand hung beside a gun butt. "You goin' to try to arrest me? Up an' talk! Are you?"

"Well, n-no not if—"

Men, pleased, yapped jeers at Marr.

"Awright then," said Red. "I'm goin', 'less, of course, somebody else wants to argy." His look glanced along faces, then he pushed through the crowd that readily gave way.

Quick words of approval flew at him. "You

done good!" . . . "Old Nims'll throw a fit!" . . .
"Yeah, one jest like Marr's!" . . . "Joe Bush—
Hepples—now kid you've raised hell aplenty!"
No one thought of stopping him. "Them eastern
tinhorns has learnt somepun!"

Buck, the range-bred stranger in store clothes,
turned to a fellow and asked admiringly, "Who in
hell is that kid?"

"Him? Red Clark! Old Sheriff Clark's boy. An
hell a-whoopin' when guns are goin'!"

"He's *who?*" said Buck with up-jerk of head
as if hit on the jaw. He turned to face the way
Red had gone. "Old Clark's—I been lookin' at—
talkin' to—"

Buck yanked at the brim of his hat, lurched
forward, making for the door with a hand back
under his coat and shouldering men roughly. His
mouth was tight-set, his hard blue narrowed eyes
glittered. He paused outside the door, looked
down the street. Red, at a gallop, was turning the
corner.

At the corner he met and passed a horseman.
Man and horse looked fagged. It was young
Johnson. He twisted in the saddle, his look
following Red as if watching somebody escape
that he didn't dare stop. Johnson faced about
and saw the crowd stirring at the Best Bet
doorway.

He struck the tired horse, came at a lagging
gallop. Buck stepped from the edge of the board

sidewalk into the dusty street, raised a hand. "Well, whoa there!"

Johnson jerked his horse, peered down. "You've come at last."

"An'," said Buck, accusing, "where all the hell have you been when—" Buck pointed toward the way Red had gone. "He was the very first feller I talked to! 'Twould have been nice if I'd knowed!"

Johnson got off the horse, moved slow, being stiff and tired, also unhappy. "I've been to Mrs. Hepple's ranch. Took word about her boy. Joe Bush and—" He tightened his fingers on Buck's arm. "Look here. I don't care how you do it, but first—before we ever start the other thing— you've got to—"

Johnson pointed the way Red had gone, dropped his voice to a whisper, sibilant and fierce as a snake's hiss.

CHAPTER FOUR

Some miles outside the town Red overtook a buckboard jogging along. The curtains were up. A nice faced, well dressed young man in the back seat was swaying and bobbing from the jar of the ruts. The young man had a slightly pained expression as if his tail bone was a little sore. Red recognized him as the fellow who had come in the stage and at once gone toward the livery stable.

Red, without drawing rein, said "Howdy," friendly-like as always to strangers on the road. The young man bobbed his head but kept both hands firm on the seat to stop being joggled more than he could help.

The driver, an ordinary looking fellow, lolled drowsily and didn't appear to be jolted at all. Red said "Howdy" to him, and the driver, raising his whip in greeting said, "Howdy."

2

It was late in the afternoon when Red passed through the sycamores, all hand-planted years and years before at the foot of the hillside below the old Dobbs house.

The house had grown from a little, window-slitted, one room adobe that stood off Indians in the early days to a great sprawling house, big as a hotel. The Dobbses had been an hospitable family, theirs a pastoral empire and generosity. In the old days, when soldiers were in the land, officers and their wives not merely visited but stayed for weeks. The wives even got bossy like they were paying a little board and had some rights to fuss.

It was a great sorrow to Mrs. Dobbs that all her children had been blighted with short lives. None were now living; and only one grandchild, who had been born and brought up back east. Mrs. Dobbs, being lonely and hungry-hearted, had by preemptory threat of disinheritance, about two months before, got Catherine Pineton to come to live with her on the ranch.

As Red appeared through the sycamores, Catherine jumped up impatiently from the hammock swing on the wide low veranda that overlooked the hillside and waved her arm.

The collies charged down hill to meet Red. They were a broad faced, strong jawed breed, savage as wolves if aroused—said to be crossed with wolves, but gentle as kittens with the family. The "family" being Mexican servants, their babies, aged parents and vague relatives.

Catherine came with flurry of skirts on the run to meet Red at the hitching rack. "Where on earth," she demanded in eager but only half-playful petulance, "have you been? I've waited hours and hours!"

Red, untying the pouch, told her, "Me I had some little business."

She fidgeted, watching the sack. The collies sniffed at her. What they really sniffed was the smell of that French poodle she carried about so much.

He waggled a hand as if aimlessly shooing flies. "Nope, they ain't a thing for you, Miss Kate."

"You are teasing!"

"No'm. Honest. You any idea where Miz George is?"

"You haven't a letter for me, Red?"

"Look for yourself." He dumped the mail on a veranda table. She fingered it, then turned, held out a hand. "Don't tease, Red. Give me my letters. At least one little fat letter! Please!"

Red stooped, gave the big collie that pawed him a playful cuff. "Duke," he told the dog, "that there is a woman for you. They never believe a feller 'less he tells 'em what they want to hear. The which is encouragin' to make us p'lite fellers lie a little." He grinned at Catherine. "Miz George in a good humor?"

"No. I made her as mad as I could this morning."

"Why you want to rile her all the time?" Red was vaguely indignant.

Catherine was a pretty girl, white, golden, lacy,

dainty, who had been brought up back east by a fastidious Pineton aunt. "Red," she demanded, "is it intelligent of Grandmother to expect me to like this ranch? This awful country?"

"Best cow country anywhere!"

"I'm not interested in cows, thank you! And don't you suppose I get tired of listening to the number of Indians that Grandmother at my age had killed right out of this window!"

"She shore done it, too!" said Red, proud.

"All very admirable of Grandmother, no doubt! But I don't care whether or not there is any of the good old fighting Dobbs or Crittenden blood in me. She makes quite a point of there not being, you know."

"Oh, the way you act gets her dander up."

"And you have heard how she talks to me. As if she were a little disgraced because her grandchild can't ride bucking horses! And I can't shoot. I don't know the first thing about skinning a cow. And don't want to! I hate these beastly wolves that she calls dogs!"

Red shook his finger at Duke, bidding him listen.

"And I love my dog Trixy! I'm afraid of snakes, bugs, and mice. I like tea and she thinks that is shameful! I shudder at her talk about what she calls 'shooting scrapes.' I think it horrid, barbarous! And she says *you* are as bad as anybody, Red."

"Me? Shucks! Huh."

"Then why do you wear those awful looking guns?"

Red looked down on one side, then on the other, as if sort of wondering what these guns were doing tied to him. "Oh," he suggested mildly, "they sorta help a little to make a balance, horseback."

"She drives me frantic, boasting of that horrible Dobbs-Hepple war and telling how 'her boys' killed men! You don't know how glad I am that you told me yesterday *you* had never hurt a Hepple in your life!"

"Yes'm, an' shore told you the truth— yesterday." Red dropped the "yesterday" with mumbled lack of emphasis. Catherine was always talking about the Hepples as if they were somehow real folks.

"And isn't it awful, Red," she went on in a flurry of earnestness, "the way men in this dreadful country kill one another!"

He fidgeted, spoke vaguely, pulled Duke's ears.

She said, "Civilized people respect the law. Have courts and judges—and prisons!"

"Um-hm. They're doing that in town now, too, I hear."

"I hate this country. I like pretty things. I like music and books. She doesn't even know that her piano is out of tune, oh, ghastly! I loathe Mexican pottery and Indian rugs. I think this ramshackled old house is horrible. And I'm not going to pretend anything I don't feel! Ought I?"

"You know," said Red with amused drawl, "I reckon they is more of that good old fighting blood in your veins than you calc'late. You are the only body, man or woman, in this whole *danged* country that sasses Miz George back!"

Catherine smiled and patted his breast with light flutter. There was always a strong, and to Red—not to Mrs. George!—pleasing smell of violets about her. "And you, Red, are the only nice person I've found in this whole *damned* country! And I like you in spite of what Grandmother says!"

"About me bein' a bad feller?"

"No. About you being such a fine 'feller' that if I don't marry some such man as you, she'll sell the ranch and give the money to a nigger orphan home! Not leave me a dollar!"

Red colored, grinned, shuffled his feet.

"So," Catherine went on gayly, "cute little pickaninnies must grow up adoring your handsome bust that will stand in their marble hall!"

Red didn't quite get the drift of that, looked puzzled, then, impulsively, "Aw shucks. Maybe Miz George'll like him fine!"

She caught Red's arm, pleaded sweetly: "When he comes, you will, won't you, try to see that the men don't take a dislike to him? I know Grandmother will like him when she gets to know him, providing," she added breathlessly, "she doesn't suspect who he is!"

"Miz George is gosh a'mighty suspicious an' quick-seein'."

"And Red?"

"Yes'm."

"You mustn't let even him know that you know who he is. I promised not to tell a living soul. But I had to have somebody I could trust to mail my letters. Didn't I? And Red, there is really so much more that I could tell you about him that I haven't really broken my promise. Honestly, I haven't. Some day you will understand."

"Um-hm."

"And please, Red, you will be nice to him, won't you? You barbarians do usually make fun of people from the East, don't you?"

"Well, look how they act."

"But he is really fine!"

Red spoke gravely, "Since you up an' married 'im, he'd better be—or stay a hell of a long way from this ranch!"

"Sh-hh-h!" She clapped a dainty hand to his mouth. "Somebody might hear! And if Grandmother knows that she would scalp me! But Col. Howland knows *all* about him, about both of us, and *he* approves. But if Grandmother knew, she'd be so prejudiced that Hal wouldn't have a chance. But you will, won't you, Red, help him?"

"You bet. But I got to catch Miz George in a good humor or it's me as will get scalped!"

"What have you done, Red?"

"Oh, I had a sorta argyment with a feller, or maybe two or three, there in town. I want to catch her in a good humor 'fore I dare try to tell my side of it."

Red raided the kitchen, laying hold on a prune pie; and, pie in hand, went to have a look at the pups.

Their mother was a savage beast, but her eyes pleaded softly for Red's approval of the fuzzy litter as she followed with apprehensive watchfulness every move he made in turning them over. Then, with only Bella to see, he took out the scrawled letter from T. Timton and re-read it, muttered in a hurt voice, "Damn their souls. I bet Hepples *are* back of it. And back of Miz Hepple—them Johnsons!"

3

Red heard the dogs yapping far down the hill and he hurried around to the front of the house. Catherine, from the swing, moodily stared into the distance.

"Somebody's coming down yonder," Red told her. "And the dogs are sayin' 'tain't home-folks."

He listened and heard the grind of wheels on rocks, then hoofs. The dogs, out of sight, barked loudly. A buckboard came into view. Red recalled the nicely dressed young man he had passed on the road.

"Gosh a'mighty, Miss Kate! I bet that's him now!"

"It can't be!" She jumped up, peered under her hand, ran forward a few steps. "Oh Red, it is. It is Hal!" She jumped up and down in glee. "But oh, how can I act as if I don't know him! How can I!"

"Better be careful. Mexican kids are smart people. They'll tell Miz George."

The buckboard wound up the hillside and stopped before the house. The dogs bounded about, barking, casting glances at Red to see if he thought these strangers were all right.

The young man stared at Catherine and looked guiltily solemn. A fat Mexican woman, very stately, and two or three girls, came to the door, watching. Little Mexican toddlers, naked as fish, came from around corners. The arrival of a city stranger these days was an event.

The driver sang out, "Oh, hello there!" as if Red were an old acquaintance.

Catherine, breathing hard and very flushed, returned to the hammock swing, clenched her hands, tried to seem cool.

The young man got out, travel-stiff and very embarrassed. "Is Mrs. Dobbs at home?"

"She'll be along soon. Come and set," said Red,

friendly, lifting a foot to the wheel hub, eying the young fellow.

"I am Harold Mason. I have a letter to Mrs. Dobbs from her old friend, Col. Howland."

"You'll be right welcome. Come and set," Red urged, keenly studying Mr. Mason's face. It was fatter and softer than the young faces seen on the range, but was goodlooking. Miss Kate's husband. Well, so far, he looked all right.

The driver was getting out some bags. Red told the Mexican girls to pack them into the house. Mrs. George would yank his head right off if a stranger guest wasn't made welcome.

Mr. Mason sat down. He was hot and flushed. He tried not to stare at Catherine, but his eyes sneaked toward her in spite of himself. The young Mexican girls stared with frank interest. Red could hear them saying in Spanish that he was goodlooking. Mexican youngsters squatted down, staring pop-eyed and shy.

Red said, "This here is Miz George's gran'daughter. Miss Pin'ton."

Mr. Mason arose, bowed. "How do you do, Miss Pineton?" A sly tinge of amusement crept into his voice. He had a hard time to keep his face straight.

Catherine nodded aloofly, not daring to trust her voice.

Mr. Mason sat down. He said, "Nice day."

Catherine looked away, her lips tight. Laughter

was right in her mouth, trying to break through. Red said, "Yeah, you bet."

The driver took a chew of tobacco, gazed about, waiting for something. Red called, "You stayin' the night?"

"I sorta calclated to."

"Over down yonder is the barn. An' bunkhouse. You'll be welcome."

"Thanky," said the driver. He climbed to his seat, shook the reins, drove off.

The collies gave Mr. Mason an embarrassing going over. Duke, a big shaggy dog, suddenly rose up with purposeful energy, put his paws on Mr. Mason's knees, peered into his face. Mr. Mason jerked back.

"Down, Duke!" Catherine cried anxiously. "Red, make him get down!"

"Aw he won't bite. He's sayin' 'Howdy'."

Catherine was frightened. "Red Clark, make that dog get away!" She knew those collies did bite.

Red yanked the dog aside, wooled him with rough affection.

"Red Clark?" said Mr. Mason, his eyes popping. "Are *you* Red Clark? I saw you ride by us from town and—" He stopped, looked a little excited and not quite sure.

Red grunted, non-committal, wondering what this fellow was up to.

"Was it *you*," asked Mr. Mason, as if holding

his breath, "who shot that gambler just before the stage got in?"

Red asked, "What gambler?"

Catherine, vaguely accusing and alarmed, spoke up. "Red, did you shoot somebody?" She just couldn't believe the things her Grandmother told about Red. He seemed so mild and good-natured.

"*Me?* Huh." He grumbled, "I'm peac'ble as an old boot." He eyed Mr. Mason as if about to accuse him of slander. "Why you say that about me?"

"I heard men talking at the livery stable. I went there just as soon as the stage stopped. Didn't even wait for lunch." That was aimed obliquely at Catherine, disclosing his eagerness to get to the ranch. "They said a Red Clark had shot—"

"Oh they's a mess o' Clarks around," Red told him. "Lots of 'em redheaded. An' somebody's shot there in town purt-near ever' day. Or ought to be!" To Catherine. "I got me some business to tend to, 'if Miz George comes, you tell her I'll be right back."

Red rode off slowly. Two or three of the collies followed with uplift of heads as if waiting for a favorable chance to inquire into his private opinion of the stranger.

Red thought, "I wonder what all is going to be said when they learn about them other gamblers?

A whole lot depends on how I break the news to Miz George. She's liable to up an' fire me. That feller messes up my chances to be dipulmatic, I'll not like him so very damn much!"

4

Red found Mrs. George on horseback down by the corral where she was reading the riot act to old Harry Paloo, which showed what a bad temper she was in, because old Paloo belonged to the family. She finished off with quirt a-dangle in wide sweep of arm and the flat statement that there wasn't a man on her range these days as was worth his salt.

She turned on Red as if about to jump him, too, then struck her horse. "Red, come back along to the house." From the sound of her voice she was sure riled. "I want to talk to you." She was off at a lope.

Red gave little old Paloo a pleading look of inquiry. Paloo shrugged his thin shoulders and raised a wrinkled hand as if giving a vague benediction for drawing her mind off him.

Old Paloo was pretty near as dangerous a man as Jeb Grimes, but looked mild, had a gentle voice. "Today over at Huskinses, a dog drug a fresh shank bone round the corner of the house while I was there. I asked for the hide, but they wouldn't show it. She says I ought've made 'em. That she will!"

Red followed Mrs. George, eyed her straight back. It wasn't a good sign when she rode with that right arm crooked at the elbow and that quirt dangling from her gloved wrist, flapping about as if getting ready to hit something.

Mrs. Georgiana Crittenden Dobbs was sixty or more. She was not tall, was rather thin, very wrinkled and gray. She could ride all day and, if any of her baronial neighbors wanted the game, play poker all night and be bright-eyed next day. When needful, she swore like a trooper. Yet the boys that rode for her thought she was not merely the best cowman in Tulluco but a perfect lady. Many people called her a "holy terror."

Near the hitching rack she hit the ground before her horse stopped, and cast loose the reins. She wore a divided corduroy skirt, old tight fitting boots of very fine leather, small spurs and a stiff brimmed hat that was fastened by thongs under her chin.

As Red dismounted she turned on him. Her tone sounded as if she were cussin' as she said, "Sheep, rustlers, nesters ain't enough! Them Hepples are putting on their war paint—who's that?" She had caught sight of Mr. Harold Mason alone on the porch. He was within fifty feet of her. Her question would have carried three hundred. Mr. Mason bounced up as if he had been shot at.

"He come, he says, with a letter from Col. Howland."

Mrs. George changed instantly. Guests were guests, whatever her troubles. She strode forward with hurrying stride. There was no dillydallying about her movements, ever. She thrust out her hand, the quirt dangling. At that moment, Red felt kindly toward Mr. Mason. His presence was softening.

Mrs. George talked fast, with a sharp sound to her voice, but friendly. "From Col. Howland? Glad to meet you. Where the devil is Kate? How is the Colonel? Sit down. Have a drink? I want two! Red, go bring whisky. Have you met my granddaughter?"

Mr. Mason was a little flustered by the snap in her voice and her sharp gray eyes. He said, "Oh, yes, I—I he—" pointing at Red. "He introduced me to Miss Pineton. She excused herself only just now to dress for dinner. From Col. Howland—a letter." He seemed pretty nervous and held out the letter. "My name is Mason. Harold Mason."

Mrs. George tore open the letter. Evening had come, but in the dim light she read swiftly and without glasses. It never took her two glances to see anything.

Red went into the house for whisky and almost bumped against the eavesdropping Catherine just inside the doorway. With her hand on Red's arm she went along the wide dark hall with him until well out of ear shot of Mrs. George, then whispered, "Oh Red, do you think she will like him?"

"Sho-ore," said Red with long drawn assurance. "He's a nice feller, ain't he?"

"Oh, *you* are nice!"

"I been tellin' folks that all my life. But some is suspicious of my facts. Go on, skedaddle. I'm going to get him a drink."

"But he doesn't drink!"

"Gosh a'mighty, he'd better if she offers it to 'im."

"Then just give him a wee little!" In the darkness she held thumb and forefinger close before Red's nose, measuring.

Away she went, a-scamper on tip-toes with skirts in lacy rustle and leaving a vague warm odor of violets in the air.

In the kitchen Red teased the girls about thinking the stranger so handsome, and asked for glasses, tray, ginger ale. He laid hold on the whisky without having to ask. He went out on the front porch carrying the tray gingerly.

There was probably no other person on earth, certainly no other who wasn't sick, for whom Red would have played servant before a strange man. No other cowboy on the ranch would have done it cheerfully for even Mrs. George.

As he put the tray down, Mrs. George said, "Fetch some lamps, Red."

He fetched, with glance aslant to see if Mr. Mason snickered. Any cowboy would have eyed Red with a grin bigger than a longhorn's loop; but Mr. Mason apparently didn't know that spurs, boots and guns weren't a part of a ranch butler's outfit. Anyhow, Mr. Mason was too tensed up over his own ticklish situation to feel like grinning at anything.

Mrs. George poured drinks, three big ones. Mr. Mason did not in any way flinch from the liquor except at following her and Red's way of gulping it down.

Red sat off by himself in the shadows, alert to change the subject if this fellow mentioned gamblers. Mrs. George rolled a cigarette, patted her breast pocket. "Match, Red." He gave her a match. She had another drink. So did Mr. Mason, but he sipped cautiously. She, half asprawl on the hammock, held her glass, smoked, gazed at Mr. Mason. He, eager to make a good impression, talked. His talk was all right but Red wanted to give him a warning kick on the shins. Mrs. George liked to talk, too.

After a time Mr. Mason was shown to his room to wash up and get ready for dinner.

" 'Pears like a nice feller," Red ventured.

Mrs. George carelessly discarded from her lap letters she had ripped open, glanced at. "Beef down again. Oh, him? Col. Howland says so." Her thoughts flicked into the past. "Colonel now.

Shavetail when I first knew him. He was in love with Kate's mother." Briskly, "Any news?"

Red cleared his throat. "Yes'm, a little. Judge Harris he got back with that girl."

"Nice girl, isn't she?"

" 'Pears to be."

"I want her out here. Kate's lonesome as a broken-legged cow. What else in town?"

"They's a new law. Sheriff Nims has got him up a notice as how you'll be arrested if you wear guns in saloons and places."

Mrs. George ripped the wrapper from a stock journal, flipped it open. "Good law." She turned a page, glanced over it. "What did you do? Stay out in the street?"

"Some gamblers there wouldn't have got so bad hurt if they'd obeyed that there law."

"You don't mean Bill Nims shot 'em?" Her tone was incredulous, her look hopeful.

"No, not exactly. They sorta jumped a feller. Easy goin' feller that was minding his own business."

"Who?"

"The first time that Joe Bush he throwed a knife an' got plugged then—"

"Joe Bush!" Mrs. George was startled and not displeased. "Well. Hm. From what I hear, he's needed killing for quite a while. Who done it?"

"Well, you see, then later on some of Bush's friends they started a fight. Quite some little noise in the Best Bet for a spell. Now gamblers ain't so num'rous as previous."

"Served them right. Pack of blacklegs!"

"Y'know, I hoped you'd sorta think so, 'cause honest to God, Miz George, I wasn't lookin' for trouble and they—"

Mrs. George slapped the magazine to the floor, stiffened bolt upright. Her wrinkled mouth grew tight-set as she gazed at him. "Red Clark!"

"Yes'm."

"You killed Joe Bush?"

"No'm. Just shot 'im. He ain't dead—or wasn't."

"Who else?"

"Bush was one. I don't know the names of all the others."

"*All* the others? How many?"

"A couple more. Or maybe three. Three, I reckon. Or four. I ain't sure, quite."

"Damn your soul!"

"But Miz George, they drawed first an—"

"You'd let the devil draw first!"

"Honest, Joe Bush he was pertendin' to be friendly, then throwed a knife. Next time—looky here!" Red took up the mail-order catalogue, showed the hole at the back of his shirt. "I happened to have this under my shirt. Round back. First I knowed, a feller plugged me. Naturally I done something. Orn't I've?"

She peered at the powder-marked hole in the

shirt. She fingered the catalogue, cast it to the floor. "Red, why the devil are you always getting into trouble?"

"Oh, I'm like a knock-kneed horse, I reckon. Allus stumblin' into it."

"Give me another drink. How many men have you shot in your life?"

"I don't know. All them I could that need it." He moved his hand up and down a holster, slowly, as if petting the thing.

Mrs. George struck her boot a hard whack with the quirt, kicked at the catalogue, shook her head, swore vaguely. "Red, damn it, you aren't just another cowboy on one of my horses. Give me another drink." He poured it for her.

She held the drink in her hand, looked straight at him. "After your mother died, you almost grew up here. You were the sweetest baby!"

Mrs. George's biggest weakness was over babies, any kind. Pups, calves, colts, or bear cubs. Often she sat holding some little Mexican toddler. She liked being tousled by baby fingers.

She drank a little, looked away toward the great shadow-blotted distance. "I'm getting old, Red. I want them about me that I like for more than just doing their work proper—What is it, Honey?"

A little thin legged bright-eyed Mexican girl came out of the shadows on the run, and said breathlessly in Spanish, "Our colt has got away and papa will be angry, and would you please,

Senora, have somebody—" her bright eyes flashed at Red "—help us to catch him?"

Red was up and moving before Mrs. George could speak. He caught up the child that wriggled gleefully. "Mrs. George called, "Hurry back here, Red. I'm not through with you by a hell of a sight!"

5

Mrs. George sat with a cold cigarette between her fingers, her hand against her cheek, thinking. The drumming of hoofs roused her, and she lifted her head, listening, then arose as the hoofbeats started up the hillside toward the house.

The horseman rode right up to the edge of the veranda and piled off. He was only a lanky brown kid, thirteen or fourteen, that worked about the livery stable there in town. The horse was in a lather and the boy's face was masked with dust.

"Miz George, ma'm," he gulped, proud of his importance as a messenger. "Here's a letter from Jedge Harris. He tol' me to come lickety-split an' I shore done 'er! He give me two dollars an' said 'f you'd say I got here afore eight o'clock he'd give me *three* more an—"

The eager kid went on talking as Mrs. George turned to a lamp, opened the note, read:

My dear Mrs. Dobbs: Joe Bush is dead and with an unaccustomed alacrity the

93

Honorable Supervisors of Tulluco have empowered the Sheriff to offer a reward of $1000 for William Tyler Clark, alias Red. This is, of course, inspired by the high estimation in which the Honorable Supervisors hold the dead blackleg's mother. I am sending this with all the speed available. No man was ever more justified than Red was in killing Bush but I am sure every effort will be made to bring him to trial and that the trial would be a farce of perjury, false swearing, intimidation of witnesses, if not indeed the furtive assassination of the prisoner.

And may I, with diffidence, venture to suggest that it would be discretion on your part to send Red away from the ranch, out of the country, until this flurry blows over. Any effort on your part to shelter him will only involve you in needless complications with the so-called Law and Order that for some obscure reason is now dedicated to the sanctity of human lives even when such lives belong to blacklegs, rustlers, horsethieves, and other common vermin. In the vernacular of the countryside, tell Red to hightail for tall timber and lay low.

I have the honor to be your friend. Sincerely. Harris.

P.S. The printer informs me that the reward notices now being set up refer in smaller type to the three or four other men Red shot this afternoon. Your keen perception will detect the significance of that typographical discrimination!

Mrs. George set her thin lips tight and held the letter above the lamp chimney until it caught on fire. She was watching it burn, but a movement from the boy caught her eye.

"Sammy," she said, in a far gentler voice than the look on her face would cause one to expect, "run around to the kitchen and tell 'Nita I sent you. Eat all you can hold. You won't have to hurry on the way back to town. But I want you to light out right off."

"Yes'm!" he gulped and bolted. He had been in the Dobbs' kitchen before. Nice and big and how them pretty girls fed a feller!

Mrs. George went into the house and came back with a tablet and pencil. She put the tablet on the table and stood up to write:

Dear Judge: For forty years I've stood up for my men when they did right. I'm sorry it happened. Joe Bush being a Hepple makes it bad. I am keeping Red right here by me. I am not going to tell him about that reward or how his being here may make trouble for me with your damn Law and Order. He would bolt just to protect me. So now if I let anybody come out here and arrest him it would be just the same as if I kept him here to betray him!

There is nothing secret about this letter. You can tell folks what is in it, or you can show it and let it serve notice to all and sundry there in town, and especially such cowmen and cow-women as may think old lady Dobbs is getting too old and feeble to hold her land, water, and cattle, that from now on gun-law rules my range, just like in the old days. Bill Nims can come out and arrest me—or try it!— any time he has a mind. From now on, like in the old days, rustlers are going to be treated just like plain thieves and I'll kill 'em on the range just like if I caught 'em in my bedroom. Sincerely, Georgiana Dobbs.

There was a postscript, thanking Harris for sending word and urging him to send out his niece.

Mrs. Dobbs laughed a little as she folded up the letter and put it into an envelope. Fighting talk always did cheer her up. She felt better, much better now. The only thing was that Harris, a cautious man, might not show it to Sheriff Nims. If not, well then she could go to town and tell the whole kit and caboodle of 'em herself!

6

Red came back, got off his horse, but stood holding the reins as if expecting to leave right away. Mrs. George motioned him to a chair.

"Set down. You haven't told me yet how that ruckus started."

Red went to a chair, dragging his spurs. He sat down, hiking a foot up across his knee, fingered the spur strap and told her, or started to; but Mrs. George cut in shrill and furious:

"Have you been carrying on with a dance hall girl? Sara Timton at that!"

"I ain't!" Red meant it. When he meant it, Mrs. George never doubted, but it made her mad that the killing grew out of such a trivial, almost not respectable quarrel.

"You were a fool. Some ways, Red, you haven't a lick of sense! Not a lick!"

He agreed, humbly.

She fell moody, took a deep breath. Her voice was low and even, had much the same tone that she used in talking to pups and Mexican toddlers.

"Red, I'm an old woman. Purt-near through riding. Troubles pile up one way and another. I'm going to tell you something. It'll make you feel bad. I want you to. Then maybe you'll try from now on to do more like I want."

"Yes'm, Miz George."

"Couple years ago the Johnsons, nice as mush with butter on it! coaxed me to borrow and buy more cows. I ain't blaming them for *that*. I am blaming them some because they promised it wouldn't make any difference whether the mortgage was paid off. Said they'd renew it. Now do you know what their excuse is for refusing to renew it?"

"No 'm."

"Old Johnson told me right after I got back from my trip that as long as I keep men that insulted and threatened him, he didn't very well see how I could expect him to renew that mortgage."

Red looked up, somber-eyed from under lowered lids. "I'll go right into town and say you fired me."

"You'll do nothing of the kind!" Mrs. George hit her knee with a fist. "I told him I'd hire whom I damned please. I told him I'd go broke before I'd let him, or any man, meddle with my business. Right now, with beef down and rustlers and nesters and *sheep!* I doubt if I could clear up the debt with every hide and hair on the range. But of course, things'll change. Beef'll go up. It just has to. Can't go any lower! But don't you think you ought to try some, a little, for my sake to keep out of trouble?"

"Next feller," Red blurted earnestly, "as makes me want to shoot 'im, I'll—I'll break his damn neck!"

Mrs. George laughed. Red was so earnest about it. She picked up her glass. It was empty but she tipped it, draining the last drop. She looked at . the back of her hand, turned it over, was looking down as she spoke. "Red?"

"Yes'm."

"Why don't you marry Kate?"

Red shifted uneasily, studied, grinned, "She ain't asked me."

"Don't try to be funny. She likes you."

"Miz George, I draw more pay and do less work on your ranch than any place I ever was in my life. But I'd cut an' run first. I get into enough trouble as 'tis."

She simply wasn't listening. "Women," she said, "like to be *made* to do things."

"I ain't going to make none of 'em do that to me!"

'Nita, the stately fat Mexican woman who had grown from childhood, and raised her own family, under the Dobbs' roof, filled the doorway and said that supper was ready.

Red started to leave but Mrs. George told him, "No, you don't. You are eating with me."

"Shucks. I'm all dirty and—and—"

"And what?"

"I'm more at home at the tail of a chuck wagon."

99

"So am I. But you are staying."

Red had often eaten with Mrs. George, elbows on the oil cloth, the food stacked between them. But a white cloth made him nervous.

Mrs. George was at ease in the shadow of a chuck wagon or at a governor's table. Since Catherine had come to the ranch the table was laid each night with fresh linen and polished silver. Wines were served. The girls brought around dishes for helpings. Mrs. George liked it. She was, she said, too lazy and tired to care for the fancy layout when alone; but this made her remember the gay old days when officers and their wives filled the Dobbs house with merriment. She was, she said, glad Kate could do something well: have dinner served nicely without fuss. Mrs. George hated a fuss unless she made it herself.

Red went around behind the kitchen and washed up, then dragged his spurs into the dining room and stood awkwardly. It was a large room, lighted with oil lamps that had painted china shades. Very pretty, he thought; but easy broke.

Mr. Mason's two big drinks had warmed him. He wasn't intoxicated at all, but his undertone carried farther than he thought. While waiting for Mrs. George to appear he said in an aside to Catherine:

"Is that servant to sit with us?"

Red's skin felt blistered. His ears almost

shriveled. *"Servant!"* And he a top-hand puncher! Of all names, including cuss-words, none would have stung more. That was enough to make a top-hand puncher want to tie a man to a bed of cactus over an ant hill and set by singing.

In another ten seconds Red would have been out of the room, and not all the horses on the Dobbs ranch could have dragged him back; but Mrs. George came clicking in. He couldn't dash out in front of her.

She had changed to a cool muslin dress with a long train and powdered her sun-blackened old face. Her wrinkled hands were as white as a baby's from always wearing gloves. She had slipped on some rings. He thought she looked mighty nice and stylish.

Mr. Mason with a kind of eager fluster placed the chair for Mrs. George, then hurried to give Catherine's a little push. Red's eyes followed him with a furtive baleful gleam. Kind of a fat face, the fellow had. Big wide staring eyes—sort of calf-like. Too particular about clothes. Not such a nice looking fellow, after all.

Red sat down and glared at his plate. He felt sweaty and wanted to scratch his back. He didn't think it would be manners to go clawing about with his fingers, so he pressed his back against the chair and wiggled a little. He did not touch the wine. He cut his steak with the fork jabbed upright and firm in the meat, took big mouthfuls and almost choked as he chewed, chewed, chewed, solemnly looking at no one.

Suddenly there was a scampering scurry across the floor, shrill loud yaps, and Catherine's poodle began clawing at Mr. Mason's knee, trying to get up into his lap.

Mr. Mason exclaimed joyfully, and a bit loud: "Why, hell-oh Trix, old girl!" and leaned over to pat and wool the frisky fluff-ball.

Mrs. George had a wine glass near her lips. Her look was as if aiming a rifle across the glass rim.

Catherine spoke up hastily. "He was playing with Trixy and—and she knows he likes her!"

Mrs. George drank the wine, did not flutter an eyelid. In Spanish she told a girl to take the poodle from the room. When the girl came back Mrs. George told her, also in Spanish, to keep Mr. Mason's glass filled.

Catherine's glances protested anxiously as she saw Mr. Mason sipping his refilled glass. She thought it nice of her Grandmother to signal attentively if the girl neglected to refill the glass promptly; but it distressed her to see Hal grow a little woozy, vague, and slightly loud. He knew he had had enough, but Mrs. George beamingly kept lifting her glass, bidding him drink with her.

Mr. Mason stumbled a little in rising from dinner. Red somehow couldn't rejoice. The look on Catherine's face hurt too much. He tried to dodge off but Mrs. George nailed him with,

"Come on, Red, we'll have coffee in the patio."

Catherine looked as hurt as if she had been hit with a whip and huddled in a deep chair in a dark corner. Mr. Mason's tongue thickened. He drank a little brandy with his coffee. Mrs. George, cruel as an Apache squaw at the torture, encouraged him to talk; and she dragged comments out of the wretched Catherine.

Red itched and writhed. He forgave Mr. Mason the "servant." Red didn't know just what had happened, something about that poodle, it seemed; but Mrs. George had surely turned cruel. People who tried to run shenanigans on her usually did get the worst of it.

Mr. Mason lay back wearily, relaxed. His head rolled to one side. He snored a little. Catherine, in the deep shadows, tried to choke down sobs. Mrs. George said, "Kate, what are you laughing at?" Catherine arose and ran on stumbling feet into the house.

"Red," Mrs. George told him, "call a couple of girls to help you get Mr. Mason into his room. Put him to bed. Then come back."

Mr. Mason was thoroughly out, limp as a rag. The girls made mild jokes. Mrs. George, gray and grim, smiled a little as she rolled a cigarette.

Red came back, reluctant. Mrs. George, with legs crossed and feet on a chair before her, lay with face up, looking at the stars. She was still smiling faintly and did not move.

Red planted himself in front of her. " 'Tain't fair!"

"Nobody held his nose and poured it down!"

"He was all wore out anyhow. Rode in the stage. Then out here. Purt-near eighty miles and him soft. He was tired to drop in his tracks!"

Mrs. George sat up, smiled grimly. "I hate people that try to deceive me—and don't!"

"What you mean?"

"You saw how that poodle knew him!"

"But Miss Kate said—"

"Lied!"

"Miss Kate?"

"They put up a job on me, Red. Pretending they were strangers. I'll fix 'em!"

"But are you sure about that poodle?"

"Of course I'm sure. I asked 'Nita before dinner where that damn poodle was. Locked up in the cellar all afternoon."

"But that Colonel's letter?" Red insisted.

"Old fool of an Army bachelor! He has known Kate from the day she was born. Knows this Mason. I can see through it, clearly. They all thought this Mason would come on a visit and be so handsome and gallant and fine that the old lady would kick her heels together in joy at having her granddaughter fall in love with him! Thinks well of himself to think that, don't he!" She rolled a cigarette. "He's just the kind—I can smell it!— that's interested in having his wife rich."

104

"Aw shucks, that ain't fair. And me, Miz George, *I* been drunk lots o' times an'—"

"I don't care how drunk he gets. I wanted Kate to see that he would get drunk and talk like an ass. She's so prissy—with her tea and poodle! I'll show her what's inside of him. You'll see!" Mrs. George snapped her fingers. "I wouldn't give that for a man that wouldn't get drunk. And I mean *drunk!*"

"Maybe he'll pan out all right."

"Not if I can help it, he won't! And Red?"

"Yes'm."

"Tell Slim Hawks to show up here at the house tomorrow morning with the buckboard. We'll haul the dogs down to Huskinses' place to look for the hide off that shank bone Harry Paloo saw there today. Haul that Mr. Mason along, too!"

"Holy gosh, why him?"

"He wants to see how we do things out west here. We'll show 'im! Besides, I'm not going to leave him here at the house alone with Kate, not a holy minute! *'Strangers!'*"

7

Lights were out when Red went down to the bunkhouse. There weren't many boys staying here now. They were out in the line camps with eyes peeled for rustlers. Only three or four, mostly old-timers, were on the home ranch.

Red saw the glow of a cigarette where some

one squatted near the door. That would be Jeb Grimes. Jed never seemed to much care when he went to bed, if at all.

Jeb got up. In long underwear he looked like a dimly seen ghost and moved with cat-soft tread on bare feet.

Jed spoke. His voice was low, almost a purr:

"I hear tell, son, you shot a gambler. That driver he said—"

"It was thisaway, Jeb . . ."

Jeb squatted to listen. His long fingers felt about on the ground, gathered a few pebbles. He thoughtfully pitched them one by one.

"Gamblers an' city thieves, son, has to have law an' order back of 'em. Elsewise they can't do their dirty work. Stands to reason. 'Cause honest men, left to 'emselves, wouldn't put up with such goin's on. But you wanta walk mighty circumspec'. That Miz Hepple'll shore try to have you killed. I," said Jeb with grave emphasis, "know that woman. Get along to bed. I'll set an' think some."

CHAPTER FIVE

The next morning as Red rode up to the house he saw a commotion among the dogs up under the spring-fed watering trough. The overflow of the trough was piped by hollow logs down into the pasture. The logs leaked, making puddles of mud.

The younger collies were bounding about, barking, digging in the mud, sniffing, jumping back. Among them was a little curly puff ball with a blue ribband about its neck. Trixy was loose. She jumped in and out, barking as much as to say, "Fellows, I'm really a good sport. I don't like to be bathed, brushed, and wear ribbands!" She was stepped on, knocked over, rolled about, all in burly fellowship.

The dogs had something under one of the logs. They looked at Red and yapped as if asking him to get off and help. He guessed it was a snake—bull snake. The dogs didn't poke their noses up so close to where a rattler lay. Besides, old Duke lay off to one side with mouth open as if half laughing. That wasn't his way if rattlers were about.

Red got off, caught Trixy, remounted. She wriggled, bit his hands but not in anger, and with quick lift of head and rasping swipe of tongue on his face apologized for her roughness.

He rode up to the front of the house.

Old Slim Hawks was there, sitting on a rail of the veranda, smoking a pipe and chewing. He eyed Red, eyed the poodle, spit, wiped his mouth with the back of his hand.

"Whar'd you ketch the mozelflickdad, hn? Thar bite is pizen, Red."

"It's been carryin' off Miz George's cows."

He took the muddy poodle into the house. One of 'Nita's daughters told him that Miss Kate had not showed up yet. He went to her door, knocked.

"Who is it, please?"

"Me—and Trix."

Catherine opened the door. Her eyes were swollen and red. "Oh, is Trixy hurt?"

"Nope. She's just been out with the boys."

Catherine put out her hands, drew them back. "I can't take her like that. She'll get everything dirty. Please, will you give her to 'Nita. And Red, you mustn't judge Hal by last night. He was tired and—and you don't think Grandmother did it on purpose, do you?"

"She hates teetotalers. I mean Miz George *hates* 'em!"

Her eyes filled tearfully. "Where is he now?"

"Don't know. But if he does like I do at just about this time of day on the morning after, he's got his head under the pump and is sayin'

108

prayerful, loud, and earnest, 'Never, no more, ever!' "

"Oh," said Catherine with tearful fierceness, "I will never forgive him! Never! But you, please be nice to him, won't you, Red?"

"I sure will."

"And take Trixy to 'Nita for me. You fearful little fool!"

Trixy yapped indignant protest at such slander.

2

Red was out on the porch with Slim Hawks when Mrs. George showed up with the humbled Mr. Mason at her heels. He looked pretty pale around the gills, sort of puff-cheeked, with big black holes in his face for eyes. At her, "Morning, boys," Hawks and Red bobbed, grinned, pulled at hat brims.

"Slim, you and Red load up the dogs. They'll maybe take out after coyotes unless we haul 'em. Mr. Mason will ride with you, Slim."

As they were catching dogs, Hawks grumbled with side look at Mason, "Usn't be agin the law to shoot 'em on sight, his kind!"

"Miz George is doin' crueler 'n that. She's taking him 'cross-country, rough road, in the sun, with a hangover—an' you drivin' wild broncs."

Hawks grinned a little at the fun he was going to have scaring this perkified galoot.

Red was tying Duke, cussing him fondly.

109

Mason came up. "I must have made an awful ass of myself last night?"

"How you mean?" Red looked as innocent as a bright-eyed babe.

"I was drunk. I'm not used to drinking. I can't even remember how I got to bed."

" 'F I ever got what you call drunk quite as you done, I'd be proud of myself. You was just all wore out and sleepy."

"Cath—I mean Miss Pineton must have thought—I haven't seen her this morning and—"

"Oh, I wouldn't over-fret myself about her. She likes you fine."

Mrs. George waited until the buckboard was far down the road. "I don't want him getting out and walking back," she explained.

When they overtook the buckboard, Mason was holding on hard and swaying this way and that. He was in pain. He had a big head. He was boil-sore and stiff from yesterday's riding.

Slim Hawks pulled his broncs down to a walk as Mrs. George reined up for a word. Red came up on the other side and asked, "How you making out?"

Mason looked weak and sick. He said, "Whew!" and tried to grin.

Red eyed the grin, studied for a minute, nodded vaguely. He leaned from the saddle, confidential:

"In a little while, no matter how fast you're goin', you just ask Slim there why the hell he

110

don't keep up with us. Then you set tight! But ask 'im that."

Mason gave Red a suspicious stare. Red nodded solemnly.

Mrs. George said, "Now pour the leather into them broncs, Slim. I don't want to have to wait for you down to Huskinses."

She and Red went ahead at a gallop. After a time she pulled down, letting the horses breathe at a walk. "Red?"

"Yes'm."

"Is that niece of Harris' pretty?"

"Umm-m-m some. When they smile they all look purty to me. She smiled."

"I believe I'll go on into town and get her. To think Col. Howland would try a trick like that on me! I bet," she said hopeful, with jerk of gloved thumb over her shoulder, "he's saying prayers!"

"And I bet," Red thought, "he's cussin' me!"

3

The house at Huskinses had once been a tavern, was two storied, well built but now some dilapidated and nothing but a kind of roadhouse with a bad name. Even the road down Monohela way had taken a short cut as if shying off from the shiftless Huskinses. Old Huskins lived there with two long nosed boys married to squaw-like women.

Red and Mrs. George galloped into Huskinses with the buckboard a couple of miles behind and out of sight over the rim of the Basin.

One of the Huskins women, the fat one, stuck her head out of the door and squawked, "Hey, Paw! Paw! That Dobbs woman is here with that red-head!"

She stood glaring, a black-eyed, lank haired, dark skinned slob in loose dirty wrapper. One of the Huskins boys pushed her roughly aside to make way for himself and came out shamble-footed.

He grinned sly and silly, said "Mornin' Miz Dobbs. Was you wantin' somethun, hm?"

The other Huskins boy, older, shuffled out with hangdog look, neck adroop, eyes up, hat down, hands in his pockets.

Red put his toes at the edge of the stirrups and set his mouth tight to keep from speaking up, sudden. Mrs. George liked to run her show her own way without other people chirruping in, helpful.

Red saw the skinny Huskins woman flit across the doorway. She set a rifle against the wall, then stood in the doorway with arms folded, looking mean, but the next instant sullenly edged to one side, making way for Huskins.

He was wearing a high crowned floppy hat but was barefooted and held a shotgun in the crook of an elbow. "Mornin', Miz Dobbs," he growled and stroked the gun butt. "I was jes' steppin' out f'r to knock over a couple of rabbits."

Mrs. George swung off her horse, dropped the reins, went right up to him. The quirt dangled on her wrist as if she meant to use it. "You had fresh beef yesterday. Where's the hide?"

"Ow, why now Miz Dobbs, you don't think I'd *steal* anybody's cows? Much less one o' yourn?"

"I ain't thinking, Huskins. I'm investigating!"

The skinny Huskins woman spoke up shrilly. "I'd like to scratch yore eyes out! 'Cause you own a few measly cows, you think nobody's got a right to eat beef 'less you say so!"

Old Huskins said, "Shet up, Mag! This ain't none o' yore put-in!" To Mrs. George, with abused humility: "You are shore welcome, since you don't trust my word, to 'vestigate all you want!"

Mrs. George flung up her quirt, brought it down with a smack against her boot. "Put down that gun while you talk to me!"

"Shore. Oh, shore. I was jest steppin' out f'r—" He stood the gun against the wall behind him.

"Now, Huskins, where's that hide?"

"Look fer it!" Mag yelled.

"Why, Miz Dobbs," old Huskins protested, fingering his beard, while the two half idiotic long nosed boys looked on slyly and grinned, " 'f I'd knowed you was comin', I'd saved that hide. But yest'dy I sold it to a feller as stopped on his way to the mines. Fer a dollar." He drew a dollar from his pocket, held out his palm. "Now ain't thet too bad. I'm powerful sorry."

"Why didn't you show it to Harry Paloo?"

Huskins straightened a little, seemed to swell some. "Why, Mizz Dobbs, me I'm a feller as can't be bulldozed. Them cowboys ain't got no business nosin' 'round my home. I don't like the way they ac', so high an' mighty! But you, now. *You,* Miz Dobbs, air a lady!"

"Right! I'm the goddamndest lady you ever saw when I catch folks chewing my beef!" The quirt snapped against her boot top. "And you are setting here on my range, doing no business at all and not a lick of work—yet eating fresh beef. So—"

"Oh my gosh, paw, looky!" the older Huskins boy bellowed, pointing.

The buckboard was streaking through a whirlwind of dust on the downgrade with Hawks pouring on leather as if he meant to upset the wagon. The broncs ran wild, the buckboard jumping at their heels. The dogs skittered and slid. The buckboard bounced and rocked on two wheels.

Near the foot of the grade, Hawks tightened the lines and began jerking as he put on the brake that smoked and squealed. He headed into the yard and ran his sweating team almost against the house before they came to a stop.

Mason sat there pale and sick, his gaze reproachfully on the back of Red's head.

Mrs. George called, "Turn 'em loose, Slim!"

Hawks untied the struggling dogs. One by one they hit the ground, ran this way and that, sniffing, and came up to Mrs. George, eying her as if for instructions. Cautiously, with far reach of nose and braced haunches they sniffed about the Huskinses. The Huskins boys looked down their long noses and fidgeted.

"Take 'em around over the place, Red," said Mrs. George.

Red reined back, whistled, and began to ride at a walk around back of the house. He called the dogs by name, turning them this way and that as he scanned the ground himself for fresh earth. He guessed the Huskinses were too lazy to have carried the hide far.

Around back of the corral there was a fresh hole half filled with loose dirt. The dogs tore into it gleefully, pawing and sniffing.

Red climbed off, found a shovel in the wagon shed, and helped dig. The ground was not hard but was stony. Red sweat and cussed. When he went deep enough to hit hard ground he threw the shovel aside and began to roll a cigarette. The dogs scratched and sniffed the loose dirt. They were sensible dogs, Duke, with tongue a-drip and earth-covered, looked up at Red as much as to say, "It was here but they have taken it off."

"Yeah," Red grumbled, "they got scairt after old Paloo spoke up yesterday." He put away the tobacco and papers.

A drawled sneer-toned voice asked, "Ain't found nothin' yit, huh?"

There stood the younger long-nosed sly-grinning Huskins, hands in pockets, looking shiftless and pleased.

Red looked him over then moved an arm. Out came a gun. Red jumped forward, rammed the gun against the fellow's belly. "Where is it?"

"Ow, don't shoot me!"

The gun's muzzle gouged. "You heard me!"

"Ow, Paw and the women drug it upstairs!"

"Dobbs branded?"

"Er course. But Paw an' Mag'll kill me if—"

"Feller, I'll give you three minutes to get around front and look innocent. Then I'll make believe the dogs trailed it into the house. Git!"

The fellow went with arms a-dangle and body hunched forward in hurrying.

"Few folks," Red mused, "are so dirty they can stand the stink of a hide in the house. These Huskinses would only think it was their socks. Only they don't wear socks."

4

Red had a hard time making the dogs come. The smell of the hide was in the dirt. He collared Duke, coaxed, half dragging him. Others followed.

Red got them to the back door. It was open. He pushed Duke into the kitchen. "Find it, boy!" In a moment they were sniffing, scurrying about, barking.

Old Huskins' startled bellow came from the front door as he faced about on the porch: "Here, what's goin' on!"

Mag shrieked, "Git them dogs outen the house!"

Red had guided Duke through the kitchen and into the big room—dining room in tavern days. The wide stairs came down into it. Red, pushing Duke along up the steps, looked down into Huskins' double barreled shotgun, twenty feet away.

Huskins roared, "Git down thet thar dog or I'll kill 'im!"

The fat Huskins woman called in anxious coaxing, "Here doggie, nice doggie. Come back, doggie!"

Duke turned his head with mouth open, panting. He looked up at Red with a kind of wistful perplexity. Red eyed Huskins and spoke slowly: "You shoot that dog and I'll kill you!"

Mrs. George, with hurried purposefulness but no fluster, pushed the fat Huskins woman out of the way, swung back her arm and her quirt lashed alongside of Huskins' face, a thong bridging his nose, raising a welt. "Drop that gun!"

The gun was fired with convulsive jerk of

finger, the charge striking high. The quirt struck again. Old Huskins howled, jumped, swung the gun about to strike at her. Mrs. George fended against the swing of the gun with upthrown arm and lashed her quirt on Huskins' face. One of the Huskins boys struck Mrs. George, and Red, with gun a-swing yelled at him and crouched to jump; but Duke went first—simply rose from the stairs, right over the banisters, in downward leap.

Mag flung up the rifle, shot at the dog, missed. Duke didn't even notice. He hit the floor and bounded straight at the back of Tug Huskins' neck, bearing him over and down. Other dogs surged into the fight, tearing at Tug Huskins.

Red, much as the dog had done, leaped the banisters. The jar of the jump put him knees down with an elbow on the floor. Mag reeled back, lifting the rifle at him, cursed him through gleaming teeth. Red jumped with arm swinging to strike the barrel aside, then whaled his revolver against her head as hard as he could. She staggered back. A hazy look clouded her fierce eyes as she fell sprawling; the rifle clattered from her hands.

The lanky Hawks had charged in, but stood interested, slightly a-grin. Mrs. George had yanked loose the shotgun from old Huskins and held it by the barrel with the butt trailing the floor as if she meant to use it for a club later on. She had Huskins backed up to the wall. She lashed him about the face and head. He huddled his arms over his face and she lashed them. He danced on one foot, then the other. He howled, pleading. She lashed his arms till he swung them wildly, then she criss-crossed the thongs on his bearded face. He bellowed, he squirmed, he hopped like he was dancing on a hot stove. Then with elbows up around his face he ducked low and made a surging lunge past her, ran out of the room, into the kitchen and out back of the house.

Mrs. George gave the shotgun a fling, carelessly. It skittered across the floor. She faced about. Red and Hawks were yanking at the dogs, knocking them about, swearing. Duke, if left to himself, would have chewed the fellow up in three snaps, but there was such a snarling huddle that the dogs had got in one another's way. The fat Huskins woman wrung her hands and howled that the dogs were killing her man. The younger Huskins stood as if half frozen, mouth agape, eyes fright-widened.

Tug Huskins was half naked, torn, bad hurt and worse scared. Hawks and Red got him and his howling woman into a room and shut the door. The dogs broke loose and bounded at the door, whimpering.

Mrs. George drew the blood-stained quirt through gloved fingers. She was breathing hard but slow. Her hat dangled back on her shoulders.

She set it straight. "All right, Red. Show me that hide!"

Red had one wild moment of doubt. If there were no hide there would surely be the devil to pay after such a ruckus. Maybe that young Huskins had lied for a joke. Red pounced on the stupid Huskins. "It's that hide or yourn! Lead the way!"

Red jerked him forward and from behind pushed him on, up the stairs.

They went through a room foul with the stench of unwashed clothes, un-sunned bedding that lay tousled on sagging springs over an uncarpeted floor. Young Huskins opened a door into a dark place. "It—it's in thar!"

"Dig it out!"

"Git a light."

"Get it yourself!"

The flickering lamp showed a kind of disordered catch-all sort of store room. In the stale air there was the unmistakable stink of green hide, very pleasing to Red's nose. "Drag 'er out!"

Huskins walked backwards, pulling the hide after him. The folded hide opened up. It was covered with dirt. Huskins went backwards on the stairs, pulling the hide down.

The hide was spread out on the floor, hair up. Branded Arrowhead.

Mason, shocked and wobbly, stood just inside

the doorway. He looked bewildered and said more to himself than meaning to be heard, "All over a cow!"

Red spun about. " 'Tain't! It's over them bein' the kind that steal cows!"

Mag Huskins had come to life and staggered to a chair. She held her head, welted to the size of a turnip and gazed blear-eyed.

Mrs. George told Red to find old Huskins. "Fetch him in here."

"Gosh a'mighty," Red thought. "He's prob'bly a mile off and goin' fast!" But he said promptly, "You bet!" and went out with hurried jangle of spurs, climbed his horse and rode about, singing out, "High-Oh, Huskins? Come a trottin'! 'F you don't, I'll turn the dogs loose! You hear me?"

Huskins limped into view. His face was ridged with welts, some already bluish to black, others bleeding. "Fer God's sake have some mercy!"

"You've had a-plenty that you ain't hung! Waltz right along in to Miz George."

Huskins went in, bulky and cringing. Mrs. George rested with a foot on the bottom of a chair and leaned forward with an elbow on her raised knee.

"Huskins!"

"Now, please, Miz—"

"You are moving. Pack and git!"

"Yes, mom," said Huskins.

121

But Mag shrieked, "We won't go! This here place ain't yourn! We got some rights. We jest ain't goin'!"

Mrs. George's foot came off the chair with a snap. She walked across the room with *shishing* rustle of corduroy, drawing the quirt between her fingers as if to make sure all the kinks were out of the thongs. Mag's blazing black eyes met with glint of Mrs. George's gray eyes. "You won't go?"

Mag's eyes glittered, but she saw something that made her afraid. Mrs. George had fought off Indians, had rode with her men to chase and hang horse thieves, had lashed the faces of bad men, had won and held the Arrowhead range. It showed in her face. Mag's glare wavered. "We'll go," she mumbled, dropped her face, sat still.

"Make a start!"

Mag got off the chair, not looking up. " 'Tain't right!" She dragged her feet, muttered. "We're goin' have justice, some kind!" Slowly she climbed the stairs.

Mrs. George turned on Huskins. "How'd you come to move in here in the first place?"

Huskins cringed, dabbed dirty fingers at the blood on his face, looked as if about to cry. "Some time back, Joe Bush thar in town he said 'twould be a'right. So I brung my fam'ly—"

"Be out of here by sundown, Huskins. Unless every hair, hide and hoof is off the place, I'll have my boys take you off at the end of a rope! Git goin'!"

Huskins wiped at his face with a forearm. "Y-yes'm," he said. He turned to the stairs, plodded up.

Mrs. George turned on Red. A corner of her mouth twitched, not quite smiling. "You, shame on you! You hit a woman!"

Red grinned sheepishly. "If she'd wore pants I wouldn't've!"

"Get outside and find that young Huskins. Tell him to get his horses and start hitching!"

5

Red had his knee cocked over the saddle horn and from horseback, as he rolled a cigarette, gave the young Huskins a talk on manners. 'Peared like, according to Red, when spoke to you ought to answer, prompt and polite, not hide away in a crib until come on.

Slim Hawks dashed out of the back of the house, saw Red and came toward him in a lurching trot with long arms flapping.

"Hey, Red, lis'n!" Hawks blurted and flung back a hand, pointing. "Sheriff's comin' up the road! Miz George says f'r you to light out f'r the ranch, ears a-floppin'!"

"Who all is with 'im?"

"Jest him. Miz George says f'r to tell you to vamoose, sorta hide yoreself in dust."

Red shook his head. "I ain't going. How you know he's lookin' for me? Maybe as how he just rode out to sweat off some fat. Then how'd I look to run?"

"But Miz George says—"

"What she says about work, any time, I'll do. What she says about my personal 'fairs 'tween me and sheriffs—hell, Bill Nims wouldn't shoot me! He knows I wouldn't shoot him. So neither of us is scairt."

6

Bill Nims fitted a saddle as if shoe-horned into it and rode big horses. He moved with a big man's slowness but wasn't awkward. He had been passing, saw the buckboard, dogs, and recognized Mrs. Dobbs' horse; and so turned in.

Mrs. George, looking stern, came out of the doorway. Nims pulled off his hat. "Howdy, Miz George?"

"Howdy, Bill."

He turned his big round face from side to side. "Something goin' on?"

"Something, a little. Get down and come here."

He swung from his horse, kept hold of the reins, walked forward with the horse stretching its neck in mild protest at being led up under the porch.

Mrs. George's gloved hand, with quirt dangling, pointed through the doorway at the spread hide. "Looky there!"

Sheriff Nims studied the brand. "Bad." His deep voice had full sympathy. Tug Huskins' howls grew louder. The sheriff cocked his head.

"Dogs jumped Tug," said Mrs. George.

The sheriff pondered. "Um-hm. I reckon the lot of 'em'll get ten year apiece for this."

Mrs. George's words exploded between her teeth. "They steal my cows, then I pay taxes for ten years to feed, bed, and clothe Huskinses!"

The sheriff didn't want an argument, not with her. He said mildly, "That there is the law."

"I've showed respect a-plenty for the law by not hanging 'em. They got to git up and git!"

"And maybe steal somebody else's cows?"

"Other somebodys can look after their own cows." She gave him a curious stare. "Has Judge Harris spoke to you the last day or two about me?"

"Why, no mam, Miz George." He waited, expectant.

Mrs. George said, "Humphf." Then, "How'd you come to be coming along?"

"Oh, I was just takin' a little ride out your way. Red to home?"

"What you want with Red?"

"Do you mean you don't know what all he done there in town?"

"Yes, I know. And," Mrs. George snapped, "I think he done right. Some ways, Bill Nims, you are a mighty big fool! One of 'em is to think you could come out to my ranch and arrest Red!"

The sheriff cleared his throat, moved his feet, wiped his face. He smiled uneasily. "Whew. Hot today, ain't it?" He moved back from the doorway, faced about.

Red, on horseback, said, "Mornin', Sheriff."

The sheriff eyed him, slow and searching. Mrs. George swished the quirt and by her look Red could tell that she was giving him Hail Columbia. Nims put his hat brim into the same hand that held the reins. He put the other hand high up against the post, leaned slightly. "Mornin', Red."

"Kinda hot, Sheriff."

"Yes, 'tis a little, Red." The Sheriff stared up at the lank sunburned lean-faced boy, range-born and bred, whose look was steady as sunlight through a knot hole. "When you was a little shaver, Red, I ust to set you astraddle of my horse's neck in front of my saddle. And now—" The sheriff straightened, slowly put a hand down inside his vest pocket, drew out a folded sheet of glazed paper. He waggled his arm, shaking the paper open, stepped forward, held it up.

Red took the poster.

$1000 DEAD OR ALIVE $1000
William Tyler Clark, Alias Red

Red gave it a glance, not more, then his eyes warily left the paper and steadily watched the sheriff. No one spoke for a time, and there was no movement. Then Red, mild and slow, asked, "Was you thinking some, maybe, of arrestin' me?"

"I come for a talk. Looks mighty bad for the son of Sheriff Clark to be on the dodge, don't you think?"

"He's been on the dodge a time or two a'ready, Sheriff. And ever'thing come out all right." Red gave the poster another quick glance, eyed the sheriff: "Since when do you call shootin' in self defense 'murder,' Sheriff?"

"Self defense has to be 'stablished in court, Red," said the sheriff, as grave and judicial as if he were a judge.

Mrs. George said, "Bill Nims!" She took a step toward him, seemed to grow taller. Her gloved fingers bent up the brim of her hat with sudden jerk.

The sheriff straightened bulkily, put on his hat.

"Bill, some ways I've always liked you a heap. You've got faults a-plenty. But ain't afraid of no man alive. There's no man I know of that goes farther than you just out of goodness of heart to help some poor body. But you are being a damn fool, Bill."

The sheriff flinched as if that quirt had swept at his face. His face turned as red as the bandana about his neck. He choked a little in pleading, "Miz George!"

"Left to yourself, you wouldn't lift a hand to arrest Red! Would you? For one thing, you know he done right. But I'll bet them Johnsons have told you to fetch Red in. So wanting to obey them Johnsons, and not wanting to rile us cowmen by trying to arrest Red forcibly, you got the notion of riding out here to try to coax Red to go to town of his own free will and have a trial. He ain't going!"

"You ortn't to talk like that to—"

Mrs. George pounded her fist against the gloved palm. "And let me tell you something else, Bill! Folks of all kinds from all sides are crowding me. But you, the sheriff, you ain't lifting your hands to help no cowman these days—'cept them Johnsons foreclosing mortgages! So—"

"But there is the Law, Miz George," he pleaded, "and—"

"Do you think I'm going to Law to keep off sheep? And rustlers? And nesters that eat my beef? And horse thieves? And cowmen that are drifting their herds onto my grass? No, by God! I'm going to hold my range with guns and men! Now you can climb your horse and start for town. I'm coming right along in after you to tell folks there just exactly what I've told you!"

Mrs. George flipped her hand. The gesture told him to get on horseback. It was very much as if she were firing a puncher, sending him off the ranch.

128

The sheriff was dripping sweat. He tried to glare at Mrs. George but her bright gray eyes were too hot for him. He mopped his neck with the bandana, opened and closed his mouth, hesitated for a time as if about to say something as he looked up at Red, who sat solemn faced, feeling a little sorry for Bill Nims. Then the sheriff climbed heavily into the saddle, reined about, heading for town.

7

It was past afternoon when Red jogged back to the ranch with the dogs following him. He went up to the house, watered and fed his horse, took off the saddle, hung it up on a peg in the open shed. He fed the dogs from a tub of beef scraps. After that he went into the kitchen, had a drink, took a pie out of the pantry and planted himself at a small table.

The stately 'Nita was awakened from her siesta by the rummaging and came in, calm eyed and slow. She saw what he was eating and said in Spanish, "You are still as much a child as when I was a maiden and loved you." She brought him a big mug of cold coffee and the sugar bowl.

'Nita has daughters as old as Red. He had pulled their hair and they had scratched his face when babies. He still at times pulled their hair.

Catherine was waiting for him in the patio and

called as he started through without seeing her, "Where is Hal?"

"He went on into town with Miz George."

"To town!"

Red squirmed a little, hitched up his belt, took a lot of pains with a cigarette. He wanted to tell her that Mrs. George was on to their little trick of pretending to be strangers, but he felt that wouldn't be quite fair to Mrs. George. Tattletaleing wasn't much in Red's line. He shook out the match, broke the stick.

"Listen, Miss Kate, you just forget about last night."

"He was drunk! Oogh." She looked down, twisted her fingers.

"Aw, he was all wore out. Me, I'll go get drunk if you want and show you how a feller really acts."

"You," said Catherine coldly, "aren't being in the least amusing."

Red shrugged his shoulders and went with rattling drag of spurs to visit Bella and the pups.

That night Red borrowed ten dollars from Jeb Grimes and rode 'cross country to a Mexican wedding. He was the only gringo there and welcome. He drank much wine, danced all night, lost the ten dollars at monte, and in the dawn rode back, asleep in the saddle.

He swiped a dozen eggs from 'Nita's crock— she never would fix eggs to suit him—and took them down to the bunkhouse. Joey fried them. The other boys had breakfasted long before. The eggs came out of the skillet looking like burnt flapjacks and were tough as leather; or, as Red thought, just right. He and Joey ate the dozen. Also he had a steak, stewed apples, and nearly a quart of hot coffee, strong as horse liniment.

"Now," he said, stroking his belly, "I'm fit for a bad job I got on my hands today. 'F I ain't back this time tomorrow, Joey, tell Jeb and the boys to mosey over toward the Cross-Box and poke around in the brush. Maybe I'll have fell off and sprained an ankle."

Red took Timton's wadded note from his pocket, unfolded the paper that tore along the creases. He spread it out on the table, reread the scrawl. "Windy and 'Gene?" he said to himself. "I don't wanta believe it, but I'll go have me a look." He lifted a lid of the cook stove and dropped the note into the fire.

CHAPTER SIX

Red rode out into the pasture, huddled the gray he wanted into a bunch, chased the bunch into the corral. On foot, he looped his rope, eyed a skittish mare, threw—and the loop settled over the head of the powerful gray.

"Fooled you!" said Red, half hitching the rope to the snubbing post.

He ran the other horses out and set about saddling The Ghost. Red cussed fluently in a soothing tone. He always talked to horses when working with them, but, not wanting to sound silly if overheard, said things that would have shocked a mule skinner.

When he climbed into the saddle The Ghost pitched a little, but not much. As the horse settled down, Red stroked its neck. "Feller, sometime when *you* been up all night dancing, I'll remember your kindness."

Red stopped at the bunkhouse, ran a ramrod through his rifle to poke out the grease, put the scabbard under his leg and struck out for the hills.

The horse didn't know the way so Red had to stay awake. He whistled some but Yankee Doodle was the only tune he could hit on with certainty. He sang a little to entertain himself and The Ghost put back his ears as if in protest.

Red pushed on, keeping off the ridges that would have shown the horse against the skyline. He was sure that somewhere out there, probably with field glasses, somebody was pretty likely to be keeping a lookout. Along in the middle of the afternoon he began to get into the timber, then turned sharply, working his way up through rough country. Twice he saw deer nosing him. To one he said, "Smart ain't you? Know I don't dare make a racket. Some day," he promised, "I'll come back along up here and skin you for that!"

In his short-legged days when it took two jumps to get saddle-high, Red had hunted all over these hills. He rounded the rocky ridge of a hogback and worked back down slowly toward the edge of the timber. Soon he reined up with ears cocked.

From far off he could hear the bellering of a cow. It told of pain and indignation. He went on, walking his horse.

Soon he got off, tied the horse and crept forward to the edge of a bluff rock ledge, took off his hat, poked his head, Indian fashion, into a bush and looked down on to the cabin and stake fence across the box canyon that made a pasture for the little Cross-Box outfit. He could see two men, so far off they looked about the size of mice, working by a branding fire on a hogtied cow.

"Nice," Red murmured grimly. "Folks is to home."

He went back to his horse, hung his spurs on the horn, pulled the rifle from the scabbard, and worked his way down a deer trail on foot. He got up close to the fence and snuggled down with an eye to a wide crack.

The men were not far from the gate made of poles laid lengthwise where they had a little pile of chips and sticks for their fire. They took a long time over the branding as was needful if they wanted to do the wrong sort of work in the right way, and changed irons two or three times.

When they were ready to turn the cow loose, one man hurried and got on his horse. A full grown cow was mighty likely to charge a man on foot after it had been branded and might have to be thrown; but this cow ran off with tail high and bellered loud.

Both men, from horseback, then put their ropes on another cow and by half dragging, quirting her rump, pull-hauling, they got her up near the fire before throwing her. The cow had to be thrown close up to the fire or it would make a long way to trot back and forth with the running iron.

The punchers seemed enjoying themselves, laughed some and made funny remarks. Red scrouged along the fence until he got to the gate, cocked his rifle and stood up. He wasn't noticed and waited a minute or two; then sung out:

"Mighty hot day for to be playin' with fire!"

The two punchers jerked up their heads then bounced to their feet. The cow, feeling the weight off her head, heaved her body but couldn't rise. She bellowed and threshed with bound legs.

"Gosh a'mighty," Red told them, "do I have to say *pul-ease!*"

At that, both boys slowly crooked their arms upwards and the smaller one called, "Well, if it ain't ol' Red!"

"Yeah. And I never knowed you liked so well to work, Windy!"

"You can see for yerself what a mistake it's been!"

"An' 'Gene there! Why damn both your onery souls! Don't us Dobbses burn our cows in a way that suits you?"

They eyed Red sheepishly.

Red went on. "Now let's not have any more hard feelin's than can be helped. But this is business. So Windy, you first! Use your left hand, unbuckle that belt and let 'er fall!"

Windy did. The belt fell, but the holster was tied low down on his leg. The gun spilled to the ground. Red wore his own holsters tied down, but he didn't think it a good sign in Windy and 'Gene. Bad men usually rigged their holsters that away.

"I'm s'prised at you, Windy. Since when have you got to splittin' seconds when you reach for a gun?"

"It flops around in the way, rasslin' cows," said Windy, apologetic.

"Now 'Gene, you shed your gun."

When the gun fell, Red added, "Windy, take some rope and tie 'Gene's arms up behind him. Do it good."

"Aw Red," Windy coaxed, "ain't our word good?"

Red kept the rifle balanced across a pole of the gate. "Not when you been lyin' like hell with that brandin' iron out there!"

Windy looked humbled and worked with the rope. "He's tied, Red."

"And if you've tied it so he can make a break, it'll be your blame if 'Gene gets hurt."

Windy touched the knots, tightening. "He is tied good. Honest."

"Now take some more rope, fit your wrists behind you in a little loop, then waltz over here to me."

"You make a feller tie hisself up!"

"Don't argy. I was to a dance last night and am sorta not in a good humor."

Windy made a small loop, fitted his wrists into it behind him, trailed the rope over to Red, turned and backed up. Red pulled the rope, then put the rifle down and tied Windy's arms.

"Set down here in the shade, Windy, and rest yourself."

Windy leaned against the fence stakes and slid down. Red made the rope fast to a stake. Then he had 'Gene come over and examined his knots. He made 'Gene sit down about twenty feet from Windy and be tied to a stake.

Red went to the cow, sat on its head, leaned far back and examined the brand. Jim Cross, 'Gene's uncle, had taken advantage of his brand, a cross in a box, to work over Mrs. Dobbs' Arrowhead into a pretty good resemblance of the Cross-Box. Red cut the cow loose, put one hand on the butt of a revolver, flapped his hat at her. Had she charged he would have shot. The cow jumped away, swinging her head far back, trying to get her tongue to where she was burned.

Red went back and squatted down, facing them, and began a cigarette.

'Gene said, peevish, "I bet it was old Rim Cramer that put you on to us. I seen him some time back eyin' the brand, nosy-like, down Monohela way. Wasn't it him?"

"Huh. I come back in the hills today over trails I used for hunting as a kid, heard a cow bellerin', poked around and smelt burnt hide." He was pretty sure that they were fretting with wonder as to how he had got back in the hills without being seen by somebody, most likely Jim Cross himself.

Windy said, "Aw Red, these ain't your cows. And we have had some good times together!"

Red walked over, stuck the cigarette in Windy's mouth, scratched a match. "If they was my cows, I'd give you two my best-sized cussin' and put you to ridin' for me till wages made up for 'em." He began another cigarette, spoke thoughtfully: "Runnin' 'em down to Monohela butchers, hm? That means you sold 'em cheaper than fellows that could steal near-at-hand Hepple cows, hm? The which means you trailed 'em across Hepple range, too, don't it? The which means the Hepples knowed what you was doin' and let you. Most likely they was some encouragin'!" Red looked up, gave 'Gene an accusing stare.

'Gene stared sullenly at the ground, not answering.

"Aw Red," said Windy, trying to be cheerful and change the subject, "it was just a purty girl as is to blame!"

Red sniffed, skeptical. Windy was a chunky little runt of a fellow with a turned-up nose and sparkling eyes.

"Yep. You see, 'Gene wants to marry 'er. She won't do it even to him, so I knowed if she wouldn't marry a handsome feller like him, they wasn't no hope for me. We both felt so bad we turned rustler to hide our sorror."

Red poke a cigarette at 'Gene. "Open your potato catcher."

'Gene was slender, good looking, dark haired. A good kid in days past but never so frank and open-hearted as Windy. Now there was a sort of mean streak that seemed to have worked through the skin since Red had last seen him and was showing on his face. He thrust out his head toward the match, inhaled.

"You know 'er, Red," 'Gene said with some trace of suspicion in his voice. "Sara Timton. She told me about you meetin' them Johnsons that day."

Red squatted down and rolled a cigarette for himself. "So you pair of idjits have, in a way of speakin', been rustlin' cows for Joe Bush, hm? Losing money at his table for to make her smile?"

"That's about the size of it," Windy agreed cheerfully.

"Um-hm," Red went on, "an' maybe Bush he sorta hinted that Hepples wouldn't object overmuch if you snuck change-branded cows 'cross their range down to Monohela?"

'Gene asked, "How do you 'pear to know—I mean *think* you know so much?" He looked mad. "Have you been goin' to see Sara?"

"I go to the Best Bet. Not to see her. Things is changed now some in town, a little, I reckon. Joe Bush he got killed."

"Who done it?" said Windy, as if almost glad.

"Who done it?" asked 'Gene as if he wasn't glad.

139

"Oh, a fool cowboy that Bush throwed a knife at." Casually, "Jim Cross around some'eres?"

Windy tilted back his head, studying the sky, not answering. 'Gene said, "I sorta forget who is around the place today."

"Suits me," Red told them. "He'll be riding in sooner or later."

Windy spoke up, earnest. "Say Red, I'm shore glad 'twas you and not ol' Jeb Grimes as walked in on us!"

"Jeb has him a habit of not taking pris'ners, and that's a fact," Red agreed.

He walked over and picked up their revolvers, poked out the cartridges, tossed the guns aside, rolled each another cigarette, took his rifle and sat down by the gate where he could watch the road up to the cabin. "You boys can take a little snooze."

Red waited a long time. He heard the drumming of hoofs and cocked his head. It was beginning to grow late. Shadows had lengthened. A rider came up through the scrub oaks. Red squatted with rifle lowered.

Windy's voice rose in the stillness. "Lookout, Jim! We're caught! *Run!*"

"You've played hell, right!" said Red and jumped up with a shout: "Pile off that horse, Cross!"

Jim Cross was about a hundred yards off, or a little more. With high lift of arm he jerked his horse to its haunches, setting it back so low the stirrups were almost scraping the ground. The case of field glasses flopped at his side. The horse threw its head high and back. Cross was carrying a rifle across his left arm. He swung it over and fired as if it were a revolver. The bullet splattered chips from the gate post about Red's head. Cross swung at the reins, swerving the horse as he kicked the spurs deep.

Red pulled down on him; fired. Cross reeled back, flinging hands and rifle into the air and slid backwards out of the saddle as the horse plunged into a clattering gallop.

"Is Jim dead?" 'Gene cried out. Then, "Jim? Oh, Jim!"

"He was a good feller," said Windy, sober.

"Now I got to leave you two fellers here a while," Red told them. "An' I'm going to make plumb good and sure you are here when I come back."

Red tied a snug loop about the neck of each. The loop encircled the stake behind, with the knot outside. He emptied their pockets, tossing away pocket knives. If they did manage to get their hands free they couldn't get at the knot outside the fence that held their necks.

He let down the poles of the gate, led out Windy's horse and while putting the poles up, said, "I'll be back soon. You can sing if you want. The dancin', it may come later."

Red walked over to Jim Cross, gave him a look, then rode off.

It was well past sundown when he came back, jogging through the darkness, leading The Ghost and Jim Cross' horse.

He watered and fed the horses first. He hadn't eaten since breakfast, and didn't now; but simply took a drink, then carried a dipper full to each of the boys.

He got a lantern, hobbled 'Gene and Windy so they wouldn't make a break for the bushes, and kept well back beyond reach so they wouldn't make a sudden jump at him. Under the light of the lantern, hung low in a tree, he made them put Jim Cross' body over his saddle and tie it on.

Red told them, sober and earnest, "Now boys, don't make me have to shoot 'cause sure as God makes big potaters out of little uns, I will." Then he put Windy on a horse, hobbled his feet under the horse's belly, tied his hands behind him. He did the same with 'Gene, but worked more cautiously because he trusted 'Gene less. He took the bridles off the horses and fastened the lead rope of Cross' horse to 'Gene's saddle, that of 'Gene's to Windy's horn, that of Windy's to his own.

"Be slow going but we got all night," he told them. Then the small caravan set out at a walk in the starlight for the Dobbs' ranch.

2

They poked along all through the night, so it was after daybreak when they got in.

Four or five men were standing about with shiny fresh-washed faces and the streaks of the comb in their wet hair. The comb was chained to the trunk of a sycamore on which hung an old mirror. They were waiting for Joey to sing out, "Take it away!"

Joey, with drooping mustache a-flutter, came to the door but did not sing out. He flipped the ripped flour sack that he used as an apron up across his shoulder and ran out among the men that moved forward with unconscious half shuffle of feet as Red rode in, leading the string of horses with men, one dead, on them.

Robertson, the old range boss, now rheumatic, limped out well in front, pulled at his beard, swept his eyes along the horses and men. Red swung off stiffly. He was saddle-tired from riding slow and was dead for sleep. Old Robertson yanked hard at his beard and said in his creaky sharp voice:

"Cross-Box, eh? Horses or cows?"

"Cows," said Red. "I left changed brands in the box canyon pasture."

Robertson glared piercingly at Windy, then at 'Gene. Both boys tried to stare back, but their eyes fell. Rheumatic pains and the anger of not being able to set a saddle had made the old foreman's temper ugly as a teased rattler's. He snapped, "Red, why ain't they belly down, too, 'cross their hosses!"

Red threw out his arm in a tired, careless gesture. "That's just why I rode over there myself, alone, instead of lettin' you send somebody—"

His glance searched out the lank dark face of Jeb Grimes, then looked at wrinkled old Harry Paloo. Red's eyes fell on another face: the bony cheeks and bright glazed eyes of that broad-shouldered Buck whom he had met by the stage there in town.

"—somebody," he went on, "as never borrowed their last dollar or slept in their blankets—with them in 'em!"

A little later, getting close to Robertson, Red said defiantly:

"I brung 'em in. Now I hope to God they get away!"

Robertson growled. In a way he didn't have much of a liking for Red who was impudent and bad-spoiled by Mrs. George. "Oh, you do, heh? Then why didn't you let 'em? "

" 'F you ever bite yourself, Mr. Robertson, snake-bite cure won't help none? Who's that puncher in store clothes?"

"Him? Name's Buck. Grub linin', so he says. 'S all I know. Come yest'dy askin' for work."

"Get it?"

"No. Times like these I don't want strangers in the saddle."

Red hung his guns at the head of his bunk, then he and the prisoners washed up, marched in and sat down on the same bench at breakfast. Little was said. It was Robertson's lookout as to how the kid rustlers were guarded.

After breakfast Red dug up a package of tobacco for them, told Joey to wake him the very first minute Mrs. George got home from town, and piled into his bunk.

When he awakened it was dark, supper was long since over. Red went into the kitchen to give Joey a cussing.

"But she ain't home yet," said the cook.

"Then you're forgiven if you give me something to eat. Anything—long as it's plenty. Where's Windy and 'Gene?"

"In the shed back of the blacksmith shop."

Red grunted, not pleased but not complaining. Robertson didn't think rustlers good enough for cowboy bunks.

"That store clothes cowboy still around, Joey?"

"Dunno. He et supper."

The fire was out in the kitchen stove. Red ate a heaping plate of the chopped cold boiled potatoes, heavy with sage, onions, steak, that Joey had fixed to fry in the morning as hash; and he drank much cold coffee.

Joey was poring over an old matrimonial sheet.

145

Such advertised offers of marriage, from widows mostly, fascinated the squirrel-faced cook. He said, turning over his paper, "Jeb and Harry Paloo, they lit out for the Cross-Box to bring in them cows. You done foolish to do that alone, Red."

Red tipped back his chair, yawned, sleep-loggy. He leaned far back, stretching his arms, turning his head slowly. As his eyes crossed the kitchen window his body grew rigid.

A hazily seen face peered through a lower corner of the pane with a revolver's muzzle moving into line. Red's yawn-stretched left arm swept the light over and off the table with a crash as he sent his tipped chair over, falling backwards to the floor, just as the gun roared through the window, shattering glass, throwing a lightning-like flash of flame.

Joey went off his chair with a yell, landed on the floor, scrambled like a broken-backed dog and was still.

Red lay as he fell, not stirring. He was unarmed, never wearing guns around the bunkhouse.

A voice called through the broken pane, eager and pleased: "That evens us, you—"

The man was so sure of his marksmanship that he misguessed why Red went over in the chair, so nearly were fall and shot simultaneous.

A moment later there was a clatter of hoofs, and a yell, challenging and defiant, long-drawn, piercing as a wolf's howl.

Red picked himself up slowly, rubbed at an elbow, called, "Joey?" No answer. Red struck a match, lighted the high bracket lamp on the wall over the stove. Joey was behind the stove, wedged in. He backed out, stammered in whispers, "W-what h-happened?" His walrus mustache looked pretty frayed at the ends.

"Somebody don't like your cookin'," said Red as he turned, solemnly perplexed and went across to the shattered pane, eyed it, trying to think.

A couple of men came running. One was Dutchy the crippled blacksmith. "Vot happen, heh?" The other, a young bronco buster. "Who shot? What happened?"

Red eyed them, nodded, grinned in a wry way. "Go look! If us galoots ain't all afoot, I miss my guess!"

"But why'd he shoot at you?"

"You heard what he said, Joey?" Red asked.

Joey denied having heard anything but the shot. All else was a blank.

"It's all your bad cookin'," Red affirmed, trying to figure why that store clothes cowboy had pulled down on him. For that $1000 reward? Maybe, but why then, "That evens us, you—!"

Perry and Dutchy had gone to look. Red soon heard plaintive cussing as they came back, old Robertson with them.

A weather-beaten, pain-marked, shrewd, honest

fellow, Robertson; also savage. He stamped into the kitchen in spite of rheumatism, said shrilly:

"Windy and 'Gene is gone! And they ain't—"

Red broke in, finished the sentence: "—a horse left within a mile! The hell-bendin' Dobbses, terrors of the range, left helpless, flat afoot! That store clothes cowboy has carried off our rustlers, run off our horses, scairt our cook purt-near to—oh, hell!" He laughed, amused, not happy.

"Why'd he shoot at you?" Robertson demanded, almost accusing. He knew Red's value as a puncher, but thought him too much over-favored by Mrs. George.

"I'm cur'us for to know. He sung out, 'That evens us!' Funny, 'cause he was nice enough there in town when I met 'im."

"Mape he vas a frien' ob dot Cho Push," Dutchy guessed.

Young Perry suggested, "Maybe he'd had a run-in with your dad, times gone by, Red. Thought to get even."

"I reckon," Red agreed, but whether with Dutchy or Perry he didn't say.

The mysterious Buck had worked it slick, like one who had done the same sort of thing before. He had first stolen a couple of horses and saddles and led them quietly off into the shadows. He had run the kept-up horses out of the corral into the pasture, leaving, as Red had guessed, the

148

Dobbses all flat afoot. After that, he had held up the Mexican, Sanzo, who was keeping watch over Windy and 'Gene, then knocked him over the head with a gun barrel and sent the rustlers on out to the waiting horses. He came to the bunkhouse, looking for Red and found him yawning in the kitchen.

"You told me as how you hoped they'd get away!" Robertson yelled, right up close to Red's face. "I hope you're happy! Sanzo is purt-near dead. May die. You—you ain't got a lick o' sense!"

He went out, limping and fuming.

3

It was about twenty-four hours later that Mrs. George, miles ahead of the buckboard, got home from town. She didn't give the dogs a cheery word as they leaped about her stirrups. When she got off she struck at them with half idle swing of quirt for crowding about her legs and making her stumble as she started on to the veranda.

It was a starlit night. She stopped short, jerked up her head. Some one was standing in the shadows of the porch, not hiding but partly hidden. It looked like Red—so much like Red that she called out sharply, faintly incredulous:

"Red?"

"Why, yes'm, sure."

149

Mrs. George came close. Her eyes were fixed in a hard look, anxious and doubtful. She reached out and touched him almost as if not quite sure that he was there. She grabbed him with sudden jerk, shook him, and began to laugh. The dogs, encouraged by her laughter, crowded near, rose up and pawed with mouths open as if laughing, too.

Red said, "You act sorta funny."

"Funny? I don't believe in ghosts, but for weeks after Dobbs died I seemed to see him at times. It was just wanting to see him, I suppose. And you—why a fellow named Buck claims there in town that he shot you in a quarrel here at the ranch. Wants to be paid that $1000! So I hear. I didn't lay eyes on the fellow. Oh, Red, I must like you an awful lot from the way I have been feeling!"

"That feller bragged some too soon, a little. It happened this away. I'd been over to the Cross-Box . . ."

"Jim Cross! And Windy? And 'Gene?" Mrs. George was hurt and angered. She flung quirt, gloves, and hat at a chair and dropped heavily on to the swing. "No doubt of it, Red. You have figured right. They wouldn't have done it if the Hepples hadn't encouraged 'em. And I purt-near believe you're right, too, in thinking Mrs. Hepple wouldn't start trouble with me unless the Johnsons nudged her into it!"

". . . and," Red finished, "we had one hell of a time catching horses afoot out there in the pasture this morning!"

Mrs. George rested her elbows on her knees, lifted her head, looked across at him. "Red, all my life I've had to fight like hell. I've won out because I had men like you, Jeb Grimes, Harry Paloo, Hawks, and Robertson behind me. I've still got 'em, thank God!" She laughed with sudden sharpness. "Be like old times again! I won't knuckle under to their damned Law and Order. I'll raise hell and keep on raising hell till the Government sends in troops. How'll you like that?"

Red grinned. "I bet nearly all the old time cowmen'll chip in and help you, too. If ever anything like we think they're doin' can be proved on them Johnsons—they'll look nice danglin' to a rope over a cottonwood limb!"

Mrs. George tossed up her hands and lay back, drew up her feet, snuggled against the cushions of the couch. In the shadowed lamplight she seemed younger, almost gay. "Bring me a drink, Red. Tell 'Nita to fix me a snack. Tell her to tell Kate there is company coming. Have something to eat ready." She rolled a cigarette, held the match after shaking it out. "Windy and 'Gene? And I once liked those boys." She tossed the match away.

Red fetched the drink. Mrs. George emptied

the glass, gave it back to him to put down. "Dora Harris is coming. She is a beauty, Red. I like her. I told Slim to drive slow so she and Mr. Harold Mason could talk."

"You think maybe he'll like her?"

"I know men! Why, even Dobbs was human. And I always thought the first Mrs. Hepple an awful fool for packing up and getting out with that young un. You don't hold a man or horse by cutting him loose to be roped by a rustler!"

She ate the snack 'Nita brought, had another drink or two, then said she would go in and freshen up a bit before the company arrived.

Red sat and thought. Pretty soon the collies stirred, barked a time or two, and started off down the road. How they knew it was the ranch wagon was more than Red could figure but there was a certain something in their barking that said so. The buckboard climbed slowly. The horses were tired.

Red took his horse and walked off into the shadows, squatted down.

Mrs. George came hurrying out and Catherine, not looking eager, was with her to welcome the company. Hawks drawled, "Whoa-up!" Mr. Mason got out, then Harris' niece. Red could see only blotches of silhouette as figures moved against the lamplight on the veranda. He could hear voices dimly, not words. Catherine and the Harris girl shook hands. Slim Hawks set some

152

bags down on the veranda. He made a gaunt angular shadow-figure and jerked his head aside to spit before giving heed to something Mrs. George was saying to him in a gay manner. Hawks wiped his mouth with the back of his hand and pushed his hat up almost off his head. Red couldn't hear but he knew Hawks was saying joyfully, "I'll be damned!" He climbed on the seat, shook the reins and began to sing, soft.

Red, walking his horse, cut down hill, got on the road and stopped, blocking the way. " 'Lo, Slim?"

Hawks pulled up. " 'Lo, you damn ghost!"

Red got out of the saddle and climbed on the seat, holding his bridle reins. "Don't try to make out you are fat. Move over. The edge of a sliver is plenty of room for you to set on."

"I got a bottle I nussed careful alongside of me."

"Who give it to you?"

"Jim, in the Best Bet."

"Did you take off your gun?"

"Miz George she said to. Awso, I got somepin f'r you. A letter with nice smellum on it." Hawks pulled an envelope from inside his shirt and held it first to his nose, then to Red's. "Smell."

"For me?" Red took it. "Who from?"

"That Sara girl. I promised not to tell nobody."

"Why'd she write me a letter if she thought I

153

was dead? One look at you and anybody could know you ain't goin' when you die to where I am."

"She give it me day 'fore yestidy. It was a'ready wrote an' she was waitin' f'r some handsome feller like me to come along from the ranch. An' I hope when I die I don't go to where you are. I don't like sulphur smell!"

Red didn't want the fellows to see him reading a letter, especially one with perfume on it, so he took a piece of candle and went to the blacksmith shop. The envelope was pink and smelled strong. The paper was pink and the writing in pencil.

Dere Red It was awful swete of you to shot Jo Bush on account of me. I hop to return the faver sometim. The other gamlers you shot neded it to. I am writin to say you had beter lookout. I here tell that feler Buck is mad at you an he has ben talkin some a lot to them Jonsons an that Miz Hepel. I dont want you to git hurt nor for eny body to git that reword that they hav got postered up for you. I shore dont. Pleas beleve Im awful gratefull. Yur true frend Sara.

Red sniffed the paper. It had a smell a little like the soap Catherine used on the poodle, but was much stronger. Very pleasant, Red thought. He read the letter again then held it to the candle, burning it. If the letter had come sooner, Buck might have been one surprised hombre before he rode off the ranch.

Thinking it over, Red decided that Sara was a mighty nice girl after all.

CHAPTER SEVEN

The next morning Red had The Ghost over to the blacksmith shop where the crippled Dutchy, with thick arms bare, a big leather apron on his belly and a meerschaum pipe between his teeth, was nursing a hind foot in his lap and paring a hoof. Red rubbed The Ghost's nose and spoke soothingly.

Hal Mason came sauntering up. He looked nervous, washed out, and pretty much down at the mouth.

"Howdy," said Red.

"Good morning." Mason looked as if he wanted to say something but had forgot the words as Red had seen kids do when reciting some poetry at a church social. Mason stooped, picked up a stick, and began breaking off little bits, tossing each down near his foot as if playing a game by himself. His eyes wavered across Red's face as he asked, "I wonder if I can have a word with you?"

"Sure can. Go right ahead."

Mason looked at Dutchy. "I mean alone."

"Oh, that Dutchman don't understand English!" said Red, loud.

Dutchy, good-humored, mumbled through

clenched teeth, holding his pipe firm, that Red was a bow-legged liar. Mason was further warned to have nothing to do with him. The warning was in pretty thick English, as well as muffled by the pipe stem, and so unheeded.

Dutchy patiently waddled to his forge, plunged the shoe into the coals, pumped the bellows, took out the red hot iron, beat it with almost dainty blows, making slight changes. He soused the sizzling iron into a tub of black water, fitted the shoe.

"Some day," said Dutchy, "you ride him from men that want to hang you, den you tank me maype for doin' the job right." He called it "shob" and beamed, flapping his hand in dismissal.

Mason came close alongside of Red and they walked off together, the horse following with slow *clump, clump, clump,* on the sandy ground.

"Where we won't be interrupted," said Mason uneasily.

"Matter?"

"Catherine has told me that she told you all about us. I mean that we are married."

"Oh, me, I been busy with one thing and another, but 'pears like I sorta remember."

"And *you* told Mrs. Dobbs!" Mason's look was accusing, but he kept his voice down, tense and strained as if afraid he would scream. His voice trembled. His hand was trembling too. He looked nervous and angered, like a man a little scared but who means to go through with something unpleasant.

Red eyed him up and down with aloof insolence. Coolly, "Well, now, how'd you guess all that?"

"Then you admit it?"

Red's eyes narrowed with much the scrutinizing look of a fellow thinking about buying a horse from a dealer he doesn't trust.

Mason was a good looking young man, all right. Nothing wrong on the surface. A bit fat of face but he had straight eyes. What lay heart-deep hadn't yet been brought to view; and Red wondered some. Except for Miss Kate's interest in the fellow, Red would have made Mason's life miserable just on the principle that Easterners, like sheep, ought to stay off the range.

He thought things over and said, "Well, feller. Since you think I've told her, why don't you just waltz up to Mrs. Dobbs and say, 'Bein' as how now you know me an' Miss Kate is married'— something like that. See what happens. She'd have your hide nailed to the barn door 'fore you could say Jack Rob'son!"

"Well, I admit that I am a little afraid of the old lady."

"Of *who?*"

"Of Mrs. Dobbs," Mason corrected readily. "I didn't mean disrespect. She is a remarkable

158

woman. But can you tell me why, if she doesn't know—*why* does she see to it that Catherine and I aren't alone together a minute?"

"Anything you want to know about cows and horses, I can purt-near tell you. Otherwise, I'm smartest when I don't talk about what I maybe don't know."

"Catherine says Mrs. Dobbs thinks more of you than anybody else on the ranch so I thought perhaps—"

"That I run an' blabbed to her, hn? Tattle-taled for to make her like me? Huh!"

"No, no, I—"

"Listen, you. She wouldn't give a bushel of me for one Jeb Grimes. The which shows her good sense. Come on, Spook." Red shook the halter, wanting to get away.

"But a minute, please. I am in a dreadful quandary and—"

"A what?"

"Mix-up. Muddle. I don't know what to do. Last night after everybody was asleep, I went to Catherine's room and we talked. Catherine thinks—do you think there will be a range war with the Hepples?"

"Hm?"

"A feud? Fights? Men killed?"

"Why you and Miss Kate frettin' so over them Hepples? Ever' since she come, she's spoke up anxious-like about 'em. 'F you all wanta worry,

worry about us handsome Dobbses gettin' hurt. Not them slabsided Hepples."

Mason turned red, looked down, stammered a little, hesitated, lifted his head. The words came out as if squeezed. "Catherine says that I must tell you. I am a Hepple. Harold Mason Hepple."

Red was rolling a cigarette. His fingers paused. His gaze lifted to the edge of his lowered hat brim. He said softly, "Keep a-talkin', feller!"

"Catherine says there is nobody else we can trust to—to help us!"

"You are old Dingley Hepple's boy?"

"Yes."

"An' married to Mrs. Dobbs' gran'daughter!"

"Yes. My mother's people are Masons and I took—"

"How you come to marry Miss Kate?"

"She is a friend of Col. Howland. So am I. We met through him. He knew all about this crazy feud. He approves of the marriage and—and when Mrs. Dobbs wrote Catherine to come here to the ranch, we had just been married. Col. Howland advised her to go and for me to come later, as I did."

Red finished his cigarette, taking much care. Across the cigarette as he wet the paper he again studied Mason's face and took a deep breath. "You all was afraid some, maybe, that Miz George wouldn't leave Miss Kate no money if she knew her gran'daughter was married to a Hepple, hm?"

"Well, in a way—why, yes." Mason was trying to hide a slight embarrassment under frankness. "There seemed no reason to throw away— she is very wealthy, isn't she?" He asked for confirmation, not facts.

"These days," Red told him, "no cowmen 'pears to have much money, 'cept your folks. Young Pinky, they say, is a spender. So's your step-maw. Do you expect to get anything when your dad dies?"

"Not that I know of. Or expect. Why?"

"Hm, just cur'us. Your dad, I hear tell, is mighty sick. Sorta crippled in the legs."

"I would like to see him. He was good to me. You can imagine how Catherine and I feel to hear Mrs. Dobbs abuse the Hepples and boast of—"

"If I was you," said Red, inhaling deep, "I'd do some imaginin' as to how poor old Miz George is going to feel when she learns!"

Mason asked, nervous and serious: "What do you think she will do?"

"I don't know. I won't try to guess. You seen her lay her quirt on old Huskins. That was a sample of what she can do. Most near the first thing I can remember as a kid, no higher than to your knee, is seein' her throw her arms 'round old Jeb Grimes and kiss him square on the mouth!

That, too, is a sample of what she's liable to do if you please her a heap."

"What did he do?" Mason asked with a glimmer of hope.

"Well, sir," Red told him in a pleased voice, "Jeb he walked backwards with a rifle in his hands for about fifteen mile, picking you Hepples out of the saddle when you closed in. Jeb was leadin' a horse. John Dobbs, bad hurt, was tied on that horse."

Mason made a sound vaguely like a muffled groan and shuddered.

"I was just a little shaver them days, but I mind Jeb never twitched an eyebrow. He didn't like your folks then. He 'specially don't like 'em these days!"

Mason forced a smile. "It isn't pleasant to hear you talk that way of—of my family."

"Feller," said Red, without anger, just speaking plain, "it ain't pleasant to Dobbses for to know Ding Hepple's boy hopes some day to run this here ranch!"

"But, good God, Red, I have nothing to do with the feud!"

"And you hadn't better have—'cept as a Dobbs man ort! I wish you hadn't told me. I don't much dislike you personal. You called me *servant* that first night and I wanted to break your neck but—"

"I'm sorry. I was drinking. I am not used to drinking. I made an ass of myself all the way 'round." He smiled a little. "I don't know what you'll think of Miss Harris, either, when I tell you that she also is in love with a Hepple!"

Red grunted, "Pink?"

"Yes, Pinky, as you call him. She and Pinky fell in love on first sight there in town."

Red dropped his cigarette, ground it with a toe. "I don't give a whoop in hell about who she loves, or don't. And I don't wish *you* no bad luck, special. But you'll have plenty if you don't hit the saddle and show some grit before Miz George finds out you and Miss Kate are married. When she finds out, too, that you are a Hepple— Gosh a'mighty, how I wish you hadn't told me! If I don't tell her, and she finds out I knowed all along, she'll skin me alive. 'F I do tell her, she'll skin you!"

"What on earth can I do to show Mrs. Dobbs that I have, as you call it, grit?" Mason asked, eager but a little helpless.

"Can you shoot?"

"I have hunted squirrels and things."

"Can you ride?"

"I have ridden, some."

"Ever have any fights?"

"Only as a school boy."

"Win 'em?"

"Not all, no."

Red mused a little, "Tomorrow, early, some fellows are ridin' over to Cocheno Valley to have

163

a talk with some sheepherders. They won't want you along. But you might ask Miz George if you can go. More'n likely she'll say 'Yes.' You'll get saddle-sore and hungry. You'll maybe get shot. Them fellers was hired to fight, not herd sheep. A man was sent over to tell 'em to up an' git. They sent the man back with word to come an' put 'em off. Which only goes to show what damn fools sheepherders are!"

"I'll ask her," said Mason and set his jaw.

Red went on, stumbling on high heels, dragging the rowels, saying things to himself. He thought, "Howsomever, nobody ever called old Dingle Hepple a coward, so his boy ought to have some grit. My dad sorta half way admired old Ding, so maybe I ain't doing so very wrong to give Ding's boy a chance to get hisself admired. But Miz George'll throw conniptions fits. She's got to remember how Dobbs was all crippled up by Hepple lead."

2

Grizzled old Robertson was giving young Perry, the bronco buster, hell. Perry stood red, helpless, and ashamed, slowly rubbing his shoulder. He had just been thrown by as pretty and well-built horse as was in the Dobbs herd.

Robertson yanked at his beard with one hand, shook his fist at Perry. "Bronco buster, you!" he snarled. "Best damn hoss—an' you let him throw

164

you! You been hired to *ride* hosses, not make outlaws out of 'em! A hoss that ain't been rode gits it into his head he can't be rode!" Robertson's leg hurt and he cussed a blue streak, flung out his arm. "Git yore duds an' git! You're fired!"

Young Perry went off, silent and rubbing his shoulder.

Robertson hobbled up to Red. "You, Red. Go pile on that Homer hoss an' ride 'im, you hear me? Ride 'im, gosh-blame-blankety-blank till there ain't a buck left in 'im! He's out thar now with his head up like he was about to crow!"

Red knew the horse, a powerful black. All the Homer strain were ferocious buckers. Red's sympathy was with Perry, who was a nice boy.

Busting broncos on a full stomach was a good way to get seasick, so Red passed up his dinner; and rode the horse. He got the worst shaking up he had had in years, knew he would be stiff and sore for maybe a week. He washed up, changed his clothes, and suddenly aware of hunger, went clattering into the kitchen.

Joey squatted on his haunches with a knife out at arm's length and was shedding tears into a pan of onions as he peeled. Red said, "You are too tender hearted for to be a cook. So how about not letting me starve?"

Joey brushed at his long mustache tips with the back of a hand. "You've stole enough grub from

165

me to know where it is. Whatever the hell has got into Perry, do you reckon?"

"Why?"

"He lit out just now with his warbag 'cross the horn. I called outa the winder at him, and he yelled back, 'To hell with this outfit. I'm goin' over an' ride for the Hepples!' "

Late that afternoon a little Mexican kid came down and told Red the Señora wanted to see him.

Red promptly roused himself off the bunk and began slipping on his boots. He was already sore and stiff and grumbled to old Harry Paloo who gently strummed his guitar:

"I miss my dinner. Now I'm liable to miss my supper. 'F I was old and useless, like your galoots, I could set around and be over-fed."

Paloo, a mild old fellow, nodded, smiling in agreement. Red dusted his hat against his leg, tossed it on his head, reached for his guns. "Since that Buck feller, I don't trust even my shadder around here. Reckon I'm gettin' skittish—like you brittle-legged, wore-out old cow-chasers."

Old Paloo hummed a love song, rolling back his head, looking at the ceiling. He was one of the best and quickest rifle shots in the country and his old hide was weighted with lead. Perhaps even now he was dreamily thinking of tomorrow, and sheepherders.

By way of dressing with care, since there was company up to the house, Red slipped on an old

166

vest, frayed at the back and all but one button off in front. That button never would come off. He had himself sewn it on with pack thread.

" 'F I felt any stiffer," Red commented, "I'd go steal Mr. Robertson's cane."

He went out with wide stiff-legged stride, clumping along as if on short stilts. In the corral he eyed the horses that were being kept up. "If you pitch," he told the horse as he saddled up, "I'll bite you to death!"

He climbed into the saddle stiffly. Every joint seemed a-creak; but as soon as he was settled, familiarity and life-long habit overcame the stiffness.

Mrs. George was alone in the patio with the collies sprawled about near her. She had on a nice dress and slippers, but her feet were cocked up on the chair's seat before her. A bag of tobacco lay in her lap and she fiddled with the tag.

"You told Hal Mason about Cocheno Valley?"

"Um-hm."

"Why'd you put him up to wanting to go?"

"You said he wanted for to see the west, some."

Mrs. George smiled grimly. "Well, I'm telling Jeb to take him. If Jeb shoots *you,* don't blame me!"

"I never blamed you for nothin'. Never will."

"Nice speech Red. Keep on, and you'll be a first-rate lady's man. You know, I think even Kate is beginning to wish Mr. Mason would top off a bronc like you did this afternoon and shoot a couple of men. Why else would Mr. Mason suddenly feel inspired to go on a long hard ride to be shot at by sheepherders? By the way, you are staying up here for dinner."

"Aw, gosh a'mighty, Miz George. Let me go back to the bunkhouse. I'm hungry. I can't eat good before people."

"Shut up. Kate has been telling Dora you seem such a sweet, gentle boy to be a terrible outlaw!"

Red fidgeted and itched. He swept a palm at his cowlick, twitched at his waist band, stood on one foot, then on the other, grinned and protested, "Aw, don't!" Then, "I bet me you was nice at their age!"

"Me?" Mrs. George chuckled. "I was a skinny, red-faced, bad-tempered terror. I had every man in the country but John Dobbs scairt of me. Maybe that's why I loved him! Let's have a drink. Get the whisky."

Red went into the kitchen, pulled one of the girl's hair and got slapped, not hard. He took a big spoon and raked some fried potatoes out of the skillet on to a plate and ate them rapidly with his fingers. He was hungry. 'Nita, not knowing he was staying for dinner, gave him the fried leg and thigh of a chicken while one of her daughters poured a big mug full of hot coffee and piled in sugar. He was eating as fast as he could, hurrying, when Mrs. George looked in.

She said, "Oh, that's what you're doing, eh? All right. But I thought you maybe had bolted." She came into the kitchen, held out her hand. "I'll take a gizzard myself."

One of the girls poked out two fried gizzards and offered them on a saucer. Mrs. George reached for the salt and ate with her fingers. "But let's have that drink." They had the drink. Mrs. George had another piece of chicken and some fried potatoes. She ate with her fingers, standing.

"Now, Red, we can eat dinner slow and finicky and them city folks will think we have got manners." She washed her hands and wiped them on a towel behind the door. "Come on. If I leave you here there won't be anything to put on the table."

At the table Red wondered if he oughtn't help a little somehow when he saw Mr. Mason hurrying to place the chairs for three ladies, all sitting down at the same time. The girls looked mighty pretty; and Mr. Mason looked funny in a black suit with long coat tails and a stiff white shirt front, big as a meat platter. Red fastened the lone button on his vest.

Red scarcely said a word. He noticed that Mr. Mason touched only the brim of a wine glass. From time to time Red caught Dora's velvet eyes looking at him as if she sort of liked him a little. He dropped his eyes, pleasantly embarrassed. Catherine, too, seemed trying to be nice to him.

Red wondered if maybe he hadn't missed a lot by not being a lady's man.

After they had coffee on the patio and talked a little, Catherine said, "Please, Red, won't you take me for a little walk in the starlight?"

He didn't want Mason to feel bad, so he said, "Why you wanta go stumblin' round in the dark?" But of course he went and found out that he had been cat's-pawed into a conspiracy. It had been arranged for Catherine to go off with him; later Mason and Dora would stroll out and meet them.

"Then Hal and I can be together," Catherine explained. "Alone."

He grunted, somehow feeling a little cheated; also very much aware of what Mrs. George's anger would be like if she ever found out he had been helping to fool her.

A half hour later as he walked away into the shadows with the graceful Dora Harris, Red felt nice and warm and a little silly. She held his arm with a kind of frank liking. The perfume she used was different from any he had ever smelled. There was a witching seductiveness about her that could very easily cause a man to make a fool of himself. He rather liked the sensation. His muscles ached and his joints creaked. Tomorrow would be another hard day. Damn dangerous day, too. He ought to have been in his bunk. But Dora was pretty, sweet, and gentle. It was nice.

They sat down on a flat rock. She took off his

hat. "That's better. Now I can see your face." Her voice was soothing and low, like soft music.

"Red?"

"Yes'm."

"You ought to be awfully proud of yourself, Red?"

"Me? Huh. What I done?"

"Everybody likes you so much. My uncle. And he really doesn't like many people! And Mrs. Dobbs. And Catherine. And Mr. Mason. You must be a nice boy!"

"Me? Oh, I am, sure. But they's one feller don't like me?"

"Who?"

"Pinky Hepple," Red blurted. "And is it so?"

"What, Red?"

"That you are in love with Pink?"

"You mean Charley Hepple?"

"Folks call him Pink."

"Yes, Red," she said, and put her hand on Red's arm, "I do love him. It was just one of those things that happen, like touching a match to powder. The moment I saw him!"

Red drew a big breath. "Um-m."

"Why, now even this dry hot dusty country seems beautiful."

" 'Tis!"

"I didn't think so at first. Do you know what it is to be in love, Red. Really in love?"

"Sure. It's like I feel toward Miz George!"

Dora patted his hand, as if approving. Then, "Why do you say Charley doesn't like you?"

"Joe Bush, for one thing. They was brothers."

"Oh, but he told me he had never, never approved of his brother, the gambler. That no one should judge him by the sort of man Joe Bush was."

Red set his teeth on edge to keep from swearing. Pinky was an awful liar, smooth and plausible, and had denied his brother, the gambler, to make a better impression on this sweet gentle girl. "Hm, how he come to say a thing like that?"

"Because Uncle says Joe Bush needed killing."

"What Judge Harris think of Pinky?"

"Oh, he misunderstands him, Red. He thinks because Joe Bush—but Charley says all his life he has been blamed because of his brother! When I go back to town, we are going to run away and be married."

"Yeah?" Red understood. It was easy for folks, when they first met him, to think Pinky a nice boy. He smiled pleasant and looked honest; was handsome.

"You don't like him?" Dora said, softly reproachful.

"Me? I'm a Dobbs man, hair, hide, and hoof."

"Then you ought to like him," Dora exclaimed, earnest and coaxing. "He is doing everything he can to prevent trouble between his ranch and Mrs. Dobbs. He told me so!"

172

Red said "Huh," and let it go at that. Catherine and her husband were coming.

"We'll have to change partners again," said Mason. "And by the way, Red, I am going with you fellows in the morning." There was some pride in his voice. "Three o'clock, Mrs. Dobbs said." He looked at his watch, slanting the face to catch the starlight. "Nearly ten now."

Red peered up at him and felt maybe he hadn't done right in putting Mason up to going along. The boy was liable to get hurt, bad hurt. It was going to be a fight; most likely a bad one. They usually were when Jeb Grimes rode down on anybody. If Mason got killed, Red would always feel mighty sorry. Still, if Mason didn't show some grit somewhere, sometime, he might just as well go off and hide in a hole, stay there and starve.

Mason and Dora walked back to the house. Catherine said, teasing but a little spiteful too, like a kitten showing claws, "I suppose you don't think much of Dora since she, too, is in love with a Hepple?"

Red snapped, "Pinky ain't a Hepple!"

"Oh. Just what do you mean by that?" Catherine was ready to be angry.

"He's a Bush. They're worse 'n Hepples any day."

"And you," said Catherine with temper a-flare, "are a cad! And a brute! And . . ."

Red got a pretty good-sized tongue lashing. He took it patiently, hazily amused that she had so angrily misunderstood. He had spoken, having it in mind that old Dingley Hepple was a fighter; but that the Bushes had a blackleg streak in them, were tricky liars, false-faced, and mean.

CHAPTER EIGHT

At three o'clock in the morning Red, sore and stiff, sleepy and feeling mean, squatted on a grain sack in the chill starlight. Three saddled horses, with bridle reins trailing, held their heads low, shifted their feet, stomped as if in fretful protest.

Old Robertson limped along with Grimes and little Harry Paloo, having a last word and coming out to see them off. He, fierce and peevish, said, "Now understand, Jeb, what we want is skelps! It's all wrong ever to have trouble twict with the same batch o' sheepherders, so make plumb sure they git their bellies full! But if you git a chanct to ask questions, speak up an' find out who's behind 'em." Robertson waggled a lean arm toward Red. "The kid here says it's them Johnsons. I don't much believe it myself, 'cause, God A'mighty, bankers in a cow country that throwed in with sheepherders 'ud be ruint!"

Jeb listened, said nothing. Robertson twisted about to look up toward the ranch house and pulled at his beard, but he, too, was now silent. Paloo took up the reins of his horse and waited, also glancing up toward the house.

Jeb Grimes looked neither to the right nor left. He rolled a cigarette, lighted it, swung into the saddle.

175

"Comin', kid?" Paloo asked.

"Me, I'll wait a little. Miz George might think we rode off a-purpose."

Robertson swung up his arm in a parting gesture as the two old lean rangemen rode off. He then turned with clumping stiffness and bent to peer at Red. "Jest who in hell is that feller Mason, Red?"

"Some kid old Col. Howland wished off on us, so I hear."

Robertson growled, stooped lower. "You know Sanzo's trick of playin' he don't know English so he won't have to talk to them he don't like."

"Yep."

"Well, he tells me he overhear'd that feller say to the girl somethin' about, 'When I git this ranch, I'll run things more like they ort a-be.' I jes wondered some."

"Yeah?" Red lifted his head in a tense vague stare. "Hm. Well, me, I'm goin' to do some wonderin', too, Mr. Robertson."

"Here he comes, I reckon."

Mason rode down off the hillside and out of the shadows at a floppy gallop. A horse had been kept up there for him. He was late, he said, because the Mexican hadn't come to saddle up.

Old Robertson's snort could have been heard as far as a bugle's toot. To his way of thinking, a fellow that needed help in saddling would want somebody around to help button up his pants.

Red got off the grain sack with weary effort, moved as if bowed and crippled. He felt just that way. He rubbed The Ghost's nose, said, "Treat me gentle, son," then climbed into the saddle. " 'By, Mr. Robertson. Come along, Mason."

Red was riled a little by that hearsay remark reported by Sanzo; so it soothed him some to notice that the way Mason set a saddle would soon make him tired and sore. They hadn't gone a half mile before Mason gasped, "Is it necessary to go so fast?"

"We got to catch them ahead."

Red pushed on at a lope. It wasn't long before they overtook Grimes and Paloo, jogging side by side. Paloo looked around, smiled pleasantly. Jeb did not turn his head. They went at a trot. Jeb would seldom push a horse faster. In the silence there was faint creak of leather, tingling jingle of spurs, the steady *chuff-chuff, chuff-chuff* of hoofs.

Mason had found the gallop hard. The steady trot became agony. To the man that does not set a saddle well, trotting is like being dragged downstairs on his tail bone.

"I've got a pain in my side," said Mason.

"Didn't you ride as a kid?" Red asked.

"Only ponies. I don't see how I can stand this pain."

He was in pain. Red didn't for a moment think otherwise, but didn't feel sorry. He suggested, "Pile off and rest. Then catch up."

Mason had a look on his face as if struggling as he rode on, then presently he drew down to a walk, fell back, was soon left out of sight behind a rise of ground, and was not seen again that day.

Paloo turned around a few times, but not Jeb Grimes. He was tall in the saddle, seldom moved his head, but that was no reason for thinking he did not somehow know what went on behind him.

2

Along about eight o'clock they reached a muddy waterhole, gave the horses a drink, opened a can of tomatoes apiece, ate some bread and cheese, and rode on.

A little before noon they came to the stake and shale fence at the mouth of Cocheno Valley where Dobbses wintered stock. The fence barred it from grazing in the summer.

Red piled off, opened the gate. They rode in. Here the valley looked as barren as if it had been burned over. The ground was gray and brown instead of black, but the destruction was complete—more complete than by fire. Fire at least left roots, and after rain grass would come up rich as ever. Sheep grazed close, and their cloven hoofs chopped the earth as if hacked by tiny grub-hoes. Also they left a stench offensive to cattle. Following wherever sheep grazed, the

178

loco weed sprang up—or so ranchers thought and said. To cowmen, a fellow that ran sheep was worse than a man that fired the range; and anybody caught firing the range was shot down on the spot, or any other spot where he could be found.

To Red's eyes it looked as if the distant valley were covered with a mess of woolly maggots. Hepple cows in the valley would have been better than anybody's sheep. Far ahead they saw a light spring wagon on the hillside and, near by, some hobbled burros.

Jeb Grimes didn't change his gait. Simply rode forward at a trot. It was like him to go into a fight, and he had been in plenty, just about as if he meant to be killed. Men with rifles in their hands began to rise up from near about the wagon. Red counted six on foot, one man on horseback. The herders had known that some day soon cowmen would come. A herder climbed to the wagon seat and scanned the country to see if other horsemen were coming down on them. It wasn't easy to believe that only three would ride in.

The sheepherder on horseback rode out in front of the wagon, raised his hand, bawled, "Stop right whar yuh air, you fellers!"

Grimes, Paloo, and Red were neck and neck at the trot, with rifles in the crook of their arms.

The herders on foot scattered a little, moving fast with the scramble of men who think maybe they have already waited a little too long. Some got behind the wagon, others scrouged down on the ground. The man on horseback slid off his horse and laid the rifle across the saddle, yelled at the top of his voice:

"Halt, damn it! Halt whar yuh air!"

It was beneath the dignity of Jeb Grimes to talk back to sheepherders. He called to Red, "You talk easy. Speak up!" Jeb swung to the right, and Paloo, as if at a word of command, veered to the left.

Red went on up to within easy speaking distance of a hundred feet or so. The fellow behind his horse looked anxiously from right to left. He knew Jeb Grimes and he knew Harry Paloo; and Red knew him.

Red reined up and called, "Well if it ain't Mike Comber! Gosh a'mighty, Mike, you allus took a bath reg'lar! How it come you turned sheepherder?"

Mike Comber up and spoke his little piece. "You fellers git out! This here is public domain, the which you got fenced illegal. Me an' my sheep stay!"

Mike Comber had been in the country a long time, worked off and on for various outfits, had a few cows of his own, a wife and some kids. As he spoke his little piece to Red, Comber's head swung uneasily toward Grimes, tall and motionless in saddle, who had reined up and looked ready.

" 'Public domain!' " Red jeered. "You never got words like them 'tween your jaws, Mike, 'less somebody pried open your mouth an' poked 'em in. Who?"

"Me an' my sheep got a right here!"

"Your sheep? Hell, Mike, we know they ain't yours. They b'long to somebody as ain't got the grit to run his own sheep on our range, so he's hired you to come an' get shot at for 'imself! *Who?*"

"They is law in this land!" said Comber, speaking some more of his piece. "You all interfere with my rights an'—"

"Mike, you're an old cowman. These ain't your sheep. This ain't your range. If your wages is big enough to make you willing to get bad hurt earnin' 'em, all right! You and these sheep are in here just to make trouble for Miz George. We know that. So if it's trouble you want, be happy that it has come! Whose are they?"

"Mine!"

"You're a liar!"

Comber shot. Red had guessed that he would and sat with toes at the edge of his stirrups. Red threw himself out of the saddle, and the bullet passed just about where his head had been. Guns opened up like a bunch of fire-crackers.

Harry Paloo could nearly play a tune on a rifle. He thought Red had been knocked out of the saddle. Paloo's first shot killed Comber's horse so as to put Comber out in the open; and his second shot knocked Comber sprawling as he tried to dodge down behind the dead horse. Then Paloo swung off and began firing across his saddle.

Red dropped the rifle without firing it and went for his revolvers. The Ghost wasn't gun-broke and began to plunge. The reins were on the ground and he had been trained not to drag them, but he plunged and sidled, kicking up a dust and almost trampling Red.

Grimes didn't draw foot from stirrup and shot with almost rhythmic timing. He was fast, steady, unhurried, and deadly. He didn't seem to notice at all that men were blazing at him. A herder had some dust knocked in his eyes, squalled, jumped up, flung away his rifle and ran. Two other men rose up with hands lifted. The other three on the ground over there by the wagon didn't move. Grimes pointed his rifle at the two fellows who were surrendering, said, "Git goin'!" and gave the muzzle a swerve by way of emphasis. They started off, walking fast, with faces jerking about in fear of bullets at their backs.

Red went over and kneeled down by Comber. "Mike, you ort've knowed better!"

Comber had been shot through the hips. He

said, pleading, "Give me a drink, will yuh, Red?"

Red took up Comber's rifle, pitched it beyond reach, then pulled the revolver from Comber's belt, tossing it aside.

"I ain't that kind! You know I ain't!" Comber groaned, reproachful. Red didn't much think so himself, but wasn't taking chances.

He went to the wagon, shook a canteen, brought it back, kneeled, raised Comber's head. Comber took a couple of swallows, coughed, looked up.

Paloo, on foot, stepping soft and looking mild, came up leading his horse. Comber stared at him, said dully, "Harry, yuh air mighty fast." He rolled his head to one side, peered at Red, took a deep breath. Red gave him more water. "I reckon I'm purt-near done for," Comber muttered.

"Why you ever turn sheepherder, Mike?" Red coaxed.

"I swore never to tell."

"Gosh a'mighty, you go an' get yourself killed just to protect on'ry sneakin' fellers! Think of your kids an' wife! Who got you into this, Mike?"

"Them Johnsons there in town."

"Them banker fellers, eh?" Red asked cool and smooth, cocking his head at Paloo and nodding. Comber moved his head in weak assent.

"But didn't you know, Mike, if Grimes and Paloo and Robertson and old Slim Hawks come a-ridin', this would happen?"

"I owed money to the bank. I got a wife an' chilern. They agreed to cross it off. But I ort've knowed, Red."

"All right, Mike. You just take it easy as you can. We'll do whatever is doable for you." To Paloo: "We'll take him along in with us. You mind roundin' up them burros?"

Grimes sat in the saddle, patient and indifferent. His job was over. The herders were done for. Tomorrow Robertson would send in some boys from the line camps to harry the sheep out of the valley and scatter them to the coyotes and wolves and such nesters as were low enough to eat mutton instead of steal veal.

Chain harness lay across the wagon tongue. Paloo and Red hitched up. They threw out stuff to make room for a pallet on the wagon bed, piled folded blankets, and spread tarpaulin over the bows to keep the sun off Comber. The burros were hitched and stood in their tracks with woebegone air. Comber was carried and lifted into the wagon, given another drink. He said, "Thanky, boys."

Red put his rope on a burro and got into the saddle. It was slow going, but there was something like a road rutted into the ground by the grub wagons that brought in supplies when men were in the valley.

"You all light out ahead," Red said. "I'll be along in when I get there."

Grimes and Paloo rode off at a trot, steadily. Red went at a slow walk. Now and then he halted to give Comber a drink. It was a hot day. He was tired, sore, sleepy. Going at a burro's walk was the hardest kind of work. Much of the time he rode with a leg around the horn and, drowsing, almost fell off.

The afternoon passed. Twilight came, then deepening shadows, and night brought out the stars. Coyotes yapped from afar off. Here and there an owl fluttered heavily, like something thrown. The burrows, sad of face and untiring, plodded on with slim dainty feet. Red yawned, rubbed his eyes. He did not dare sleep in the saddle. The burros had to be guided.

It was away after midnight when he pulled into the ranch. All was quiet, but as he swung off a big-bodied shadow with a beard came limping, stick in hand. Robertson had waited up.

"How is he, Red?"

"A'right I reckon. 'Pears to be asleep. I thought Miz George would like to have a talk with him."

"I ain't seen her so mad in years as when she heard it was them Johnsons."

"You ain't seen her have so much cause, neither, I reckon. I'll go roust out somebody to help carry 'im in. Then water and feed these burros."

Red went into the bunkhouse, shook up Slim

Hawks and Harry Paloo. They slipped into their pants and boots and came stumbling out.

Old Robertson said, "Go along back to sleep, boys. He is dead. Bled to death, I reckon."

3

The next morning Red was having a talk with Mrs. George under the sycamores in front of the bunkhouse. Her quirt moved fretfully and she was angry; but he repeated in good-humored stubbornness, "I'm goin' along to town with you all. You got to let me go—or fire me. You fire me, I'll tag along!"

"Red Clark, I don't know what's got into you! With that reward on your head—"

"Shucks! I shot them Johnsons' gamblers. Paloo and Jeb shot their sheepherders. You're takin' Paloo and Jeb. You got to take me, too. I wouldn't miss hearin' you talk to them fellers for a hundred dollars!"

"But if they try to arrest you there in town?"

"You're plannin' to get in after dark. I won't be seen—much. Anyhow, I'm going!" Red stooped and pulled at a collie's ear.

"I never in my life been so over-rode this way before! I ought to fire you as a matter of principle!" She was exasperated, but also a little forgiving. "'Course, there'll be enough boys along to make Bill Nims mighty polite about asking you to get arrested. For that matter, there's

186

likely to be warrants out for Jeb and Harry, an' even me!" She chuckled a little. "But I don't think you ought to go. For one thing, they'll be hardly anybody left around here but Robertson and Dutchy and Joey."

"And are you takin' Hal Mason to show him some more about us out west?"

Mrs. George grinned, bright-eyed. "My worries about him are over, I think. He rode back yesterday and went to bed. Had a pain in his side and was stiff. I wish you could have seen Kate's face! Done me more good than a rise in beef." She took Red's tobacco from his shirt pocket and asked for papers, then rolled a cigarette.

"I bet you never had a saddle pain in your side. I get 'em sometimes when a horse pitches, stubborn."

"But you don't climb off and go to bed!"

"I sure would if I done what I feel like."

"But you don't. That's the point."

"It all comes from me havin' been such a cute baby!"

Mrs. George swung the quirt at him. "You've changed plenty. By the way, I think Dora Harris is good for Kate. They are out riding now. Both wearing my skirts. I'm glad Kate has at last got up gumption enough to straddle a saddle."

"Mason with 'em?"

"He is not. He's up to the house setting on a cushion. His tail is sore. I wish it was blistered!

I'm thinking up a letter to write Col. Howland!"

Mrs. George got into the saddle and rode off. Red went down to the musty harness room and worked on his cartridge belt. Some of the loops were unstitched. There was an old stitching machine that he didn't know much about, so he talked to it as if trying to bully the thing into good behavior. He had the belt fixed and was rubbing away with neatsfoot oil when the doorway was darkened.

Dora had come up on horseback. She said, cheerily, "Good morning, Mr. Clark!"

The floor of the harness room was two feet above the ground. He strapped on the belt and stood in the door at a height almost face to face with her. She looked past him, leaning a little. "Are you alone, Red?"

"No'am. I got a purty girl here talkin' to me!"

"I am glad you think so." She smiled and slipped a hand from its glove. Her tone was low and serious. "Red, Mr. Mason asked me to mail this without letting anyone know, when I returned to town."

"Huh?"

"Look at the address."

Red looked:

Mr. Dingley Hepple,
H P Ranch,
Tulluco.

"Well, I'll be damnedified!"

"Red, I hope I am doing right. It seems odd that a guest of Mrs. Dobbs', just from the East, would be writing Mr. Hepple, secretly. You know how I feel about the Hepples, but I love Mrs. Dobbs and Catherine. And if there is anything underhanded being done, I don't want to have—"

"Him knowing about you and Pink, he reckoned you wouldn't mind mailing his letter."

"But I do mind if—what shall I do?"

"Give it to me."

She did, and Red promptly ripped it open. "Why, Red!" He didn't answer, simply read:

My dear Father: I know you will be surprised to hear from me after all these years, and more surprised to find that I am in this country. I hear that you are not well and I do want to see you very much. I have always remembered you with affection. Mother died about two years ago. Col. Howland said that since this was the country of my birth, I ought to return. If you want to see me, please write to H. M. Hepple, Tulluco. There are some important things that I want to talk to you about. I think I can explain why that old feud must not be revived under any circumstances. Your loving son, Harold.

Red tore up the letter.

"Why, Red! Was it something dreadful?"

"Nope. It wasn't. 'Bout a feller old Hepple used to know what went East. But like you said, a guest of Miz George's has no business writing Hepples, times like these."

"Red, I know, just *know,* that Charley Hepple is doing everything he can to prevent trouble, and—"

Red grunted, non-committal, eying her. He thought it a dirty shame for a nice girl like this to be so bamboozled by a no-good scoundrel like Pinky.

"I must be going. Catherine will wonder where I am."

After she turned the horse, Red looked at the scraps of paper in his fist and pondered. One way, there wouldn't be much wrong in a fellow writing his dad that way. Mason 'peared to have some good intentions about the range trouble; but, in Red's mind, it was wrong of him not to cease altogether from thinking of himself as a Hepple. He was now nothing but a Dobbs man.

"Besides," Red mused, "I done him a big favor. He don't understand about things. Old Dingley, being sick-a-bed, Miz Hepple would read that letter. If she finds out Dingley's boy is around in this country, writing to his dad, she'll maybe figger he wants to horn Pinky out of some cows.

190

And that Buck feller is likely to take a shot at him through a winder. Jeb says he knows she had something to do with his coming out here after me."

4

That evening Red, just about dark, carefully avoided the ranch house when he went up to see how the collie pups were making out, but Catherine caught him. She crowded into the shed where the savage Bella was stretched out, blissfully relaxed as the puppies suckled her breast.

Catherine was wearing her coolest don't-touch-me manner. "Red, why did you play that mean trick on Hal?"

"I didn't play any tricks of any kind." He turned a pup over on its back, scratched its belly. "These here pups—later on when they are bigger, I'll show you how Bella teaches 'em. I'll kill a rattler and bring it in, then she'll—"

"Red, you know you did!"

"I know I didn't."

"He said you rode fast when he asked you not to!"

"Listen, you!" His rudeness gave her a start. "Miz George sent me and Jeb Grimes and Harry Paloo to Cocheno Valley on some work. Mason wasn't ready when 'twas time to go. They went on. I waited for 'im. It was my job to catch up with 'em. I wish to God he hadn't told me he was a Hepple—"

"That's just it! You dislike him and want to make Grandmother dislike him! You do things to make him ridiculous! You can't forgive him for being a Hepple!"

Red said, "Bite her, Bella. Go on. She needs learnin' more'n your pups ever will!"

"You aren't being in the least amusing, Red!"

"I ain't tryin' to be!" He faced her, spoke sharply. "I like you. I'd like you even if you wasn't Miz George's kin. But bein' who you are, I'd most near break my neck to have things like you want. But you got me in a pickle. Miz George won't never forgive me if she finds out. And she will. You can't fool her long. Far as I know, or think, Mason ain't really a bad feller. He wanted to know how to make Miz George like 'im, and I told him the best I knowed. He'll have to be like the men she likes. Ride and shoot and do as told, and work like hell. He'll have to be a Dobbs man—and at the showdown, fight his own kin folks!"

"Never!"

"And if he done all that," Red went on, imperturbably, "she prob'ly wouldn't like him overmuch. Hepples fought her from the time she was a girl, just married. They tried to ruin her ranch. They burnt her range. They stole her cows. They shot her men. They near murdered her husband—"

192

"She did as much to them!"

"She done more," Red admitted proudly, "since she licked 'em! That ain't the point. She hates Hepples like I hate a polecat that's climbed into my blankets while I'm asleep. She won't forgive 'em. She won't forgive anybody that does forgive 'em. And your husband is a Hepple. You are goin' to catch hell. And I'm goin' to be some splattered too with fire an' brimstone. And 'tain't my fault if your husband can't ride. Or if he gets drunk. Or if he goes to bed 'cause his settin' place is sore. Or—"

Catherine slapped him, hard, with resounding smack squarely on the cheek. Without a word, but with eyes flashing, she backed out, turned, slammed the door of the pen.

Red rubbed his cheek, grinned, laughed. "Oh, no, they ain't no good old fightin' blood in her! I bet before long her pet Hepple crawls under the bed to get away from her, and she'll poke him out with a broom stick and break it over his head! Bella, you're the nicest lady I know. Though at that, I bet these pups' daddy is a wolf—the which to proper collies is just like a Hepple!"

CHAPTER NINE

Mrs. George rode into Tulluco at nightfall with four horsemen behind her. They kept off the main street where there were a lot of people milling about and cut 'cross lots to a flat adobe house with a long porch at the front. The windows were lighted, so folks were home and it would be about supper time.

They all climbed down, but Slim Hawks and Harry Paloo stayed with the horses. Mrs. George took Red and Jeb Grimes with her. Their boot heels and spurs made a racket on the porch floor. Mrs. George knocked on the door with the butt of her quirt. She beat fast and hard.

It was opened by Milton Johnson. His face was cold, sly, and mean; a broad face, pinched at nose-tip and not covered with much flesh. His mouth was thin and his ears stuck out. He gulped a little at seeing Mrs. George and especially at Red who was supposed to be dead since nobody had brought to town a correction of Buck's story from the Arrowhead. Old Grimes being there, too, made it harder for Milt Johnson to swallow easy. These weren't nice people to quarrel with, and Mrs. George looked quarrelsome. Just beyond the porch he saw two other men, guessed who they were.

Mrs. George said, "I come to see your dad, Milt."

Milt Johnson said, "Sorry, Mrs. Dobbs, but dad ain't to home. He went—"

A strong heavy voice called from within the house, "Who is it, Milt?"

"So!" said Mrs. George stepping in.

"He must have just come in the back way," Milton explained with no embarrassment at all. "You are always welcome to our house, Mrs. Dobbs." There was a reserved alert suspicious stare in his cold eyes. He seemed inviting in Mrs. George only.

Red pulled off his hat and almost bumped into him as Milton was making to close the door. Grimes kept his hat on. He paused and looked hard at the young banker. Grimes' black eyes had a kind of bright glaze, like opaque polished stones. He didn't say a word but he had given a threat.

Mrs. George stamped through the big room where supper was being put on the table and to a doorway where old Johnson stood in mystified glower. But old Johnson put on his best manner with, "Hello, Mrs. Dobbs. Was you wanting to see me?"

"I come for a talk."

Mrs. George marched by old Johnson and into the next room. Red followed, dragging his rowels. Grimes, somehow in silence, gave Milt Johnson orders to get along in there, too. Grimes pulled the door shut and stood before it.

Mrs. George pushed up the stiff brim of her hat and turned on old Johnson. He was big boned, broad, not tall, wore baggy clothes. He was sixty or more, coarse of feature, thin of mouth, with sunken pale eyes. His forehead sloped back. Behind his back folks called him "Toad" Johnson. His voice was deep. Mrs. George's was shrill and her gray eyes were on fire: "Johnson, your sheep are off my range! Your herders killed or run out! And I am here! Start talking!"

She drew the quirt thongs between her gloved fingers, taking out the kinks. Old Johnson sucked in a deep breath and swelled up. He stared hard, held his breath and looked sort of funny and helpless.

"N-now Mrs. Dobbs, I—I—I can explain! Th-they wasn't *my* sheep a-tall! Not a-tall! I—agent—merely acted as agent and—"

"Whose?"

"Why, Mrs. Dobbs, a banker has to have things confidential and—" Just as he thought he was getting along fine that quirt whizzed past his nose. He stepped back and looked scared. Milt Johnson wet his thin lips with a smacking sound. He opened his mouth as if about to say something, but didn't; just left it open as if to help his breathing.

Mrs. George said, "It is my business to know who is trying to ruin my range and the agents of them that do it will catch just as much hell as anybody else. Out with it!"

Old Johnson backed up and she followed, step for step. He was well against the wall and she was just a good quirt's reach away. He knew she was liable to horse-whip the tar out of him and there wasn't much of anything he could do about it. His face got splotched with pale spots and his eyes jumped about as if looking for a good place to duck.

Mrs. George swung back her arm, the quirt straightened out behind her. The banker flung up his crooked arms before his face and said quick, "Young Hepple and his maw!"

Mrs. George let the quirt fall. She looked as though all the breath had been knocked out of her. There were some things one cow outfit wouldn't do to another, like poison waterholes and run sheep. What took her breath was the admission of this cow-country banker that he had thrown in with Hepples to help ruin her.

She said slowly, almost low-voiced: "A cow-man's banker running sheep!" It sounded as if she cussed him with the worst words known to the range.

Milt Johnson licked his thin lips some more and said oozily, "Business is business, Mrs. Dobbs, and a banker must—"

Grimes spoke with bubble-like softness. He said, "Shut up!"

And there was silence until Mrs. George said in a tired hurt way, "I don't know what's come over this country."

Red had to take hold on himself with both hands to keep his mouth shut. He didn't dare speak up. He glared at old Johnson as if trying to give him a lot of good reasons for worrying. Johnson's anxious eyes lit on Red's face and skittered into an overhead glance. He appeared to remember that Red had said he would kill him, and Milton too, if they tried to run a shindy on Mrs. George. The shindy had been run, and Red looked purposeful.

There were heavy steps outside the room. The door opened with a shove, and Grimes spun about. It was Bill Nims and with him, tagging along, mild and unobtrusive, was little old Harry Paloo.

Sheriff Nims looked hot and worried. He stared at one Johnson, then at the other, as he blurted in his deep voice, "Word's just come the Monohela stage—Cramer is killed, and the messenger! Your big shipment—they got it!" Then, grudgingly, "Howdy, Mrs. Dobbs." He stared at Red who was supposed to be dead. "What you doin' in town?"

"I brought him!" said Mrs. George.

The sheriff took off his hat and rubbed a hand over his sunburned forehead. It was going to be bad if folks knew Red had come to town and not been arrested after so much hullabulloo. But the sheriff switched back to the robbery with:

"Four men, I hear. Masked. The messenger showed fight an' they killed him from behind the rocks down at Tipson Grade. They killed a lead horse. Then they shot old Rim Cramer with his hands in the air!"

"Thirty thousand dollars!" said Milt Johnson and shook his head.

"Bad, awful bad!" said old Johnson.

Red eyed the Johnsons and thought that for money-lovers they were standing up pretty well under the shock. Maybe Mrs. George had scared them so bad they couldn't suffer much.

Old Johnson seemed to think he could buck up some with the sheriff there. He cleared his throat and took a deep breath. He said, deep and slow, trying to show that he was firm and calm, "Sheriff, there is a man you want to arrest!"

Sheriff Nims looked at Red and said, troubled, "Yes, I ort."

"An', Sheriff," said old Johnson, getting back some confidence and speaking louder. "Even if Mrs. Dobbs here is an old friend, she is breakin' the laws. She killed some men on public domain and she is protectin' that there outlaw, Red Clark, so—"

Mrs. George grinned, cold and savage, slapped her boot with the quirt. "You're damn right I'm protecting that outlaw! Red, you light out for home. I'm staying in town. I've got some

199

business with Bill Nims, right here and now. He's going to stay and listen to me. So, Red, you don't need to push your horse none, hurrying."

"But, Mrs. Dobbs, them stage robbers, I ort—" the sheriff protested.

"Done the crime in Monohela County, Bill. I'm going to talk about robbers and such right here in Tulluco. First off, Bill Nims, you are a cowman. I want you to listen to what these Johnsons have been up to!"

She leveled her finger at old Johnson and started in.

Red went out to the horses.

Slim Hawks chuckled as he said, "Me an' Harry told Bill Nims that Jeb an' jest a couple o' fellers was in thar talkin' to ol' Johnson. I bet he nearly busted his bellyband when he saw you an' Miz George was them fellers!"

"Tell you about the hold-up and Cramer?"

"Yep. But why them Johnsons sendin' that money down thar?"

"To swap coin for dust. They's big money in it. I rode guard onct for a bank as done that up to the mines at Lelargo. Miz George she sure give 'em hell—an' is still shovelin' coal! My orders is to light out for the ranch. S'long."

2

Red rode out of town, taking a way that avoided Main Street. The Ghost, being gray, was likely to be looked at, but few people knew the horse anyhow.

He gave some thought to the stage robbery. The only reason, ever, for shooting a driver was if he recognized the highwaymen as somebody who were thought to be good citizens, or to ease a grudge. Drivers weren't hired to fight.

"It's goin' to be hard on Mamie. I bet you she goes and hugs that pig an' cries."

Red wasn't taking the road home. He had insisted on coming to town with Mrs. George chiefly because he did want to hear her light into them Johnsons; but he also had something else on his mind.

Because it was a starry night and The Ghost could be noticed at a distance, Red pulled down into arroyos and worked his way in the general direction that would bring him up behind the Golden Palace. He knew the town and surrounding country as well as he knew the Dobbs bunkhouse, every dip and rise, almost every sage, at least every patch of cactus.

He took a lot of time because he wanted it to be late before he went to the hotel, otherwise somebody might see him.

A little more than a hundred yards back of the Golden Palace it was just plain desert; but on such a bright night it might look funny to see a horse staked out there. Red didn't like walking, but there was a good-sized gully about a quarter of a mile off. He rode The Ghost into that, found a suitable rock, carried it into the gully and made the horse fast so he wouldn't go climbing up the bank to graze.

"You behave yourself, Spook. An' don't go whinnyin' to the purty mares you can't see up there in town."

He smoked some cigarettes, loafed about until he judged it was almost twelve o'clock, then went up near the hotel and waited a while to make sure nobody was about. Then he climbed the veranda rail and tip-toed with light rattle of spurs through the entrance.

An oil lamp, turned low, burned in its bracket on the wall at the side of the stairs. Red went up the stairs, hurried along the corridor, knocked lightly at Harris' door.

"Who is it?" Harris called in thin sharp tone.

"Me, Judge. I got to see you!"

"Who are you?"

Red spoke low. "Red Clark!"

There was a muttering of reproachful oaths, a squeak of bed springs, the scrape of a match, the nearly noiseless scuffle of bare feet and Harris, lamp in hand, opened the door, held the lamp high above his head and peered. Then he stepped back, pulled the door wide, said, "Hurry up in here, you damn fool. Somebody may see you! What the devil you doing in town?"

Red came in with shuffle of feet, pulled off

his hat, grinned, looked uncomfortable. Harris, a small thin man, wore a long tailed white night gown that came below his bony pipe-stem ankles. The thin hair of his sparrow-like head was rumpled. He said encouragingly and anxious, "What's wrong, Red?"

Red began a cigarette. "Listen, Judge. I come about somethin' that ain't none o' my business a-tall, but—" Red took a hand from the paper and pulled at an ear, at a loss for words.

Harris put down the lamp and took up his own sack of tobacco and brown papers. "Go on, Red."

Red looked a little sweaty and uncomfortable. "Judge, your niece is shore a nice girl!"

Harris smiled with tolerant twitch of thin lips. "I think so, Red. And am glad you do."

" 'Tain't *that!*" said Red, embarrassed. "An' I feel like a damn tattler. But—" Red hesitated, then blurted—"her an' Pinky are plannin' to run off an' get married!"

Harris jerked back his head, peering. He dropped the unlighted cigarette, and struck his palm with small bony fist. What he said was sulphurously blasphemous, and mostly self-blame. It appeared that Dora being so lonely, he hadn't minded her dancing in the dining room to Bucky's fiddle, though most of the dances had been with Pinky. "I told her he was no damn good!" said Harris. "But women are fools, Red, just plain unadulterated fools over good-looking men!"

"Listen, Judge." Red inhaled deeply, spoke earnest. "Me, I make quite a point of never hidin' what I do. So 'f it comes to a showdown, you just up an' tell her 'twas me as told you! I'd rather she hated the sight of me than—"

"Tell her nothing!" said Harris, with trembling fingers beginning another cigarette. "I'm glad you told me. The damn worthless lying pup! And tell me, Red, what about that fellow Buck who claims—"

"Huh. Shot from the dark through a winder— an' missed. Then run like hell."

"Has Mrs. Dobbs gone on the warpath yet, as she threatened?"

"She shore has. Sheepherders' scalps is danglin' to her belt. I left her over to the Johnsons skinnin' them bankers alive. You'll hear plenty tomorrow, but me, I'd better be goin'."

"You had that!" said Harris, urgently. "And I want you to know that you couldn't have done Dora a more important service. Nor me a bigger favor!"

3

Red ran down the stairs and in the hall came slap-dab up against Pinky Hepple hurrying into the hotel along after one o'clock in the morning.

Red looked him over with new interest. Pinky was sure enough a good looking boy, sort of blond though his maw was dark as the Queen of

Spades. As usual, Pink was wearing a lot of range finery, but now it was dust covered and he looked tired and a little skittish.

" 'Lo, Pink."

Pinky gave a jump. His lips curled back in a cat-like snarl and his arm twitched but didn't go toward his holster. He knew better. "Oh, you! I thought you was dead!"

"Hope you ain't disappointed none too much. Why you starin' at me so hard?"

The look on Pinky's face showed that he was deciding what it was best to say. He didn't want a quarrel, not face to face and alone. Red could lick him with fists, cuss words, or guns; and Pinky knew it. "B-Buck said he shot you!"

"He tell you?"

Pinky said "No," so quick and earnest it sounded just like a lie. "But I heard it said by folks."

Red inquired as mildly as if asking for a letter at the post office:

"Buck happen to be 'round town, some'eres?"

"No. I mean I don't know. I—I just rode in. Maw keeps a room here. I was going to wash up before going up town."

Red barred the stairs by standing in Pinky's way and looked him over. "Was you thinkin' some, maybe, of taking it out on me on account of what I done to your brother, hm?"

"Red, you know me and Joe wasn't good friends much."

Red said, "Huh." He knew Pinky was backing down. He knew that blandly earnest look on Pinky's face didn't mean a thing. His eyes ran up and down Pinky's finery, now dusty and spotted with some sweat stains, like he had rode a long way in a hurry.

Pink's boots were fine leather, ornamentally sewn with colored thread. He wore chased silver spurs with silver jinglebobs to make more tinkle when he walked. He didn't do cow work, much less in brush, but wore fancy chaps that were fringed and lined with silver buttons. His was a pearl handled revolver and had a couple of naked girls carved on the pearl grip. Holster, cuffs, hat band were hand stamped. He wore a silk neckerchief and a deer-skin vest. Looked just like an Eastern goof's notion of what a cowboy was like; and he always had money. Good punchers never had money only once in a while and didn't keep it long. Otherwise they wouldn't have been good punchers.

"Well, Pink," said Red, critical, "you shore do look sorta tired and wore out, like you'd come far and been hurryin' some."

"What I do ain't none of your business, is it?"

"Might be," Red suggested with the sort of mildness that irritated folks, "if you do it on Dobbs' range."

Pinky's voice exploded into a pleased sneer-tone:

"Well you can just tell old lady Dobbs that—"

"*Miz* Dobbs, Pink!"

"—that we—"

"*Miz Dobbs!*" Red snapped.

"Well, Miz-zus Dobbs then, that us Hepples have squatted down over where them Huskinses was livin' and are moving cows into the Basin! Our men are already there! That's sorta puttin' one over on you all, ain't it?" Pinky grinned, glad to give unpleasant news.

Red asked, soft as pie, "You seen Huskins' face? How you like to look like that?"

"No chance!" said Pinky with triumphant jeer. "We got fightin' men on our side!"

"Honest, Pink?"

"You'll damn soon learn! Too bad you didn't come a-ridin' for us that time my maw asked you. I got to go wash up."

That was a request for Red to stand aside and let him pass.

"Um-hm. By happenchance is one o' them fightin' men you got ridin' for you named Buck?"

Pinky said instantly, "No. I don't know anything about Buck."

"So you got fightin' men on your side? Now ain't that too bad for us pore little Dobbses? Me, I'd be plumb scairt, Pink, 'cept I happen to know you are as much of a liar as a side-winder is a wiggler. But if they is a lick of truth in what you say about squattin' down at Huskinses, then you

Hepples are sure hankerin' for some bad luck!"

Red stepped aside, gestured, bidding Pinky trot along up the stairs. "Miz George gets done with you, your face won't be pink. Be black an' blue!"

Pinky's handsome face took on a spasm of meanness. He was a natural born liar, with soft smooth face and deceptive look; but he didn't have much self-control, and Red knew how to torment him. A look of fury flared over Pinky's face; but he didn't get so mad as to forget that Red was a killer.

"Git along. Let me see how you look a-walkin' up stairs. Toddle, Pink!"

There was nothing much that Pinky could do about it without starting a fight, so he went up the stairs sullenly, and when he peeked a little over his shoulder, he saw Red keeping an eye on him. Red had no good opinion of Pinky playing fair in a shooting scrape.

4

Red jumped the veranda and started on a run for his horse. He was thinking that if Hepples had moved in on Huskinses' Place it would be well for him to ride wide on his way home. He could be shot out of the saddle—and somebody would collect a thousand dollars for doing it.

Then he thought of Mrs. George and the boys. If they went jogging up and the Hepples were laying for 'em—Red stopped in his tracks. He faced about and started the other way, back toward town, not yet deciding what to do, but sure that somehow Mrs. George ought to know. The Hepples hadn't moved in without being prepared to fight. Red didn't put ambushing above them. Not when it looked like Pinky and his maw and the Johnsons were running things. In his day old Dingley Hepple would always come a-rarin' right out in the open; but he lay abed, paralyzed some.

Maybe Pinky had lied and maybe he hadn't. Red felt Mrs. George just had to be warned.

He judged it was between 1:30 and 2 o'clock. The air was mild with a pleasant tang of chill. Stars were bright. He walked over to where he could have a look down Main Street. There was only an occasional figure or two staggering through splotches of light in the wide-open doorways of the saloons. People were not in the street but the dim hum of loud voices, far off, and music came from the Best Bet. The gamblers would be busy at their games.

Red kept in the shadows and went to the corner across from the Best Bet. People over there seemed to be having a good time. He wondered where the devil Mrs. George was. It wasn't likely that she had rode for home already; and if she stayed in town, she would surely have put up at the Golden Palace. He had idled about, watching the veranda, and hadn't seen anything of her. If any of her boys were still in town they

209

would most likely be over there in the Best Bet.

Red felt he ought to have a look. From across the street he could see only shadow-shapes that moved through the thin smoke haze. Now and then he could hear the shrill laughter of some girl sounding as if she was having a good time. He wondered if Jim was on duty. Jim roomed and boarded with Mamie's mother; and if he weren't on duty, Red could go there and have Jim go find Mrs. George.

Red told himself there was no use acting like a scare-baby, so he walked across the street, stood to one side of the bright doorway and looked in. Jim wasn't there; but 'Gene Cross was, and dancing with Sara. She had gone back on the floor as a dance girl after Joe Bush was shot. Windy was there, too, but not dancing.

Red thought it was mighty funny for them to be there. They sure wouldn't be there enjoying themselves if they knew that Mrs. George, Jeb, or Harry or Slim were in town. He had an impulse to walk in and say, "Hello," because he very much wanted some words with them. He didn't have much of a grievance because they had got away, and he wouldn't get up much of a sweat to catch them again. In his heart, Red blamed their rustling and all on to 'Gene's uncle. He wished he could get them off alone because he wanted to ask them about that fellow Buck.

A couple of men were coming to the door so

Red stepped back and hugged the shadows. The men were miners. Before they got out of earshot, Red heard one say he had lost over three thousand dollars in two days. "Nuthin' to do now 'cept to go back tew the mines!" That helped Red to understand a little how the gamblers could afford to pay big money to somebody to be allowed to run crooked games.

He edged round for another peek at the doorway and saw Sara leading 'Gene with an arm about his waist to the bar. Her face was bright and flattering with enticement. 'Gene made a not quite sober flourish and called, "Drinks for the house on me!" A vague buzz of commendation went up. Sara looked pleased. She got a cut on the money he spent for drinks. It took much money to buy drinks like that. Red wondered some as to what 'Gene and Windy could have been up to. "Something not honest, I'd most near bet," he said reluctantly. Somehow Windy, who was a cheerful fellow, now looked a little down at the nose and was quiet-like, as if not happy.

CHAPTER TEN

Red headed for the house of Mamie's mother. Jim, for years, had boarded with that gaunt hard-working widow when he came to Tulluco.

She lived in a small wooden house with a picket fence to keep stray cows and horses from the garden. Red wondered if there was a dog. Mamie had a passion, like fierce motherhood, for pets. Horned toads or horses, anything, even the pig; but Cramer's giving it had helped her to love that. Nobody lived within a stone's throw of the house which was right at the edge of town; but Jim, being a little fat, thought the walk did him good.

Red went to the gate and hoped that Mrs. Miller wouldn't see him. The old woman had a rifle and didn't mind living alone when Jim and Mamie were away. He knew where Jim's room was and meant to tap on the window.

A sharp voice spoke through a front window and Red saw the end of a rifle come out into the starlight. "Who air you?"

"Red Clark, Maw. I come to see Jim."

"Land o' Goshen! I plumb near shot you, Red. It just goes to show! Mame? Mame, wake up. Red is here for to see Jim!"

Mamie said, "Red?" and almost screeched, "Then he wasn't killed!"

"Don't 'pear likely," said Mrs. Miller.

Both women came to the door to let him in. Mrs. Miller's husband had died soon after coming to Tulluco; and, though a widow with a young un, she wouldn't put up with anything that looked like charity from anybody, but had washed, sewn, waited table, clerked, until Mamie had got big enough to go to work.

As kids, when Mamie and Red got into mischief, Mrs. Miller spanked both with stern impartiality. Mamie, being stubborn, just wouldn't cry; and Red, a prideful boy, couldn't cry if a girl didn't; so as Mrs. Miller didn't think a spanking or a switching did any good unless it brought yells and tears, the two kids had been well tanned.

Mrs. Miller pulled down the blinds which were made of heavy wrapping paper and lit a lamp. There were some gray streaks on her hair, but still a lot of brick red too. Mrs. Miller had a gaunt face and Mamie looked just like her.

Their heads were frowsy from sleep but not their eyes. Mrs. Miller pulled a light blanket off the foot of the bed and put it around Mamie because it wasn't proper for a man to see a girl in a nightgown.

Mamie asked, "Why are you to town, Red?"

He guessed they hadn't yet learned of the stage robbery and killing, so he didn't speak of that, but told how it came about that he had to try to get word to Mrs. George.

Mrs. Miller awakened Jim, who slipped into his pants, poked his nightgown down inside the waist band, pulled his broad colored galluses up over his shoulder, took up an unlighted cigar butt and came in, fingering his mustache tips.

The women both at once retold what Red had said. Jim tried to make his mustache stay curled and twisted hard as he said, "You oughtn't be hangin' around town, Red."

"I gota get word to Miz George. Be bad if Pinky wasn't lyin'."

"I sold out my interest in the Best Bet. I don't like how things is run here in town. I still work there extra, but don't hang around down town. But I'll dress and mosey up to see what I can find out for you. You can pile into my bed."

"I got a horse staked out in the 'royo back of the hotel. I can't leave him."

"We've got a stable, Red," Mamie told him.

She called it a stable but it was a shed where she had once kept an old broken-down horse as a pet. According to Red it had died of a broken heart at thinking of all the comfort it had missed by not finding Mamie when it was a colt.

"Maybe folks'll be peeved at you all if they find out I sorta holed up here," Red suggested.

Mamie and her mother spoke at once. Mamie said, "Folks can go to the devil!" and Mrs. Miller, "What else air friends fer than to help a body?"

"I'll go get The Ghost."

214

Jim dressed with his usual care to look neat as if the social elegance of bartenders must be maintained even at 3 o'clock in the morning.

As they walked off together, Red asked if he had heard of the stage robbery. Jim said he hadn't heard because he had come home in the afternoon, and Mamie wasn't working at the restaurant any more. Some miners had seen the pig and paid to have it roasted. When Mamie found out it had been killed, she gave her boss a plain good licking with some scratches about the face thrown in to help him wish he hadn't done it. Now she had the promise of a job at the Emporium the first of next week.

Jim said, "Mamie ain't purty but she would look different if dressed up. A good man couldn't have anybody better to look after him."

"Um-hm. I think pore old Rim Cramer sorta looked forward to that. She'll be mighty broke up. 'Nother thing, Jim. You see if Sara can't get out of 'Gene and Windy where that feller Buck is. I seen 'em in the Best Bet spendin' money."

When they separated, Red gave the town a wide circle. He hadn't walked so much since once when he was thrown, miles from camp. Red would explain that he was a good rider only because he hated so to have to walk.

He rode The Ghost to Mamie's shed and carried in a bucket of water but there was no hay. Mamie said she would get some from a Mexican in the morning, also a bucket of oats, and for Red to lie down and rest while waiting for Jim.

He pulled off his boots, pants, and hat, hung his guns over a post of the bed and was soon asleep. When he awakened he didn't know it was broad daylight because the shades had been drawn and pinned tight. The women had wanted him to sleep. They both had the motherly feeling that a lot of sleep, like a lot of food, was good for a man. It was pretty near noon when he roused up.

Both the women were solemn faced and Mamie had been crying. She had learned about the robbery and Rim Cramer. And about something else too. Mrs. Miller told that in a tone scornful with disbelief:

"Ol' Johnson was shot in the shoulder last night an' he says you done it!"

"I'd be willin' for to take the blame if it was through the heart!" Red told her.

"No, you wouldn't! It was from the dark jest as he was comin' out the door. Ol' Johnson an' young Milt, too, says you swore to kill 'em! An' Depyty Marr, he says he caught sight o' the feller an' 'twas *you*. 'Long about two o'clock. It's all over town that you done it! Folks say you know 'twas Johnson as put Bill Nims up to posterin' that reward for you an'—"

Red was unimpressed. He said, "Maw, I'm hungery. An' what of Miz George? Jim find 'er?"

"That's plumb funny, Red. They was no trace of hair ner hide o' Miz Dobbs an' them boys in town last night. Jim he come back to the house to say so, then went off up town again to find out more if he could."

"Huh. Didn't them Johnsons say she paid 'em a call?"

"Jim didn't hear about it if they did. There is whoopin' excitement over ol' Johnson bein' shot, 'specially as fool folks think 'twas you!"

"If Marr saw me, or thinks he did, why wasn't I killed?"

"Marr is a depyty," said Mrs. Miller shrilly, "because them Johnsons want 'im. Not 'cause Bill Nims does. He arrests boys that throw rocks in winders."

"An' evicts folks as can't pay mortgages," said Red and sat down to a stack of flapjacks that he flooded with blackstrap.

2

Along about the middle of the afternoon Jim came back to the house and the women served dinner. There was, said Jim, a big whoop and stir over the stage holdup and murder, and excited talk over Johnson getting shot.

"He ain't bad hurt a-tall," said Jim. "Has got his arm in a sling. But its cur'us how many sensible people 'pear to think maybe you done it!"

The women stood by making bitter comments

217

on such persons as would think a thing like that.

Jim said he had heard that Mrs. George and her boys had rode out to the Nims' ranch last night. Red nodded, understandingly. "Her and Sally Nims was always good friends. An' a good cowman, the same as Miz George. Did Miz George lead Bill along by the ear for to be present?"

"No. The sheriff and some folks is ridin' out around lookin' for tracks of the stage robbers who maybe headed up Tulluco way."

Jim ate his dinner, smoked on a cigar, talked some more, repeating what he had said. Red fretted and wondered if he oughtn't to be riding since Mrs. George was still paying him wages; but Jim gave him a look that meant there was something more to be told when he got a chance. So to pass the time he and Red played seven-up while Mamie helped her mother with the dishes. Then both women decided they would go up to the store, buy a little something for supper and hear what the talk was.

As soon as they had passed the gate, Jim tossed the cards aside, screwed tight on a mustache tip and said, "Sara wants to see you, Red."

"How she know I am in town, Jim?" His tone was almost accusing.

Jim put a match to his cold cigar, puffed. "She is smart. When I asked her to find out from 'Gene and Windy about Buck, she looked at me a while then up an' said, 'If Red is where you can tell him what I tell you, he is where I can tell 'im myself. At least I won't tell nobody but *him*. And I know plenty!' "

"I don't wanta see 'er."

"Don't blame you, son. But she won't tell me anything."

"She know anything?"

"Maybe she does. Maybe she don't. She is a woman and you can't tell." It was hot in the room. Jim took off his coat, laid it over the back of a chair, wiped his neck. "Maybe she is lyin' to make you come. Use your own judgment."

Red said, "Yeah," doubtfully. "I ain't got no much of what you call judgment when it comes to women."

Jim sighed, chewed his cigar, fingered the cards. "One thing, though. She'll purt-near know whatever 'Gene and Windy can tell."

Red smoked a cigarette nearly to the end before he asked, "If I agree to see her, how'd I work it?"

Jim cleared his throat. "She said you could come around back and up stairs to her room between nine and ten tonight. She has got a room alone since the girl she lived with has gone to Monohela. Ace of Hearts is tacked to the door. I'm workin' tonight. Do I say you are comin'?"

Red studied for a while. "I reckon."

219

3

Mamie and Mrs. Miller came from town breathless and angry. 'Peared like nearly everybody in town seemed to think Red had shot Johnson. "But most of 'em think you done right!" Mamie threw in.

Also Mrs. George had just rode in with Grimes, Paloo, and Hawks. They had spent the night at the Nims' ranch.

"I hear tell," said Mrs. Miller, "that she is mad as a wet hen over thinkin' you shot Johnson—"

"Huh," said Red, untroubled, "she don't believe that."

"I hear tell she had a talk with Depyty Marr and—"

"She is smart. If he says I done it she won't believe 'im. But has she heard, do you reckon, about Hepples at Huskinses' Place?"

"I hear tell she is stayin' in town tonight," said Mamie.

Jim put on his coat. "I got to go to work. I'll see as how she gets word. I'll eat supper up town, Maw. An' Red, do I tell the party as how you'll come? 'Bout nine or little after."

Red ate a big supper. Troubles didn't much bother his appetite. After supper he poked the shells out of his guns, had a look and reloaded.

Mamie said fiercely, "You'll be careful, won't you, Red?"

"That is how I keep myself lucky. Somebody may have heard as how I am ridin' a gray horse. Can I have a bucket of water an' some soap? I'll show you how careful I am!"

Red took a bucket full of soapy water and bluing and went out to the shed. He rubbed the mixture on The Ghost. A white horse was conspicuous.

He felt a little queer and almost uneasy about riding around to see Sara because if people found out they would sure misunderstand. Somehow, too, he seemed to remember Sara as a prettier girl than he had ever thought when looking at her. The nice letter she had sent him helped the mental picture. Last night he hadn't got a very good look, but she had seemed mighty pretty then, too.

He said to himself, "Miz George won't believe me on oath about that Sara girl. But I wanta know about Buck. I owe him a sorta debt. I'm pernickety about payin' debts."

Red rode around back of the Best Bet and left his horse tied to a wagon that was near a scraggly cottonwood on a vacant lot. He hesitated a little about leaving his rifle. Somebody was more likely to steal the rifle than the horse; but a rifle would only clutter his hands.

He didn't have a watch but he knew it was somewhere around nine or after. He stood in the shadows for a time, just waiting. He didn't at all like going up stairs over the Best Bet. When he was hunted he liked to be out in the open. "Dead or alive" was a bad order. He could be shot down on sight, in the back even, and the fellow that did it might not be much admired but he would be paid.

Near the back of the Best Bet he could hear the hum of voices broken by the staccato sounds of laughter and shouts. He looked through the narrow open back door. There was a dense cluster of men about the faro table. The lookout had his hat pulled low and stared down intently from his high chair. Somebody must be bucking the bank, hard.

Red went up the back stairs. They were of pine, seemed pretty flimsy, and were built up outside of the old adobe wall. He opened the door. Here was the smell of unpainted pine, and also the perfume that girls used. The addition was so new that the pine looked fresh except on the level where sticky hands had groped for support and matches had been struck. The hall was narrow and there were rooms only on one side. A dim bracket lamp was about half way down the hall. On the door of the third room he saw an Ace of Hearts.

He tapped lightly and there was no answer. He tried the door. It was unlocked. A lamp, turned low, was burning. He went in slowly and closed the door.

The bottom of the lamp rested on the edge of a sheet of pink writing paper that hung down from the table. It had been placed where it must be noticed, and one word in large letters was written there and underscored: *"Wait."*

It was a small room. The walls were thin unpainted pine. There was no closet and the dresses hung on nails. A mirror was above a pine kitchen table. The table was covered with wrapping paper that had a cut-out pattern for a fringe. There were little bottles and a big powder box on the table and much powder spilled on the dusty floor. One straight back cane-bottom chair was at the table before the mirror and another beside the bed. A pair of worn red satin slippers lay overturned under the bed which was covered with a turkey red tablecloth for coverlet.

Red sat down cautiously with as much gingerliness as if afraid the chair might give way. He pushed back his hat, faced the door and waited.

He heard the hall door close, the running patter of tip-toes, and Sara opened the door, breathless. She had made herself as pretty as she knew how and wore her best finery. She pulled the door to, said, "Oh, Red!" laughed and threw her arms about his neck before he could move.

It wasn't unpleasant, but he thought he oughtn't let her. He wriggled his head out of her hug so he could speak easily and said:

"What of that feller Buck?"

She laughed, squeezed harder, and asked teasing: "What of that feller Red Clark?"

Somehow Sara didn't look quite as pretty as he had been thinking she was. She was closer than she had ever been before and he saw, as he had never noticed before, that there was stuff on her eyelashes, stuff on her cheeks, stuff on her mouth, and lots of powder. The strong perfume smell was almost too much when she had her breast against his face. A little way off, when one was inattentive as he had been, these things weren't noticed. He knew too that she was what is called a "bad woman" and he was a little afraid of being friendly with bad women because they were smart, reckless, and made trouble. He sort of more than half way believed also that she had tricked him into shooting Joe Bush. Bush needed shooting, but Red didn't like having been tricked.

She patted Red's cheeks and swore at the Johnsons whom she said had caused the reward to be put up. Red didn't think it sounded good for any woman, except Mrs. George, to swear. Mrs. George made it sound all right.

"I'm awful sorry you didn't kill old Toad Johnson last night!" Her tone was just about as if she were offering condolence for the death of someone in his family.

"I didn't do it!" said Red.

Sara was on his lap. She drew back her head,

studied his face, pulled his nose, laughed a little, then jerked his head against her neck, holding him tightly. "You don't need to lie to me about *that,* you silly boy!"

"Aw, damn it, I don't shoot folks from the dark!"

"But Toad Johnson—"

"Not even the Devil, I wouldn't!" said Red, earnest. He wriggled uncomfortably. "But what about that Buck?"

Sara got off his lap and bounced down on the bed, making the springs squeak and put a hand on Red's knee. "Them Johnsons has hired him, Red, to lead the fighting for the Hepples. I hear tell he is a killer and mean, and 'pears like he had it in for you all along."

"How that come? I never seen him before that day here in town when he first come."

"I don't know. 'Gene and Windy says so. They are working for the Hepples too. They have been blowing advance wages. Three hundred dollars!"

Red said, "They are liars. Why pay all that when real fightin' men would ride for forty a month an' no advance?"

"Red?" She leaned close, as if the better to study his face, and said low and hurriedly, " 'Gene is jealous that I like you!" Red looked blank. "And I do!" Pause. "Don't you like me, just a little wee teeny bit, Red?"

He said, "Sure," evasively. "But this here is

business. Hepples ain't smart but they ain't goin' to pay—"

"That's what 'Gene and Windy told me when they rode in late last night. And they had the money, too. They come to town with Pinky. He's down there now betting stacks of chips that high—and losing! 'Gene and Windy are staying out of sight tonight, some, because that old Jeb Grimes is up at the front of the bar. He is drinking and Jim sure looks worried."

"Gosh a'mighty, they's reason for to be worried if Jeb is—but he promised Miz George—I wonder what can have happened? But what about that Buck?"

"Oh, I could have killed him myself, Red, when 'twas said he had killed you. But he stayed from town. Out to the Hepples I hear. What happened between you and 'Gene and Windy? 'Gene is mighty mad at you."

"I caught 'em change-brandin' Miz George's cows."

Sara knew that rustling was a bad crime but she didn't really feel it was so terrible. She shook her hair, making it fly. It was dark and curly. She thought it looked better if bushy. She took Red's cigarette from between his fingers, put it into her mouth, drew back her head a little, narrowed her eyes, smiled.

"Red Clark, there is a thousand dollars reward for you!"

She seemed teasing, yet with something serious under her words. He said, "Um-hm" and didn't feel quite sure. There was no telling much about women, her kind anyhow.

"So you," she said, leaning forward, "had better kiss me—nice!"

He grinned, felt shy, shifted his feet—and leaped to his feet, overturning the light chair and taking a backwards step as the door was flung wide.

Sara screamed and jumped from the bed. 'Gene had taken off his boots to slip up on them. He had been drinking. A leveled gun was in his hand. He said, quick and mad:

"I've heard talk about you an' her, so—"

He shot point blank. Sara, with head up, had flung herself before Red with arms out stiffly behind her as if with far backward reach hedging him in. She crumpled forward without a word; fell just about as one of her dresses that was hanging up might have fallen if a nail had come loose.

It looked like 'Gene, anyhow, had meant to kill her, too. He was over-hasty to be quick about shooting again and his aim was bad. His gun and Red's went off together. Red killed him on his feet and shot him a second time with the same gun as he was falling. A playing card would have covered both holes in 'Gene's breast.

"You goddamned fool," Red said with a sound

as if bad hurt, "when we was friends! She wasn't nothin' to me!"

He dropped to a knee and pulled at Sara. Her head moved as if her neck were broken and her eyes were open in an unseeing stare. There was blood coming from her breast. He knew the sounds of the shots would bring men but he thrust the gun into its holster, heaved up Sara in his arms, laid her on the bed. 'Gene, with the drop at point blank range, could not have missed him. Sara had taken the bullet and Red felt all choked up in realizing that.

He jumped over the dead body of 'Gene and down the hall. His boot heels stamped. He opened the door to the stairs. Already there were three or four men crowding at the bottom of the stairs with faces lifted, and one man was already half way up.

Red drew his gun, shouted, "Out of the way!" and jumped down the stairs. He struck against the man who was half way up. It was Deputy Marr who had probably expected to find merely some drunken miner showing off by making a noise up there. Marr rocked back, off balance, against the banisters and the banisters broke. Red, cat-quick, whaled the barrel of his revolver over Marr's head even as they toppled. They fell together. It wasn't far, some seven or eight feet, but Red was jolted pretty hard. Marr had been unconscious when he hit the ground, and would have a welt on his head big as a goose egg for days to come.

Red scrambled up into a crouch, cocked his gun, tried to get his breath. His words came in pauses, but they had a warning edge: "Keep off—all you—not a move!—or—" His second gun seemed to spring into his hand, muzzle on.

Red began to back off, edging around so as to make a break for his horse a hundred feet away. People just seemed to swarm out of shadows on all sides. His name was spoken shrilly. Every man there had stared at the posters offering the reward for him. There was also Johnson's verbal promise of increased reward. Nearly every man among them was armed. A thousand dollars was a lot of money, and the name of having killed or captured Red a lot of fame. It looked bad for him.

All of a sudden a horseman came tearing down through the alley with a yell that simply lifted the hair of old timers who knew what the Apache war-whoop was like. Some people who didn't move fast had to fling themselves back as if knocked over, for the horseman came as if the Devil himself were in the saddle and would have trampled them. He was tall and straight and had a rifle half lifted as if it were a revolver. He rode through the crowd, yanked up his horse, called:

"Red?"

Red said, "Yeah!"

"Where's yore hoss?"

Red pointed. "Over yonder apiece!"

Jeb Grimes turned his horse about, faced the crowd. "Has anybody," he inquired soft-toned, clear-voiced with that curious bubble sound in his throat, "got them some objections to me an' Red here takin' our time about doin' our departin'?"

Nobody spoke up. Some eyes shifted to watch Red cut catty-cornered across the vacant lot where his horse was tied. Others stared fascinated at Grimes, who backed his horse, followed slowly but faced the crowd.

People who knew him said soft and warning to those about them, "That there is old Jeb Grimes and he's been a-drinkin'!"

"Take yore time, son," Grimes called as if he was pleased and hopeful that somebody might start monkeying with him.

Red didn't take much time but gathered up the end of the rope in loose coils and hit the saddle. Grimes turned his horse and came up alongside. He ordered severely, "Walk 'im now! Never run when folks chase you. Makes 'em swell-headed with feelin' important!"

Some people had run up the stairs and an excited fellow who liked to give bad news shouted down from the landing that Red had killed a man and that Sara girl.

Grimes was riding at a walk, a slow walk at that. "Did you do that, son?"

"Gosh a'mighty, no! 'Gene Cross shot the girl, him bein' crazy jealous. I killed him. She saved

230

my life. Where the devil did you come from, Jeb? And how did you know 'twas me?"

Grimes pulled a pint bottle of whisky from his pocket, drew the cork with his teeth, held it out. Red took a drink and was tempted to let the bottle fall and break; but he was afraid Grimes might simply face about and ride back for another. Grimes reached out for the bottle, put in the cork and returned it to his pocket without having a nip for himself. He wasn't going to spoil his nice edge by overdoing it.

Red tried to jog a little faster, but Grimes wouldn't have it. He said, "Whoa-up, son. We got all the time in the world. We ain't workin' for Miz George no more!"

"What in hell?"

"You're fired an' I quit."

"You, Jeb? Quit?"

Grimes looked over his shoulder, sniffed. "I smell me some trouble." It sounded just like as if, being hungry, he sniffed steak frying. "Be a shame to have 'em wear down their hosses chasin' us. Mebbe we'd better ride back to 'commodate 'em."

"Nobody's in sight. Come on. Why'd you quit, Jab?"

Grimes was staring backwards. "Best way on earth, son, for to keep folks from follerin' you is to chase 'em."

"All right," Red agreed, humoring him, "if they

start followin', we'll chase 'em. But why did you quit?"

" 'Cause Miz George has lost her mind. Gone plumb clear crazy, son."

"Miz George?"

"Yes, Miz George. She come to town 'safternoon an' heard you shot Toad Johnson an' talked with Marr, an' listened to a lot of fool lies an' argyments about why you—"

"She believes that, Jeb?"

"She said she just couldn't put up longer with all the trouble you made. She said she didn't quite know just what to think. I tried to tell her just perzactly what she ort to think, the which was that if you ever took the trouble to shoot Toad Johnson he would be dead, not struttin' around with his arm in a sling a-offerin', I don't know what all. Oh, well, one thing led to another, so I up an' quit. She purt-near wept."

"Then got mad?"

"Then got mad," Grimes admitted. His words bubbled softly, and he was a little amused. "Told me I was no good anyhow. Never had been worth my salt. Was glad to be rid of me. All of the which I agreed to polite as I knowed how an' that made her madder. Then I went over to the Best Bet an' was havin' me some drinks with Jim when we heard shots. He said 'My God, that's Red! He's up-stairs!' So I poked a bottle in my pocket, hit my hoss, an' rode around back for to take some part in whatever doin's was done. An' here we are, son, just two punchers a-ridin' out lookin' for a job. My hoss is fresh. Who's yourn?"

"The Ghost."

Grimes peered. "The Ghost? What kinda likker have I been drinkin'?" He raised his look to Red's face. "You 'pear natural, but if this is The Ghost—he has got The Ghost's build but—"

"Soap an' bluin', Jeb. Where we headin'?"

"Oh, we'll ride out some'eres, have a drink an' sleep, git up, have a drink an' ride off some'eres. Shh! Lis'en. I hear 'em comin'!"

Red had keen ears but he hadn't caught the sound of hoofs before Grimes spoke. In a few minutes a bunch of hard-ridden horses came to view out of the dimness. Red said, "They think I shot that girl!"

Grimes said, "Come on, son!" and wheeled his horse, drove home the spurs, gave a yell wild as any Indians', let the reins fall on the horse's neck, and went at full gallop straight for the pursuers. He opened fire with the rifle.

Red followed, spurring hard and swearing at Grimes' madness—if it were madness and not a well-founded contempt for such people as must huddle together to chase a man or two. There were a few wild answering shots, some scared yelping, then the astounded pursuers turned tail, scattered, went hell-for-leather straight back up the street.

Grimes reined up. Red went plunging on ahead before he could pull The Ghost down. When he came back, Grimes was reloading his rifle and, for one of the few times in his life, grinning. He patted the side of the butt, called his gun "a good girl, an' like most women, allus ready fer to argy!" He pulled his bottle, took a swig, passed it to Red.

"They think I shot that girl, Jeb." Red was apologizing for, almost approving of, the pursuers.

"Now mebbe they'll go back an' think some more," Grimes suggested. "Le's go on about our business."

4

As they rode, Grimes told about going to the Nims' ranch. "Her an' Sally Nims talked up near all night. That runnin' sheep is some rilin' to cowmen. Miz Nims she rode over today to see her father. She says if Bill ain't plumb honest, she'll skin 'im alive."

"You hadn't ort've quit, Jeb."

"She hadn't ort've listened to Dep'ty Marr. To me he's jest a louse off an' Injun."

"But Miz George is in a fight, Jeb. That Buck has been hired, and of course men like 'im, to clean us out. You are her best man."

"Know it," said Grimes, matter-of-fact. He nursed the rifle in the crook of his arm and rolled

234

a cigarette. "Have 'nother little drink, son?"

"Not yet. Listen, Jeb. Did she or Jim tell you that Hepples have moved in on that house where them Huskinses was kicked out? They are bringin' in cows, of course. Why else would they squat down in our Basin?"

A match was flickering before Grimes' eyes. He drew back his head a little, faced Red, asked almost in a whisper, "What you say, son?"

"I bumped into Pink Hepple at the Golden Palace. We said 'Howdy' an' such-like. He got a wee peevish over me makin' a remark or two an' up an' said I could tell Miz George that Hepples had planked fightin' men down in the Basin, over to Huskinses."

The match flame was right at Grimes' fingers but he shook it out, not dropping the stick until the flame was dead. He put the cigarette in his mouth, rode in silence for a time. Pretty soon he pulled something from his pocket, gave it a fling. It was the bottle of whisky. He struck another match, lit his cigarette.

"Well, son, looks as how you an' me was a-ridin' again for Miz George, hm?"

Red cussed him, pleased and joyful.

As they jogged on, Grimes said, "Nice o' them Hepples, ain't it, son, for to come over clost where they'll be easy found? I hope Miz Hepple she come along. I been waitin' a long time now to up an' say 'Howdy' to her!"

Red was tempted to pry a little with some questions, but decided not to. Grimes might turn sour and silent.

In about an hour or so they saw a horseman against the skyline on a hill quite a piece ahead. The man was flogging his horse. He rode sort of lumpy and awkward.

"Whoa-up, son. We'll wait here in the gully. He comes from the way we are headin'."

They drew off to the side of the road, waiting. The horseman seemed a heavy man and floundered in the saddle. As soon as he saw Red and Grimes waiting ahead he left the road and started 'cross country.

Grimes called, "Halt!" in a way that made Red jump a little. It was always as surprising as an unexpected shot to hear Grimes' velvet voice explode with power and sharpness.

The fellow flogged the harder as they took out after him, angling to cut around them; but it seemed about all he could do to stay on the horse. When he saw he was being headed off, he tried to double back and turned too sharp. The horse slipped and fell.

By the time they rode up, the horse had got to its feet but the man was on the ground, swearing outlandishly. Red said, "Gosh a'mighty, Dutchy!"

Dutchy's round eyes popped in his round fat face. He tried to get up and grabbed his crippled leg, swearing. There was no understanding him for he was jabbering German. When he remembered and tried to speak English it was so excited and broken that about all Red could make out were the cuss words with "Hebbles" and "dod Buck" thrown in every now and then.

"Calm yourself some!" Red urged.

Dutchy went on jabbering, but presently they began to get the story. Then it was Red who used the cuss words. Grimes squatted on his haunches, silent and attentive.

CHAPTER ELEVEN

That morning it had been shortly after breakfast up to the Dobbs house when Duke lifted his head, growled deep in his throat and stood up.

Mason sat with elbows on knees and had a kind of silly grin, expressive of bliss, as the two girls, with arms about each other on the hammock swing, giggled in confessional ecstasy. Catherine had just confided her own secret about being married to a Hepple.

Duke growled again and the hair rose along his back. Other collies stirred, threw up their noses, listening.

"What's the matter with those dogs?" asked Dora.

Duke gave a sharp bark, high-pitched, and bolted down the hill with a half dozen dogs following.

Dutchy, fat and crippled, limped around the corner, pipe in mouth and little round blue eyes peering. He mumbled, "Zumpody iss combin'." Dutchy had been working on the leaky water tank behind the kitchen.

The dogs, now out of sight, set up a kind of frenzied yapping. Dutchy shook his head, doubtful.

Far below down the hillside, moving through

the sycamores like a flight of shadows, horsemen could be seen. They came clearly to view on the winding road. The horses labored on the up-grade under the thresh of quirts and kick of spurs.

"Dey nod our poys," said Dutchy, uneasily.

The snarling dogs sprang savagely at the riders' legs, snapped at the horses' noses. A collie was knocked over, trampled, lay howling piteously. The eight horsemen came on.

"Gott!" Dutchy bellowed, flapping his arms as if to shoo them, "you girls ged ind der house. Dot feller Buck!"

"And—and old Huskins!" Mason gasped.

Catherine whirled. She looked taller, her face was thinned and pale. "Why don't you men do something!" She seemed accusing Dutchy mostly but her eyes were fixed on Mason's face as if in sudden tense appraisal.

The horsemen, now near the house, began shooting the dogs. They couldn't dismount with those brutes ready to come at their throats. Catherine shrieked, "How dare you!" and moved as if to run forward among the dogs, but Dora caught her. "Oh don't! Don't! You would be hurt!"

Duke's head was almost as high as the saddle horn, leaping with hopeless effort for Buck's throat when Buck shot him. All the men were banging away, partly at the dogs, partly for the noise.

Buck rode right up to the end of the veranda, yanked up his horse with hard high jerk of arm. The revolver was still in his hand, but his hand hung low at his side and without menace. He was grinning, savage and pleased, looked longest at Dora, said, "Well, folks! Howdy!"

"Gott!" Dutchy blurted. "You are pandits!"

"Well now," said Buck with friendly sort of jeering, "ain't that just like a damn Dutchman! Folks ride in for a visit, soc'ble like, an' you call 'em hard names!" Buck swung his arm, shouted at his men: "Round 'em up, fellers!"

The horsemen stormed on around the house, shooting into the air. They were making sure nobody would escape from the house. Two jumped off and turned back 'Nita and her girls, brought them through the house and out on to the veranda.

"Here's all we found, Buck," said a pot-bellied man who had a wide-jowled, flat moon-like face.

Old Huskins piled off his horse clumsily. His bearded face was scabbed, looked grotesquely like an odd attempt at disguise.

They were all a hard looking lot, none younger than Buck, none so broad chested, and all seemed none the less scoundrels because they grinned as if having a good time. Only Huskins looked as if he wanted to hurt somebody for the pleasure of it.

A lean old thin-faced fellow with broken teeth

drawled, "I reckon, Buck, from now on Dobbses won't hold thar tails so high in the air, hm?"

Buck stood with hat in hand. His lips were twisted in a kind of malicious good humor as he looked at the girls. "None of you all is goin' to get hurt. Shore a pleasure for to meet you again, Miss Harris!"

Dora held her breath, stared with gentle dark eyes in a daze of uneasy astonishment. She remembered him well enough from the long ride in the stage, and with no dislike. "W-why are you doing this?" she asked timidly.

"Ho, lots of reasons. *You,* maybe, are one of 'em!" Buck grinned. He seemed trying to be nice.

The pot-bellied man thrust out an arm, pointing toward the bunkhouse and corrals down in the valley. "How 'bout them thar, Buck?"

"I'm plumb forgetful when I talk to purty girls! Sam, you all go on down an' do what you come for. 'F you need my help you won't be worth a damn! So me an' Hank'll stay up here. He's a lady's man, too!"

Hank was the old withered scrawny man with broken teeth and tobacco-dribbled mouth.

The pot-bellied Sam yelled, "Hit yore hosses an' come a-humpin'!" The men whooped, partly at Hank's being a lady's man, partly in sheer glee at the easy success of the raid. They strung out in a furious gallop down the hill, old Huskins behind with elbows flapping like broken wings.

Catherine straightened until she seemed to rise on tip-toes. She threw back her head with a jerk that shook the blonde curls, spoke angrily and her voice did not tremble: "What are you doing here!"

"Me?" Buck grinned. "Oh, come now! Me, I'm havin' a good time mostly—or meanin' to! That right, Hank?"

"You girls are lucky," said Hank. He had a voice that sounded as if his vocal cords were raveled. "And," with intent to please and reassure Dora, "he has talked a lot about how nice you air!"

Buck reached out for Dora's hand. She drew back, staring timidly. "Aw, I won't hurt you!" His voice wasn't rough, was almost mild in its coaxing. He took the hand, patted it. Dora's was a gentle nature, with none of Kate Pineton's fire and fierceness; and she seemed to feel it was better to act submissive than to anger him.

"Hi, looky, Buck!" Hank called and pointed.

Buck faced about and stood with mouth parted in intent watching of the far-off midget-like figures in the valley below. The horsemen had pulled down before a limping figure with beard flying and rifle lifted that came hurrying out to meet them. Old Robertson scorned to take cover. The pot-bellied Sam rode forward with arm lifted, palm out, as if to parley. A shot was fired, then another. Robertson, taken off guard, had been shot by one of the men behind the pot-bellied fellow. He fell forward, lay like a tired man asleep.

"You Gott-tam gowards!" Dutchy blurted, rocking back with crippled sway on his short leg, glaring. He clapped the meerschaum back in his mouth and stared with blue-eyed anger at Buck who paid no attention at all. But Hank, with a hand on his gun's butt, walked over to Dutchy, jerked the pipe from his mouth, threw it down, tromped on it, slapped him. "Shet up or I'll larn yuh—"

"Aw," Buck called casually, "keep yore shirt tail in, Hank!" There was an easy authority in the way he spoke as if he were used to being obeyed.

"You call us cowards agin," said Hank, showing his broken teeth, "an' I'll blow a hole through you!"

"That," Catherine snapped shrilly with a sound that was almost like Mrs. George's angered tone, "would prove you weren't a coward—wouldn't it!"

Hank glared at her and met a fierce stare. It was his eyes that moved first.

Down in the valley the horsemen had dismounted and were scurrying like looters through the bunkhouse and kitchen. Two men came out of the kitchen dragging a man in his undershirt and a white apron. Joey was nearly dead of fright. He was tied to a sycamore.

A man on a bareback horse, riding with a halter, bolted from behind the stables. It was the Mexican, Sanzo, making a break to carry word of the raid. Yelps went up and men began shooting rapidly. Sanzo, shot through the back, slid off. A man jumped into a saddle and took out after the horse, shooting. The horse stumbled, hit in the leg. The fellow rode up and killed it, then galloped back toward the bunkhouse, yelling as if he had done something to make a noise about.

Smoke began to appear through a bunkhouse window, then flame.

"They jes' ain't goin' to be no Dobbs ranch no more!" said Hank.

Men were running about through the smoke, carrying fire to the kitchen, stables, corrals. The crackling roar of the dry timber came like a sound of high wind. There was little, or no smoke, after the fire took hold, but a high sweep of flame and even the air on the hilltop was for a time as if it had come from an oven.

The stately 'Nita watched the fire with a look as if her own home were burning. Her hands were wrapped tightly in her apron but she made no sound. Her daughters huddled against her and wept. Dutchy cussed under his breath.

"We're burnin' this here house, too, 'fore we leave!" said Hank, evilly pleased and showing black broken teeth.

"No? No? You aren't, are you?" Dora asked of Buck. She was so breathless that her voice sounded soft and coaxing. Instinct seemed to warn her how best to hide her fears and get on the weak side of this ruffian.

"Aw don't you fret none, Honey. *You* ain't goin' to be hurt!"

He didn't see the look Catherine gave him. It was scornful and challenging, as if she would rather lose her head than soften a word or glance.

The men in the valley had ridden into the pasture, roped horses, then cut the wire fence and drove out the horses they didn't want, scattering them over the country.

Catherine clenched her fists, held her arms straight at her side, moved so as to stand directly in front of Buck. "Why are you doing this? You! If you are just plain thieves, rob the house—and go!"

Buck looked amused. "Kind of a cross-patch, ain't you?"

"What's the meaning of all this?" Her voice was edged with increased sharpness.

"Why, ain't you heard?" He was vaguely mocking. "Range war has come! You Dobbses are wiped out. We are Hepple riders—makin' a clean sweep! A damn sight cleaner sweep, by God! than even them as hired us bargained for!" He laughed as if somewhere behind his words there was a good joke, not yet disclosed.

245

Catherine was so angry she looked frozen. She said coldly to the unhappy Mason, "Since these men are from *your* ranch, why don't you speak up!"

Buck perked up his ears. "What you talkin' about?"

Mason was pale. He moved a step nearer. His mouth was so dry his tongue sounded thick and his voice trembled, but he lifted his face with a steady look:

"I am Mr. Hepple's son and this is m-my wife!"

He put out an arm, meaning to take Catherine's waist protectively but she turned aside, stepping off as if she scorned support.

"You're who?" Buck frowned for a moment in a kind of wonder as to why a thing like that would be told him; then he laughed. "You Dobbses are smart, ain't you? Huh! I won't swaller that one. I know more about this country than you think. I know all about the Hepples!"

"But B-Buck, it is true!" said Dora. Using his name was desperate flattery and her fears made it sound shy.

"What you talkin' about, honey?" He still thought Dora the prettiest girl he had ever seen.

"He *is* Mr. Hepple's son and he and Catherine *are* married!"

"Ho, ho, you can't fool me. And if *you* can't, nobody can! From what I hear tell, old lady

Dobbs 'ud poison any Hepple as set foot on this ranch! Besides, now that Joe Bush was killed, they's only Pinky that is the son—"

"Oh, but please listen!" Dora exclaimed. She somehow felt it must be better to have Buck know Harold Mason was a Hepple. Hastily, with panting nervous eagerness, she told the story of the marriage and its secrecy, of Harold Hepple coming to the ranch as Mason.

Buck slapped his leg. "I'll be damned if that ain't some joke! Not only on old lady Dobbs but on your step-maw, too! She'll be mad enough to bite herself when she learns you'll maybe want a share of Pinky's cows—an' hern! Ho, ho, here her and the Johnsons are a planning to get the Arrowhead from old lady Dobbs an' you've already got it, so to speak! Ho, ho, ho! I'll be damned!"

Buck laughed some more. It struck him as good and funny. "Well, here comes the boys. Now we'll all enjoy ourselves a little." He turned toward 'Nita. "You trot to the kitchen an' cook up somethin' good. Make it plenty! Hank, go 'long and see they don't bolt. Them's purty girls, so watchin' 'em will be a pleasure!"

The men were clattering up, jumping from horses, roughly good-humored.

Buck told them, "This feller here with the sick calf look is ol' Ding Hepple's boy and married to old lady Dobbses' gran'daughter!"

Sam, the pot-bellied, asked, "You goin' to take him over to see his step-maw, Buck?"

"That might be a good idee," Buck agreed with thoughtful side-shift of glance at Mason.

Sam swaggered close, leered at Catherine. "Kinda nice, ain't you?" Her hand, without any warning, whacked his face. The smack had the sound of two leather straps snapped together. Men guffawed. Sam looked a little sheepish, rubbed his jaw. "She's got the kick of a two year ol' in that paw of hern." Then, with glint of malice, "But I'd damn soon tame you if you was mine!"

"You," said Catherine, sweeping their faces with a look that included all of them, "are a fine lot of two-legged things to call yourselves men! You—" her look fixed on Buck "—are a coward and look it! You knew the men were away from the ranch! You wouldn't have come otherwise! You'd have run, run! just as you did that night when you shot at Red Clark from the dark through a window—"

That was not the way Buck had told it to folks. "Shet up!" he snarled. "Oh I'll—"

"I won't shut up! You coward! You were afraid of Red! You shot from the dark—"

Buck said, "I'll shore shut yore mouth for you good!" He lurched at her with raised fist. Catherine shrank back, then stopped and straightened as if too proud to run. Buck struck her with open hand across the mouth.

Dora screamed, "Oh, don't! Please don't!" and hid her face.

Mason, wild and helpless but brave, rushed at him. "She is my wife, you dog!" His fist wavered in awkward swing at Buck's face. Buck knocked him down and kicked him again and again, glad to have someone on whom to work off his rage.

Catherine flew at Buck with fingers set claw-like. Men grabbed her, pulled her back. They held her firmly and grinned with a kind of admiring tolerance of her spunk. She begged them to make Buck stop. A big fellow with both hands on her wrist shook his head with a kind of warning. "No, miss. We know 'im! An' we don't meddle when he's mad!"

Buck didn't feel proud of himself. He had worked off his temper, but Dora was staring at him with fear and reproach. He seemed oddly submissive in wanting to please her.

"I don't like Hepples!" he said as if somehow vaguely justifying what he had done. "I'm s'posed to be workin' for 'em. But them bankers hired me to. They knowed, for one thing, I had it in for Red Clark. They knowed, too, I don't mind making trouble for folks! Hepples are no good. None of 'em. There's that Pink—he thinks he is goin' to marry you. But he ain't! I wouldn't let you marry into a no-count outfit like that. And you wouldn't want to if you knew what all I know about 'em. 'Sides, what marryin' is done to you, me, I'll do it!"

He was quite good-humored again and patted Dora's hand, then put an arm about her, pulled her to him. She neither yielded nor resisted; but there was such reproach in her eyes that he said, "She hadn't ort to rile me. I'm a good feller if I ain't riled."

Mason got off the floor all bent over. He was bleeding, half sobbing and stumbled into a chair, blindly. Catherine dabbed at his face with a small handkerchief and stood over him in a kind of protective rage, helpless but unafraid. Some of the men peered at her with furtive admiration, spoke one to another out of the corners of their mouths: "That girl's got grit, feller!" . . . " 'Tain't many as'll sass Buck!"

Buck didn't like the sudden solemn feeling that had come over everybody. "Hey, what's the matter with you all! Come on, let's get into the house. We're goin' to eat soon. And, by God, drink now!"

They moved into the house. Mason was half dragged, stumblingly. He was hurt, and hurt the deeper by his helplessness. A man, not unkindly, held to one arm; Catherine to the other. Mason sat down and she stood with an arm about his shoulders.

Men searched through the house, especially old Huskins. With clatter of cowhide boots he ran from room to room, emptying trunks and dumping drawers on the floor. He said loudly that he had a right to whatever he could get out of that old Dobbs woman. Men grinned, eying one another with secret understanding, and called, "Pop, be shore an' don't overlook nothin'!"

When he had gone through the house he went nosing about outside and opened the gate into the shed where the savage Bella nursed her pups. His yells brought men running and they found him on his back in a corner wildly flailing the air with his heavy cowhide boots. The dog had torn his clothes half off and leaped this way and that, slashing at him with ripping teeth as a wolf strikes. They shot Bella. With her back broken she crawled at them with teeth bared and snarling; and when a bullet went through her brain she lay flattened out with a look as if still ready to jump. When Huskins got to his feet he ran and jumped on her body, cursing.

"I'm goin' to tromp to death ever' god-damn one of them pup-dogs!" Huskins bellowed, and started toward the shed.

One of the men caught him by the shoulder and flung him back. He said with slit-eyed menace, "You just ain't!"

Huskins went limping into the house, belly-aching about his bad luck, and the men tormented him with pretended seriousness that Bella had had all the signs of being a mad dog.

Wines and liquors had been found and were brought out by the handful and in baskets. Dutchy's fat body and the way he lumbered tickled some of the men. After they had a few drinks they laughed at his crippled waddle and it amused them to make him play waiter. All were soon nicely warmed and a little tipsy. Their loosened tongue haphazardly disclosed that nearly all them had been on the dodge, and some still were. They had been attracted by the Monohela mining boom to this part of the country and raked together to ride for Hepples. Many of them had rode with Buck before.

One fellow poked at the piano, thumping the bass keys as if trying to imitate thunder. Another cocked his feet above his head and sang, "Oh, bury me not on the lone, lone prairie." Voice rose in a higher pitch, good-natured. They had no uneasiness whatever about loitering in the Dobbs house. Once in a while somebody would go out and have a look and come back. There was no other guard kept.

'Nita and her daughters were fixing dinner. They worked sullenly, scarcely speaking. Some of the men pawed the girls who said nothing, made no protest, were as impassive as dummies.

'Nita, quite as if getting a package of salt, opened a dark little closet door high over her head and took down a box of rough-on-rats. Dutchy saw what she was doing. He furtively wrenched

252

it from her hand. In his thick broken English, half whispered, he told her not everybody would be poisoned at once and that those who weren't killed would be murderous. She made no reply at all, but simply turned to the stove, poked in wood.

Buck had pulled Dora on to his lap and was trying in what was a respectful way for him to tell her some more about how much he liked her. She had none of Catherine's fierceness and he mistook her passive fright for a kind of yielding. He drank much whisky and she, pressed, took a little wine. She felt in need of something because she was faint and seemed choking.

Buck told her she mustn't think any more about Pink Hepple who was a bad feller and sure to be hung! Both the Johnsons, he said, were sweet on Mrs. Hepple who was a pretty woman and swell dresser, but sure a bad one. " 'Specially if she don't like you!"

Pinky had told Buck all about how his maw had worked them Johnsons to a T. She told old man Johnson that she was nice to his boy Milton so he would like her for a maw when old Hepple died; and she told Milton that she was nice to his dad so he would like her for a daughter when old Hepple died.

Buck slapped his knee and thought that was pretty good. "Regular Hepple trick—like sneakin' into the Dobbs house by marryin' the gran'daughter!" Buck said it was Mrs. Hepple who had coaxed the Johnsons into throwing in with her son, Joe Bush, for to let gamblers run games like they wanted. "Bad lot, all of 'em." Buck even sounded indignant. He said, "I like you too much not to make you do what is good f'r you!"

Dora smiled nervously. She was desperately anxious to keep Buck in a good humor. All he saw was the smile and that pleased him.

Them Johnsons, Buck explained—repeating, he said, what Pinky had told—at one time and another had dished out purt-near twenty thousand dollars to Mrs. Hepple. Naturally, they didn't want that money to come out of their pockets. They thought stockholders in the bank ought to help pay for her clothes and Pinky's gambling. They had a talk with Pinky and explained how to work it slick. They would put a little money in an express box, make up the weight with a gunny sack full of iron, and send it on the stage to Monohela and say it was $30,000 in coin. Pinky and some friends were to hold up the stage. The few hundred dollars in the box would be for Pinky and his friends to spend. The Johnsons could then explain the bank shortage and have some thousands left over to hire men to fight Dobbses.

"Pink he got them two kids, 'Gene Cross an' Windy Jones, for to throw in with him. But none of 'em knew anything about holdin' up a stage. So they got 'em another feller—"

Dora was listening in a kind of anguished breathlessness. He could tell by her look that she suspected him of being that fellow. So he said, "—feller, whose name I don't know for to help 'em."

The shotgun messenger thought he was guarding $30,000 and showed fight. They killed him. Then they saw that the old driver looked like he had recognized somebody and 'Gene Cross, who was anyhow suspicious that Rim Cramer had tattled some about Cross-Box rustling, killed him.

"So Pinky is shore to be hanged," Buck told her, gleeful. "And I want you to go with me. After I get through here in Tulluco—and when I settle up some little business over to the Hepple ranch, I'll be through—I'm goin' down to Mexico where I've got friends, and get me a ranch. I am going to take you along."

"Please, I—I—oh, you mustn't make me—"

"Oh, I'll be good to you. I'm a nice feller thataway!" Then he laughed, looked across at Mason. "An' I'm shore goin' to take him along to the Hepple ranch and show him to her. 'Twill help me argy her into raisin' my wages some!" He grinned, sinister and ironic. "Tonight," he said, "we'll stop over to that place old woman Dobbs druv Huskins off of. Then tomorrow—"

Some of the men, in prowling about, had released Trixy from her closet. She came into the room and barked wildly. Men were amused by the furious little puff ball and poked out their boots, tormenting her into a frenzy. Her yapping was so shrill and persistent that Buck turned from trying to talk nice and persuasive to Dora and said, "Shut that thing up!" A man kicked the poodle as hard as he could, sending her some ten feet through the air and against the wall. Catherine shrieked and ran to her pet, crouched down. Her tight-set lips trembled. The little poodle had a leg broken and whimpered with pleading lift of tiny head as if trying to understand.

Buck, telling Dora what a fine fellow he was, pointed to Mason as an example of what a man oughtn't be like. Mason was bleeding about the face and had some bones nearly broken. Buck called him a cry-baby.

"Now me, I onct crawled more'n ten mile with a busted leg across the desert without a drink of water! An' never whimpered none!"

Catherine stood up, hugging the poodle to her breast. "You are nothing but a big brute anyhow!" she screamed at him. "And a coward! If I were a man I would kill you!"

"Huh, it's been tried by men!" said Buck, complacently.

"You tried to kill Red Clark when he wasn't looking and—"

"I got a right to kill him any old way I can. His dad killed my dad and—"

"Your father needed killing then!" Catherine's voice was shrill and furious: "Needed it if only for being the father of such a thing as you!"

He shoved Dora off his lap. Catherine's tongue had cut him again. He glowered, looked mean.

"Coward!" she shrieked.

"I ain't afraid of—"

"You are afraid!" Her tongue was loose again.

He yelled at her to shut up. She wouldn't shut up. She said anything and everything that swirled into her mind. He had seemed to wince most at mention of Red; so she said, "You are afraid of Red Clark! He would shoot you like *that!*" She stamped a foot, showing how quick Red would shoot. "You know it, you coward! To shoot from the dark through a window—"

Buck's men grinned furtively, amused to see him, a bad man if ever there was one, tongue-lashed by a girl, a pretty girl.

Buck's temper again exploded. He cursed her and jumped up. Dora screamed and snatched at his arm, pleading. She might as well have caught at the shoulder of a wild horse. "Ho, onct ain't enough, huh?" He struck her.

Catherine rocked back, but kept her balance, stood firm, not flinching.

Mason weakly came up out of the chair. There was a mad dazed look in his eyes. He could scarcely see. He could scarcely stand. He was trembling. He swung wildly. Buck knocked the blow aside with almost casual toss of forearm.

"And you ain't had enough yet either, eh? I'll shore give it to you now!" He drew a gun. Catherine dropped the dog and flew at him. He threw her aside and struck Mason over the head with the gun barrel. Mason fell as if shot.

"Oh, you have killed him!" said Catherine as if she had lost her voice and could no more than whisper.

"I ain't. But I shore will if you don't shut yore damn mouth!"

She threw herself knees down over Mason. He was bleeding from nose and mouth and lay on his side as if dead. She called to him. Her hands fluttered about his face and breast, searching for signs of life. Her courage, her devotion, her prettiness, made Buck, who again didn't feel very proud of himself, say, "Too damn bad you don't love a *man* 'stead of sissy feller like him!"

That was like putting a match to powder. She was on her knees and her head went up in a way that sent her yellow hair flying. "He's braver than you!" The gleam in her bluish gray eyes was like the glint of bright metal. "You are ten times stronger, so he is ten times braver than you ever could be because he isn't afraid!" Her wild look flashed about on the stolid-staring faces.

"You beasts! Beasts! You let him beat a helpless boy like this! You let him strike *me!*" Their eyes swayed blankly to avoid her fierce look. "Strike women!"

Old Huskins was half drunk so he didn't feel the pain of the dog bites now. His pockets bulged with stolen stuff. He growled, "I'd smack 'er again, good, Buck!"

Buck whirled on him. "Keep yore goddamned mouth shut or I'll—" He drew back his fist and Huskins shrank away, blinking.

One fellow mumbled vaguely, "Aw, let's be ridin'!" One studied his dirty fingernails. Another stared from a window, suddenly interested in scenery. Buck took up a bottle of whisky from the table, drank with long gurgle, handed it to man nearest, said, "Drink." It was like a command.

Dora put her arms about Catherine. "Darling, come with me!" That seemed a way of escape from the room for Dora, too.

"I won't leave Hal!" said Catherine.

"An' you ain't goin' to get out of my sight!" Buck put his hand on Dora's shoulder, trying to be gentle. "I liked you from that time in the stage!"

Dora trembled. Her nature was not defiant. She used his liking for her to coax Buck into letting Mason be carried into Catherine's room.

The men who carried him, because of a kind of abashed admiration for Catherine's spunk, were almost gentle. "Careful of the kid," one mumbled to the others.

Catherine demanded a pail of water and towels. Dutchy was told to fetch them. Then Catherine banged the door to.

The men began to drink again and grew half way gay. It was a good joke for them to make old Huskins shell out all the loot he had picked up, and, saying it was share and share alike, they divided everything among themselves. He whimpered and cussed, and was jeered.

Bacon and beans and stuff out of cans were piled on the table and men crowded about, hats on, elbows on the table, snatching like dogs out of a common platter. They gulped old wines.

After they had eaten they were ready to ride. Buck stuck to his notion about packing young Mason along. Dora, in a kind of timid desperation, tried to talk him out of taking any of them and mentioned the dangers he would run in handicapping himself with "prisoners."

Buck was contemptuous. "Anyhow," he said, "you ain't no prisoner. You're goin' to be my wife." He made Dutchy bring an empty tin can and to show how well he could shoot, threw it out of the door. He hit it once in the air and again before it stopped rolling on the ground. "Why," he demanded, patting the gun after reloading, "ort I be afraid of anybody?"

There was some talk of firing the ranch house

before they rode off. The lean Hank and the pot-bellied Sam insisted, but Dora's coaxing had the most weight. Buck said, "Anyhow, we done more now than them bankers'll like since they feel it's their property we burnt!"

Mason was dragged out. He was sick, hurt, helpless, and begged not to be taken. "I just can't stay in a saddle!"

"We'll tie you in!" said Buck.

"And I," Catherine announced fiercely, "will go wherever my husband goes if I have to follow on foot!"

Buck eyed her with frank admiration. "Women like you are shore scarce." He turned to Sam. "Get a horse for her, too."

They rode off, with nightfall not far away.

As soon as they were gone, Dutchy began trying to find a horse. One of the Mexican children brought in an old horse that had been tempted by a pan of oats to within reach of a loop. Then Dutchy set out for town.

CHAPTER TWELVE

In trying to avoid Grimes and Red, Dutchy had fallen with his horse and hurt his bad leg. As he told his story he rubbed at the leg. Red cussed a little, listening. Grimes said not a word; just rolled a cigarette a time or two and squatted, patient.

Dutchy tried to get up. His fat weight was too much for the injured leg.

"But can you set a saddle if we heave you up?" Red asked. Dutchy, swearing, said he could try. "Then if you go at a walk, maybe you can stick an' get to town."

Red and Grimes lifted, pushed, heaved while Dutchy, bulky and awkward, clawed at the saddle and struggled to climb up. Grunts of pain came out of him. "We hurtin'?" Red asked.

"Tam der hurt!" said Dutchy. "Ged me ub!" He squealed like a stuck pig but told them to keep on shoving; and so got into the saddle, rubbed his leg, swore.

Red patted Dutchy's good leg. "I never knowed the time would come when I'd admire Dutch bullheadedness so much. Now you take it slow or you'll spill off."

"Whad you feller goin' do?"

"Us? Oh, me an' Jeb'll sorta poke around some an' have a look. That right, Jeb?"

Dutchy rode off into the darkness.

Grimes swung into the saddle, pulled his horse about, not speaking, and headed at a jog trot 'cross country straight as a bee line for Huskinses Place.

2

A couple of hours later and a mile or two from Huskinses, Red ventured, "Maybe they'll have somebody on guard?"

Grimes said, "Mebbe," just that, nothing more; and it was the first word he had spoken since they left Dutchy.

They rode on at a quiet trot. Grimes very seldom ever put a horse into a lope.

After a time Grimes began a circle. Red understood that he was working around so as to come up to the house from the back.

About a half mile off they saw the glimmer of lights in the house. Folks were up. Grimes pulled down to a slow walk so hoof beats wouldn't carry through the night stillness. He drew the rifle from its scabbard, laid the barrel in the crook of his left arm and rode with reins loose, letting the horse pick its way but heading toward the dark blotches that were sheds behind the house.

Red would have preferred to do a little cautious sneaking. This riding up in starlight, slow and casual, was hard on his nerves. Anybody, or many, could creep out there in the shadows and shoot a couple of times, all of a sudden. But Red would have choked before he let Grimes know how he felt about it. So they went on, stirrup to stirrup, and Red peered tensely at shadows.

Grimes put out his long arm, pulled at Red's reins, stopping. He said in a quiet voice, "We'll walk from here."

Red got off, shook himself, hitched up his belts, and started to take his rifle, but changed his mind. It would be merely useless weight.

Grimes murmured, "Let's look over their horses first."

He stepped forward with a kind of gliding stride. So far as Red knew, Grimes had been on horseback nearly all his life but he wasn't bow-legged and didn't walk with a wriggle and stumble, and was as erect as if on parade.

They went to the small corral, looked over. Six horses were there, some lying down. They swung their heads, twitched their ears. One got up slowly but stood still. Grimes counted and said, "That's too bad."

Red knew what he meant. Dutchy had reported eight men in the party; and there should have been at least eleven horses here since the two girls and Mason had rode off with them. On top of that, there had probably been some men left here at Huskinses when Buck went to the Arrowhead.

"Now, son," Grimes explained low and easy, "I'll walk around front. You go up the back way here, but wait for me. It is for me to say 'Howdy,' first."

Grimes stepped along to the edge of the shed, gave a look toward the house and walked out into the starlight with his rifle in the crook of his arm. He seemed quite consciously to have the feeling that it would be other people's bad luck, not his, if they caught sight of him.

There was a glimmer of light at a dusty window up stairs, a glow from the front windows down stairs; none from the kitchen.

Red went in a hurry for the back door. He felt his skin squirm a little at the thought of how anybody standing in the dark kitchen doorway could shoot him down; and he very frankly admitted to himself, humbly, that he didn't have much of what is called cold nerve when put up alongside of old Jeb Grimes. But he had some shame at feeling scairt and it helped to make him go right on, boldly.

The kitchen's outer door was open; the inner closed. A muddle of loud voices came from the front room, with anger in the loudest tones as if a quarrel were on. Red tiptoed quickly across the kitchen and found the door closed but not latched. He pushed cautiously. It was an old heavy hand-made door and swung without a squeak, opening an inch or two.

Red saw a young man half way up the stairs and over a leveled gun facing those below him. His face was distorted with a determined look, almost frenzied. Red recognized him as young Perry, the bronco buster old Robertson had ordered off the ranch. It sort of made Red mad that an Arrowhead puncher, even if fired not quite justly, should have thrown in with Hepples. But when he heard how Perry talked Red's feelings changed.

Perry was cussing as he said, "You ain't comin' up! You just ain't! Not while I'm alive, you ain't! I'll kill you if you do an'—" He was a little hysterical but fierce.

Men were talking to him, their eyes on that gun. Three men, one of them old Huskins, were together at the foot of the stairs. They glared, venturing a foot on the lowest step.

Two other men were sprawled in chairs, looking on as if at a show and with a kind of evil amusement taunting the fellows Perry had stopped. One of the on-lookers was a pot-bellied man with a flat moon-like face. He had a sneer sort of grin and jeered, "You all look handsome, I must say, lettin' that kid stop you—after you won 'er!" The other, a wrinkled starved looking old man showed broken teeth and tobacco-slobbered mouth in grinning: "He's jes' tryin' to save 'er for himself!" The lean old starved fellow had his arm on the table and a pack of cards in his hand.

Huskins, with some rags tied around his leg where the dog had bit him, stomped about and bellered, "We'll kill you, kid! We won 'er fair an' square—an' playin' poker was yore own notion!"

A bareheaded wild looking young fellow was yelling, "We ain't scairt! It's only we don't want to hurt you!"

Another man had one foot on the lowest step and kept pretending that he was about to rush, but talked, saying, "Don't be a fool, kid!"

Perry kept right on saying, "You ain't comin' up! You just ain't!"

" 'Twas you," Huskins bellered some more, "said let's play poker for 'er, an' now cause you lost—"

"Ol' Pap there he won 'er!" said the pot-bellied man, amused. Then the pot-bellied man straightened a little in his chair, let his hand fall to his side, shouted in a kind of boisterous good humor, "I'll show you how!" He had drawn his gun unnoticed and as he spoke he shot from the side of the chair. "Now," he yelled, "go git 'er!"

Perry, hit in the breast, pitched forward headlong down the stairs. His cocked revolver fell from his hand and the jar of the fall let the hammer strike. It exploded harmlessly on the floor but made men jump. A woman screamed as Perry plunged down, flopping with wild swing of legs to the bottom of the stairs. The men there stumbled back as if from blows.

Red's glance went high up the stairs. Catherine's blanched face peered down with look of terror.

Red kicked the heavy door wide and lurched

forward. He said, "God damn your souls!" and was shooting before the words were out of his mouth. The first bullet went into the moon-faced man's pot-belly; and, as he sprang up, really falling, but very much as if to rush, Red shot him again.

There were squeaks and yaps of surprise, blurted oaths. Huskins howled, "Oh, that Red!" The old skinny man scattered the pack of cards in a convulsive toss of hand as he sprang up, knocking over the chair behind him. He drew and shot quick, and without looking around swung his left arm at the lamp on the table behind him. The swing missed and Red shot him. The lean withered old fellow went down, shooting. His mouth was wide open as if to bite poisonously with blackened tooth stumps.

There was blaze of guns. Flame tips jabbed at Red. Smoke boiled explosively above gun muzzles. Red jumped to one side, getting his back to the wall. He shot as a fighter uses his fists, all instinct and fast. Bullets splattered the wood behind his head.

The black-headed wild looking young fellow crouched as he backed off with two guns out and both blazing, then pitched forward, hit in the heart. Red's mouth was half open, his lips drawn back. The look of an unconscious grin, savage and joyful, was on his face but his eyes had a hawk-fierce glare. Huskins stumbled to take cover at the side of the stairs, drew awkwardly at his revolver. His first shot, over-anxious, hit the floor not far from his own feet; his second went off at the ceiling as he fell with the top of his head blown off. Red, with a snap shot through the two-inch space between the banister supports, hit him high on the forehead.

Red's hat jumped as if snatched and as it went he jerked his head to one side, instinctively as a fighter dodges. A bullet smashed the wood where his head had been and there was a kind of frenzied petulance in the cry of the lean withered old fellow: "Why can't I hit the—" He was on the floor, half under the table, dying but still murderous. He gripped a rung of the overturned chair with his left hand, rested the revolver on his wrist, squirmed flat, drawing a bead.

Catherine shrieked, "Look out!"

A rifle roared through the open front doorway. The old withered fellow simply flattened out still more, face down. His grip on the chair's rung loosened. The gun slipped from his fingers, turned on its side, lay cocked with its muzzle on his left wrist.

Grimes stood in the doorway with smoking rifle waist high and looked about. His eyes were a little narrower, their look more of a gleam than usual, but otherwise he might have been coming in from a rabbit hunt to sit down to dinner. He stepped in, moved through the smoke haze, stood before Red, and his glance went up and down, seeing if Red were hurt.

Red waggled his guns, grinned nervous and gulped a deep breath.

"A-whew, but it was nice to see you! These here are empty!"

"Son," said Grimes calmly, "you done good." Then, with reproach, "But why didn't you wait like I said?"

Red pointed. "There is why!"

Catherine was coming down the stairs a slow step at a time with trance-like movement. Her hand slid along the rail as if fearful of letting go.

"Why you here alone?" Red asked.

She didn't answer but moved slowly and trembled a little. Her pretty face looked as if it were frozen in a dazed stare. "Perry?" she mumbled.

"He's dead, I'm purt-near sure," Red told her, trying to sound gentle. "When they fall like that—" He went to the foot of the stairs, kneeled. Still kneeling, he looked up, nodded.

Catherine came on down the stairs, closed her eyes, reached out, took hold of Grimes. He steadied her to a chair. She leaned forward with forearm against her face, over her eyes. In a moment or two the forearm dropped as if she hadn't the strength to hold it up. She straightened wearily, muttered, "Terrible. Oh, terrible!" and looked blankly toward Perry's body.

"Where's Buck and them?" Red asked.

Catherine swung a listless hand. The hand dropped as if it were too much effort to point. "He heard me ask Dora to coax him to let me and Hal go. So he left me here alone. Alone with those awful men. I could hear them talking. Perry—Perry made them play poker for me. For hours and hours, then—oh, why did he have to be killed after being so brave and honorable!"

"He was a nice boy, Miss Kate. But he made a big mistake in talkin' to them kind of fellers— 'stead of shootin'!"

She didn't appear to be listening, but sighed and brooded. When Red asked, "Where'd Buck and them go?" she answered in a dazed voice, "To the Hepple ranch. He said—said I'd never see Hal again."

Red looked expectantly at Grimes. Grimes nodded slightly. The glance had asked, "Do we take out after them fellows?" and the nod said, "We do!"

"Miss Kate," Red explained, "I'm sorry, but me and Jeb has got to be ridin'. We'll put you on a horse an' you can light out for town. 'Tain't far. Miz George is there. You'll be took good care of."

Catherine stared at him. "You are going— where?"

"We sorta have to have a little word with that Buck feller. He's got some wrong notions as need tendin' to."

"You are going to follow him?"

"Kinda, a little."

Her eyes cleared, brightened, "I am going with you!"

"Oh, no, you ain't!"

"I am going to follow my husband! I would follow him to the ends of the earth."

"I bet. But you don't ride good an' we'll—"

"I can hold on!"

"You'll be jolted an' awful wore out."

"You can tie me on! That is what they did to poor Hal!"

"No'm."

"I promise there won't be a whimper out of me."

"We ain't goin' to take no girl, Miss Kate!"

"If you don't take me, I'll follow! I will go!"

"You can't keep up and you'll get lost, sure."

"Very well, then, I shall get lost!"

Red looked appealingly toward Grimes; but Grimes was aloof and his dark lined face as expressionless as a mask.

"Now, Miss Kate, please. You can't stand hard ridin' like we'll—"

"I will stand it!" For an instant her look and her tone were very like Mrs. George. "Hal is brave. I am proud of him! He tried to fight for me. And he is to be more admired because he tried when he was weak and helpless against that big murderous brute! I am going to him if I have to walk!"

272

Red swore. He used highly colored oaths, help-lessly. "You just can't and ain't!"

"I just will!"

"Listen here." There was a rough snap in his voice. "Much as I like you, Miss Kate, I ain't goin' to ride slow on your account. And you know damn well you can't keep up with us. So do you wanta do somethin' that'll maybe keep us from catchin' 'em? We are goin' to wherever the hell them fellers are because they got to be learnt they can't make trouble for Miz George and not wish they hadn't!"

Catherine's pale tired face had an expression of petulant anger but she did not say anything. There was fierceness in the way he had spoken. She moved a hand, pushing the loosened hair that hung about her face, and still looked determined; but she said, weak and slow, "Perhaps you are right."

Dawn had come. The lamp was burning on the table but its wick was now just a tiny flame that seemed to give no light. The windows and doorway were grayishly transparent with the cold glow of early morning.

Grimes went out to feed their horses and saddle up for her. Red walked over to Perry's body, straightened his arms, put his feet together, unbound Perry's neckerchief and laid it over his face. Catherine sat dully staring toward Perry, brooding sadly.

3

Red prowled about and found grub. He brought some crackers, cheese and a dish of cold beans and offered them to Catherine. She shuddered, glanced up reproachful, looked away, "I couldn't."

He leaned against the wall and began to eat, just chewed and chewed and chewed on the dry food with a preoccupied air. He swallowed two or three times, cleared his throat:

"When you see Miz George, tell her for me I don't have to have wages to ride for the Arrowhead as long as they is trouble. Jeb he is the same. Tell her, too, I never shot old Johnson— but I sure as hell am goin' to, next chance I get!"

He started to take a bite of cheese, stopped:

"Tell her Jim of the Best Bet can explain why I went to see Sara and 'Gene shot 'er tryin' to shoot me. She jumped right square plumb out in front of me."

Red examined his hunk of cheese as if studying where next to take a bite, raised it to his mouth, had another thought:

"Tell 'er, too, as how she'd better tell folks in Tulluco to wait till I've settled with this Buck before they crowd up on me tryin' to collect a thousand dollars. After that they can play hide and seek with me and most liable not be bad hurt."

He stuffed cheese into his mouth with one

274

hand, crackers with the other, and chewed and chewed, still preoccupied with thoughts. Soon he swallowed some more, then spoke again, serious:

"Your husband is a right good feller from how Dutchy talked. Nobody as I ever heard tell, ever called old Dingley Hepple a coward and his boy takes after him, some. But you want to stand off quite a piece when you tell Miz George you two are married. Then you'd better back off some more before sayin' he is a Hepple. She'll go right up like a scairt bronc an' come down stiff-legged in a way to jar your back teeth. And that's a fact!"

Grimes picked what looked like a gentle horse, saddled it, mounted and shook the horse up with a few pokes of the spurs. The horse didn't pitch, so he rode around front. Red went to the door, stuffing the last of the cheese into his mouth. He turned to Catherine, beckoned, said:

"A'right. You'd better be makin' a start."

She got up, dead tired and weak. Grimes and Red both gave her a hand up into the saddle. She pushed at her skirts, tucking them in under her legs more as a gesture than really caring.

"You know, I been thinkin'," said Red. "Dutchy will have got to town purt-near by now or before. Miz George an' them will be right along out, quick. You may meet 'em on the way. Don't tell *nobody* me an' Jeb is headed for the Hepple ranch 'cause then folks'll know where to look for me and try to get that thousand dollars."

Catherine looked down at Grimes, who stood tall and calm. She looked at Red, again at Grimes. She spoke to both. "Promise me you will kill that man Buck? *Promise?*"

Grimes merely nodded slightly with bare drop of eyelids.

CHAPTER THIRTEEN

Grimes and Red switched their saddles to horses in the corral that were branded H P and rode, leading their own. As soon as they were warmed up, Red was eager to gallop some but Grimes held to a trot. Grimes believed the trot the fastest way to cover long distance. A horse, he would say, couldn't gallop in a day farther than a man could walk, but no man could walk in a day as far as a horse could trot.

They took the old road toward Monohela which led near the Hepple ranch, over forty miles south. Red tried to talk but Grimes had nothing to say; so Red shut up and wished he could sleep, but he couldn't at a trot. He tried singing but it didn't go well, so he shut up and played like he, too, was a sour old timer.

A little before eight they came upon a covered wagon by the roadside. The man was breaking camp, just hitching up. He looked pretty much like a sleepyhead. A dirty yellow dog with ragged ears lay under the wagon. A woman with two small children about her skirts was putting things in over the end gate. The wagon was pointed south. Both were tired, shiftless-looking folks and stared at the cowmen.

The man said, "Howdy," not cheerfully.

Grimes reined up. "Howdy." He looked at the man a moment or two, then inquired in a soft voice, "Camp here the night?"

"Shore."

"Did you folks see some men ride by, a woman with 'em?"

The woman came forward with a rush, over-turning one of her children. It got up stoically and teetered after its mother. She was saying breathlessly:

"An' that woman was a-cryin' like all get out! Pepper growled 'long about midnight. We keep 'im tied up on account of coyotes. When he growled I raised up an' listened. I heard hosses comin'. I nudged Bub but he was all wore out an' sleeps like a log. But I raised up an' peeked over the side board. They was ridin' all strung out. Six 'r seven men an' a woman. She was cryin' somepin turrible. A feller he was a-swearin' at 'er! It made me hoppin' mad but I couldn't do nuthin'. Who was they, mister? I've wondered powerful!"

Grimes said, "Thanks, lady," and started on. Red paused with, "They stole that girl!"

The woman gasped, "Oh, great God A'mighty!" Bud dropped his jaw, almost letting his tongue hang out.

"I hope to God you boys git 'em!" the woman screamed; then, "But they's only two o' you!"

Red waggled his hand at Grimes who was

riding on, and he grinned a little as he bent in the saddle, sort of confidential. "You ain't guessed right a-tall. There goes a half dozen all by hisself!"

2

Red fidgeted at the trot but kept his mouth shut. Grimes knew best. On they went with faint jingle-jingle of spurs, squeak of leather, steady beat of hoofs, mile after mile. They met men and passed under staring eyes. Grimes, tall and straight and stern, looked like somebody. One glance and people knew that he was a range-bred fighting man; and when they said, "Howdy," Grimes gave a look, raised his hand a little in acknowledgment, said nothing, and rode on.

About noon they stopped, changed horses, turning loose the Hepples to wander home or to be stolen. Red was glad to be free of a lead rope. He stroked the still bluish Ghost's neck. "You still look sorta sin-tainted, Spook. Come on now. Show that barrel-bellied lop-eared ewe-neck Jeb's settin' on how to trot!"

The Ghost was fast and strong, but Red had been wilfully insulting. Grimes' horse was ewe-necked but barrel-chested, lean of belly, tireless.

Red turned a lot of remarks over in his mind and at last selected one as likely the best to get a reply. "Your idee, Jeb, maybe is not to get in much before dark, hm? Sorta be able to ride up close before them folks find out we ain't Hepples ourselves, hm?"

"Live an' learn," said Grimes.

Along toward the middle of the afternoon they saw, far off the road, what looked in the distance like smoke. Grimes jogged 'cross country straight for it.

A small herd was on the trail.

They reined up on high ground and eyed the herd. Looked mighty like the Hepples were sending cows into the Basin. Red guessed there were about five or six hundred, and counted five horsemen.

The Hepples naturally didn't expect any trouble on the trail; thought they had already seized and were holding Huskinses' Place, the key to the Basin. These cows were being moved about as casually as a beef cut on the way to market.

Grimes rode forward, trotting, with Red alongside. Three men came along up to meet them, no doubt thinking they were Hepples, perhaps bringing word of some kind. When they saw the Arrowhead brand they reined up stiffly, backed their horses a little, separating so as not to be bunched if a fight started.

Grimes rode right on up to almost within arm's reach of the nearest man and looked all three over with a quick glance. Red sized them up as just punchers, the sort he had rode with, bunked with, scuffled with, nearly all his life. Would have maybe been all right fellows except for the Hepple brand on their horses.

"Who's trail boss?" Grimes asked, soft and clear, eying a bronzed young fellow.

"Me," said the bronzed young fellow, setting his jaw. He didn't mean to stand any sass from Dobbses.

Grimes eyed him quite a long while, then bubble-soft, asked:

"You maybe are drawin' wages to fight Dobbses?"

The trail boss looked like a pretty good man and, as trail bosses are supposed to have, had some sense. He said, "We are drawin' wages to ride for the H P, take care of Hepple stock an' do as told. Right now, orders they is to take these cows into the Basin, the which is bein' done."

"My name it is Jeb Grimes. The Basin it is Arrowhead range."

That wasn't much to say but it meant a lot. The trail boss knew about Jeb Grimes, and knew that Grimes had said, "If you still have got any notions about pushing these cows on into the Basin there is going to be a fight, here and now."

The trail boss spoke soft. "All I know is that my orders is—"

Grimes said, "Jest a minute till I say somethin' more." His voice was cool and soft as a little brook running over pebbles. "Some folks from yore ranch 'peared to be followin' orders yestidy when they rode in on the Dobbses, knowin' scas'ly nobody was to home. They killed the foreman. They killed a cowboy. They burnt corrals and bunkhouse. They stole some hosses. They carried off a couple of women."

"God A'mighty," said the trail boss.

"Me an' this kid here," Grimes went on, "is down here lookin' for the rest of them we didn't catch up with last night over to Huskinses' Place."

The two punchers with the trail boss spoke up. One said, "We never heard!" The other said, "Women?"

Grimes went on eying the trail boss. "I have made you quite some speech. Now, do you turn that herd an' head back south, or do you want me to do it for you? Speak your piece!"

That was that and plain as the spot on an ace-card. They all knew Jeb Grimes by name, knew him better by the look in his eyes, the softness in his voice. What Red knew, and they didn't, was that Grimes had sized them up as honest looking punchers who were drawing wages for just cow-work, and he had given them a choice. They could fight or back down.

The trail boss showed some color under his bronze. He didn't want to back down and maybe be jeered later on by men who most likely would have turned tail and bolted if Jeb Grimes merely leaned forward and spit at them. The trail boss was studying some when one of his boys spoke up:

"Women? You say them fellers carried off some women?"

"I said it."

"That feller Buck an' them?" asked the other boy.

"Them."

"Who was the women?"

"One was Miz Dobbs' gran'daughter. Other, some relation of Jedge Harris there in town."

"An' burnt the ranch?"

"Bunkhouse an' corrals."

"Me," said the youngest puncher, "I ain't goin' to uphold no doin's like that! An' I didn't like the look, nohow, of them men Buck brung."

"Me neither," said the other.

The trail boss asked, "What happened to them you fellers caught up with?"

"They are dead. This kid here shot 'em. His name it is Red Clark."

Red felt a little embarrassed and a little pleased, too. He tried not to grin and he didn't want to set sober and stern like he thought himself a bad man, so he began to roll a cigarette as if he didn't hear well and hadn't took notice.

They all stared at him, hard. His name was known; and the reward for him, too. It was some surprise to see that Red was just a kid, like most any young puncher, without more trappings and fixin's than two heavy guns; and that he didn't stare like he was trying to scare somebody.

The trail boss said to his men, "Boys, it shore does go against the grain to be told by a rival outfit what to do with our cows. When I draw wages, I foller orders. But me, I won't back up no bunch from any man's outfit as steals women."

Grimes nodded, turned his horse a little to ride by them, lifted his hand in grave slight gesture of parting and went on at the trot with Red at his stirrup. Neither looked back.

As soon as they were well away from the herd, Grimes touched his horse into a lope, a hard one; and as the gallop kept up, Red, pleased, nevertheless jeered, "Here me, I was allus taught to think a feller went faster—trottin'!"

"We got to git there first, son. One of them boys may try to ride ahead an' say we are a-comin'!"

3

The Hepple ranch house lay ahead in the twilight. It was a sprawling squat adobe, roughly built with deep-set narrow windows. A few old cottonwoods rose scraggly and wide-reaching close up to the house. They were said to have rooted from green corral posts, hauled in and put down in the early days when old Hepple was a young man, unmarried, and he had his corral right up close to where he slept on account of Indians.

Grimes rose in the saddle, stretched his neck in far peering. Red too stretched his neck and made out a bunch of eight or nine saddle horses standing near the front of the house.

" 'Pears to be quite some folks about, Jeb?"

"Son," said Grimes, mild, "you have got perception a plenty!"

He pulled his horse down and again jogged on just as if riding into a friendly place, except that the rifle came from the scabbard and lay in the crook of his left arm. Red felt of first one revolver, then the other, loosening them in the holsters so they would come smooth.

He could see, or thought he could, a dim shadow or two move between the trees. No use in saying something about that. If there were any movement, Grimes' hawk-keen eyes would have seen; if not, Grimes might get the notion that Red was skittish a little. So he kept stirrup to stirrup with Grimes and said nothing.

When they were within something around a hundred yards of the house a man stepped into view with a rifle in his hands. His voice was sort of insolent and sure, as if it were a good joke to have these two punchers—he must have thought they were Hepples, just coming along in to the home ranch—ride into a trap. "Pile off an'—"

That was as far as he got. Grimes simply twitched his horse with knee pressure a little to one side, and shot. It looked as if he didn't take aim at all. That was the only way Grimes would parley with fellows who had done so much of what wasn't right.

The man went into the air like a buck that is shot just as it jumps, flung the rifle and sprawled out as if he had been thrown.

The instant he shot Grimes had yelled cheerfully, "Come on, son!" He drove in the spurs and rode straight for the trees, shooting as he went. He let out a yell that was like—that was!—an Apache war shriek. His horse thundered forward with furious bound on bound.

Red rode after him, plumb dead sure that if Grimes had stayed up a week of nights, thinking hard, he couldn't have thought up anything foolisher than to charge at a 'dobe house when some bad men were in it. But the range code Red had lived by ever since he could toddle away from a cradle said that you had to stay with a friend, damn fool or not, when he headed for trouble. So Red sort of braced himself for the shock of the bullet that would knock him out of the saddle, drew a revolver, rode headlong, and shot a time or two just to be taking part in the goin's on.

But Grimes' damn foolishness somehow always had some bold commonsense back of it. Now, headlong and whooping like mad, he rode down on that bunch of saddled horses, jerked off his hat, flapped, struck, yelled, stampeding them. One horse that hadn't been trusted with "ground hitching" was tied to a tree. Grimes drew a revolver and shot the horse as it plunged, rearing, to follow the others that had been left with reins trailing.

The bad men might be behind 'dobe walls, but they were on foot. They would have to stand and fight. They couldn't rush out, hit leather and ride.

There was a rapid popping of revolvers, and angered yells shrill with surprise, as men from within the house rushed through the doorway to see what was going on.

The horses had been turned and Red was on their tails, driving them hard, making them snap their trailing reins under their feet as they ran. The firing behind him was so hot that Red flung his head about to have a look. He saw Grimes' horse, with empty saddle, plunging off in a wide circle after the other horses.

"They've downed old Jeb!"

Grimes was flat on the ground at the edge of the cottonwoods, right up within easy stone's throw of the house; but his rifle was going off with a kind of rapid regularity as if he counted between shots. Shadows were leaping with a kind of frantic waver about the lighted doorway. There was a lance-like flash of guns, much mad yelling and some of it sounded a little scairt. At such close quarters, even in the dark, and even if himself bad hurt, Grimes could almost shoot off a man's nose.

In no time at all, Buck and such of his men as hadn't already been dropped, had enough of trying to shoot it out with Grimes at close quarters. They went hopping into the house and slammed the door to. Now if they wanted to get away without fighting they would have to sneak out back and cut 'cross country on foot, which to high-heeled horsemen would be about like walking barefoot over hot cinders.

Red pulled up with jerk on jerk of reins. He figured Grimes had been knocked out of the saddle and lay there making it a fight. He had driven the fellows into the house and they were some cautious about making a noise even now because the flash of guns showed Grimes where to shoot.

But it seemed to Red that Grimes was in an awful bad hole. Those fellows might sneak out, circle, get at him from the back and sides, many shooting at once—that is, if there were many left.

Red didn't do much thinking. In a jiffy-flash he swung loose his rope, jumped off, put a noose over The Ghost's head, tied the end to some sage, whipped out his rifle and started back toward the trees so he could squirm to where Jeb was, get down alongside and help him argy.

Red ran low and went zig-zag. A gun flashed at him from a dark window. The bullet went high.

On the instant there was a second shot and a howl. Old Grimes, wary and watchful, had shot on the instant at the flash in the window.

Red, even if anxious and tense, couldn't help grinning some as he thought those fellows in the house probably knew by now that they had been monkeying with somebody a lot more dangerous than themselves. Red worked his way cautiously from one splotch of sage or cactus to another. He thought it would be pretty bad if he got crippled and old Grimes was crippled, too.

He angled over to line up the cottonwoods between him and the house and crept along. Somebody from a far corner of the house took another shot at him. The bullet splattered dirt about Red's foot and Grimes answered it with the promptness of an echo.

Following that, suddenly, as if a plan had been figured out by Buck's men, there was a burst of rapid fire from a window and now darkened doorway. It looked like the fellows that were left were trying to swamp Grimes with lead. And Grimes' rifle did not answer.

Red had the ghastly feeling that one of the bullets must have clipped Grimes through the head. Red swung belly-down on the ground. The trees were a little in his way, but he put some shots through the air just to let the fellows know that he, at least, was still in the fight. The trees were even more in the way of the men who were shooting back at him because he was nearer the trees. Then the fellow up at the corner of the house broke cover to make a run forward and get behind a tree himself. Red could see the shadow detach itself from the solid blackness of the house and with a blur of scurrying 'cross a starlit patch. Red shot twice, fast. Then Grimes' rifle banged. The old plainsman had been playing 'possum. The scurrying shadow straightened, tottered, fell, stirred on the ground as if trying to crawl, then lay still.

A fellow within the house yelled in angered shocked scared tone: "They got Body!" and his voice ended in a kind of nervous whoop as Grimes shot at the window through which the voice came.

Red could hear some angry cussin' in a frustrated tone going on in the house. It sounded to him like Buck's voice. He was cussin' his luck. It was sure bad. Red felt like yelling at him, sarcastic and jeering; but he didn't. He scrouged slow and cautious up to a tree trunk not fifty feet from where Grimes was and called softly, "You hurt, Jeb?"

"Bad hurt," said Grimes. "They busted my leg an' I been hit twict more."

"Gosh a'mighty! Jeb?"

Grimes answered, full of pain, "I'm purt-near done f'r, son. You'd better back off an' light out!"

"Yeah," Red growled, "when hell's snow-bound I will, maybe!"

"I'm all sick an' dizzy," said Grimes, and groaned.

Buck, listening, heard that too. He yelled, savagely. "They's only one left out there!" as if the one would be easy to take care of.

It made Red mad and he shot pretty fast, just sort of making a noise to let Buck know this fight wasn't over yet, not by a whole lot.

Red stopped shooting and began to crawl over to Grimes. Buck and the fellow or two left with him were quiet, too, as if putting their heads together for a plan to get at Red. It was so quiet that Red could hear a woman crying. Buck swore irritably at her, "Aw, shut that bellerin'!"

Red squirmed over to almost arm's reach of where Grimes lay all spraddled out, hugging the ground, almost as flat as if dead; but his gun was up on a bent elbow for a rest and his head was cocked as alert as a rattler's in a coil. He was in the deep shadow of the trees so there wasn't much of anything that could be seen of him from the house.

Red peered close, tensely anxious, then gurgled in a joyous whisper, "You damn old hypercritter, you! Ain't you shamed to lie like that to some bad-worried bad men!"

Grimes hadn't been hit at all. He had simply thrown himself out of the saddle and rolled over behind a tree so as to be right up close to the house. It was his way of showing contempt for this bunch of bad men that had rode in on Mrs. George's place, shot her dogs and men, burned her bunk houses and carried off women. His notion of making a fight was always to let other folks shoot at him just about as much as they liked as long as it gave him a good chance to shoot at them.

Now Grimes didn't make a move or say a word, just moaned a little, low and hurt, as if he couldn't help it and all the while lay there watchful and ready.

Everything was pretty quiet for a time except that the woman in the house was still crying, and the cottonwoods rustled their leaves as if they were a little nervous over all this shooting. The stars were bright and it was a soft cool evening.

Red sprawled out, too, trying to be ready, and watched at the corners of the house, with rifle aimed. But his elbows got tired, his neck felt strained as if ready to break. He had to move his legs a little, easing muscles. Old Grimes didn't stir. He was steady as a log, patient as an Indian.

There was a sudden racket in the house. Guns went off together as if folks in there were shooting at each other. There were the screams of more than one woman, some yells and blurted cuss words. It sounded like a lot of people were badly scared and some were being hurt.

Red cocked his ears with, "Now, what the hell?"

But Grimes, who could think quicker than most people could wink, was on his feet and running forward with, "Come on, son!"

Red jerked himself into a scrambling lurch, dropped his rifle, taking a revolver in each hand. He understood all in a flash that Grimes had figured that with so much racket and commotion stirred up in the house, Buck and whoever else was left with him would be too busy for a moment or two to be watching close.

It was a hundred feet or so from where they had been lying to the house; and it seemed to Red a mile. His legs were working fast but felt as if they were dragging. He ran clumsily, trying to keep on his toes, but his long dime-pointed heels hit the ground and the jingle of his spurs sounded to him like bells that rang an alarm. All that anybody there in the house had to do was poke a gun through a window and shoot fast.

The heavy front door that Grimes had splattered with lead was half open. Grimes did not pause. His rifle was pointed forward as if he had a bayonet on it. He struck with his shoulder the door and went through. It was almost dead dark with a dim hazy glow coming from the doorway of a room far down near the end of the hall.

As he passed a side door a gun from within the unlighted room flashed at Grimes. He wheeled, stepped into the doorway, faced the darkness and with rifle butt at his hip shot instantly at what seemed the stir of a darker splotch of black in the unlighted room. There was a muffled grunt, a soft sliding sound, the clattering bump of something like a revolver.

"Got 'im," said Grimes, soft and cool as if he had shot a bobcat outside Mrs. George's chicken pen.

Red, with both revolvers out, was crouched alongside of Grimes and peering tensely for the movement of any other dark splotches in the room when he heard a woman's sobbing scream, partly a cry for help, partly a wild shriek of warning there in the hall. Red, looking another way and crouched in an awkward position to whirl quickly, gave a lurching stumble as he turned with startled jerk of body. A flame-tipped streak flashed at him from the end of the hall.

Red, off balance and stumbling, nevertheless shot instinctively with arm outflung, but even as the hammer was falling he wrenched his arm back to pull off, miss, shoot wild, for there, silhouetted in the dim glow at the end of the hall, he saw that he was shooting at what looked merely like the distorted figure of a woman. There was a woman's long skirts and head, with hair wildly disheveled. One hand was out in a frantic reaching as if for something, anything, to grasp; but, such was the instant's blurred grotesque impression, the other arm and hand seemed a man's and held a revolver. Also a man's hat appeared just above the woman's shoulder and was partly concealed by her neck. The woman screamed wildly.

It was Dora. Buck held her tightly before him— was hiding behind her. She struggled crazily, was fear-crazed; but had scarcely more force against his strength than a fluttering canary in a cat's mouth; yet her helpless hysterical struggling jarred Buck's arm as he fired again and again and again, rapidly.

Bullets slapped the wall beside Red, but he stood with the look of a man who could not move. He could, and knew he could, have shot fast and not missed once in twenty times the mark that Buck's face made above her shoulder; but in that vague light, and while Dora writhed and tossed her head this way and that, Red simply felt paralyzed. He did not dare shoot. All of which Buck had counted on, craftily.

But Grimes stepped from the doorway, turning. He frowned for an instant in peering to figure out what a woman was doing there; then, apparently without aim, shot. The bullet took a hole right out of the crown of Buck's hat. The roar of the rifle between the walls of the hallway was instantly followed by another. Woman or no woman, Grimes was going to shoot it out then and there; but Buck jumped sideways, whisking Dora with him, and vanished into the dimly lighted room.

There was a moment's hush after the noise of the guns; silence except for the quick clatter of Buck's sharp-pointed heels and scraping click of spurs as if, burdened with weight, he ran unsteadily, and the vague loudness of his baffled oaths. There was no other sound throughout the house. Dora's voice was stilled as if she had fainted, or been killed.

Grimes, wary, unhurried but not in any way hesitating, walked along the hall and paused in the dimly lighted wide doorway that opened into the dining room. The floor of the dining room was two steps down from the level of the hall.

The lamp on the dining room table had been turned low. The smell of powder smoke was strong in the room. Some of the recent shooting had been in there.

A man yelled from across the huge room at Grimes, "He's hid in that closet! Look out!" Another man's voice shouted, "Drug the girl in with him!" Then a woman, amazed and shrill, cried out, "Who are you fellows!" It sounded a little as if she somehow didn't like what was happening.

Grimes did not answer, so there was some more silence. The smoke shifted, thinned, rose; and Red's eyes began to get used to the dim light. Grimes held his rifle waist high and pointed toward the door of the closet where Buck had holed up.

Red went across to the table and turned up the lamp. It had been dimmed so the fellows who moved about in the room wouldn't cast shadows for Grimes to shoot at through the windows. The table was set for supper and there were two lamps on it, but one had been blown out. The lamp Red turned up did not fill the room with light. He lighted the other.

"Gosh a'mighty!" Red mumbled sort of sucking in his breath as he made out four or five people tied up on the floor, backed up against the wall; but Mrs. Hepple was tied fast in a rocking chair.

Out away from the wall were two men on the floor that looked dead. One, all huddled up with face down and knees drawn up, was Hal Mason.

Red blurted, "What the gosh blamed hell's been a-happenin'?" His voice sounded loud and almost as if he had said something he hadn't ought've. There was so much hush and staring from the people who were tied up; and nobody said a word for a moment or two.

Then one of the cowboys that had their hands behind them and ropes about their legs and waists—the same who had called to Grimes to look out, that Buck was in the closet—asked, "Good for you fellers!" And the other said, "F'r God's sake let us loose so we can help do somethin' to that—" His cuss words decorated Buck's name with a lot of feeling.

A fat Mexican woman lay on the floor, tied up,

and also a Chinaman in a blue blouse and black pants. Mrs. Hepple called, "Oh, Red! It is you! I am *so* glad. Let me loose, please." Her tone coaxed, not very pleasantly, and she was eying him with black-eyed stare, but seemed to convey that she liked Red fine, just as though he hadn't shot her gambler-son and she, in turn, hadn't most likely helped put Buck up to try to murder him. The Mexican woman had a black-eyed stare, too; but it was fixed on Mrs. Hepple and looked just about as if there were a mask over her heavy face and the eyes peered hot and angered from behind that mask.

The Chinaman seemed too scared to wiggle.

Grimes called cool and soft-voiced, "Turn them boys loose, Red, but not that woman!"

Mrs. Hepple knew that he meant her and not the Mexican woman. She rocked back in a kind of surprise and her black eyes lighted with a flare of temper. The more she stared at Grimes the queerer the look got on her face. Her eyes popped and stretched almost saucer-size and her mouth opened like she was trying to yell and couldn't. Then she said, sort of hushed and scared, *"You!"* It was plain enough that she recognized Grimes as somebody she had never wanted to see again, but he didn't even look toward her.

Buck, through the heavy door of the closet had come to life and was trying to talk. He yelled with a kind of assurance, "You out there! You got to let me walk out of this house and give me a horse or I'll kill the girl!"

Grimes said, "Suit yoreself!"

Red bounced up from where he was untying the punchers and begged, "But my God, Jeb, Dora—he'll murder her, that fellow!"

"Shut up, son. 'F he gets out an' away he'll murder somebody else. Lots o' somebodies. Let 'im kill 'er if he wants. 'Twill be the last he ever does."

"But Jeb!"

"Shut up, I told you!" said Grimes, harsh and stern. "I won't make no bargain with 'im."

Buck could hear. It made him mad because his plan wasn't working the way he had figured it ought. He yelled some cuss words and began to shoot. The reports were muffled. Some splintered spots appeared in the door. Buck had a bad temper and had lost it. He was blindly trying to shoot through, hopeful of hitting somebody. Red jumped a little to one side. Grimes did not move. His rifle could have smashed clear through the door and made things hot in the closet but he didn't shoot; just said with a low pleased sound, "He keeps that up, he'll suffocate hisself in thar."

The punchers were squirming on the floor and swearing, begging Red to hurry and turn them loose so they could do something. He went back to them.

As one, with Red's help, was shaking off the

coils, he jerked his thumb toward Hal out there on the floor. "That city kid, he wasn't tied good and got his hands loose. He wiggled to a gun one o' them fellers you all killed had dropped an' he was waitin' for Buck an' them to come back in here. When Buck come in, *her* there!—" the puncher turned fiercely toward Mrs. Hepple— "she yelled, 'Look out, Buck!' "

Mrs. Hepple screamed, "Oh I never!"

The other puncher said, "Why, you shore as hell did!"

"I never!" she yelled. "You just didn't hear right! I said, 'Look out!' to the boy because I knew they would kill him!"

"You are lyin' yore head off!" said one of the punchers in a slow amazed tone.

The other went on with: "That there kid he started shootin' but he was a mighty pore shot an' they just flocked lead into him, an' that purty girl who had been cryin' an' wasn't tied jumped up an' that Buck he whaled her over the head. Then you all come a-bustin' in, an' Buck he jerked the girl up an' carried her before 'im out there into the hall—hidin' behind a woman, the dirty—"

"An' 's now hid like a skunk in a hole!" said the other puncher.

"How'd he catch you all?" Red asked, working at knots.

The puncher spoke fast and angered. "Me an'

Clem here just come a-ridin' in this afternoon an' they had a man out there watchin', so we, not expectin' trouble, was stuck up an' hogtied like a pair of calfs! They picked themselves some good hosses, turned loose all the others an' loafed around here like they owned the place. We didn't see Miz Hepple a-tall till you fellers rode up. Then Buck an' them acted mad an' brought 'er in here an' tied 'er up. But now, me, I think it was just a put-up job between 'em to make us think she wasn't in with Buck an' them! Look how she acted when that pore kid there was a-fixin' to kill Buck!"

"Gosh a'mighty!" Red murmured, peeking at Mrs. Hepple as if a little afraid of her.

Her lips flashed in movement, words came scornful and furious as she jerked her head at the Mexican woman, then at the Chinaman: "Why don't you accuse them, too, of being in with Buck! They weren't dragged in here and tied up till after I was!"

"They was busy fixin' supper!" said the puncher. "Was yanked in here so they wouldn't do no mischief after you all started raisin' so much glorified hell out there!"

Grimes told the punchers to go get an ax. One went on the jump while the other helped Red to have a look at Hal. His face wasn't fat any more. It was thin and white as paper except for bruises. He was breathing in soft little panting gasps, and was bleeding. He had been all sore and worn out anyhow from the beatings yesterday, the hard riding since; and now had been shot twice, once in the shoulder and also in the leg above the knee. The shock of the bullets had numbed his nerves so that he wasn't feeling pain yet; but he was near dead from exhaustion anyhow.

The puncher and Red lifted Hal to a big wide swinging couch, covered with Indian blankets. Red talked to him, low and encouraging, but Hal was in a kind of stupor with eyes wide open. "Good leather, kid," Red murmured as he ripped the shirt from about the wound in the shoulder, having a look.

Red went across to the fat, stolid Mexican woman, talked to her in Spanish and began to cut her loose. She seemed stupidly sullen and stared as if distrustful; then suddenly asked, "You are the son of The Sheriff?"

A lot of people, especially among the Mexicans, still meant Red's father when they said The Sheriff. In other parts of the country bad men might not have thought it worth while to notch a gun if they killed what they called a "greaser," but it had sure been bad luck, while The Sheriff was in the saddle, to trouble honest Mexicans in Tulluco.

The Mexican woman said, "They killed Señor Hepple in his bed. *She* had them do that. She is a devil-woman! They talked in Spanish and did not know I listened. She wanted Señor Hepple to die so the ranch would be her own and it would look as if the bandits had killed him."

Red said vague things under his breath and twisted about for another look at Mrs. Hepple. The Mexican woman hadn't hushed her voice at all, and Mrs. Hepple was not more than two long steps away but she had not heard a word. Her eyes were again fixed on old Jeb Grimes. Now her face, even if it did not have a wrinkle, didn't look at all pretty. It was all out of shape with just plain fright; and the look in her eyes made Red think of how a crippled snake stares, hoping for a chance to bite.

The Chinaman was huddled down like a bunch of rags with a wax head. Red cut him loose and told him to bring towels and water.

The puncher that had gone for the ax came back on the run with two. Red started across the room and Mrs. Hepple called to him, partly coaxing and partly as if giving an order: "Help me loose, Red. This rope hurts and—" Her voice changed to a quick low tone, slightly hoarse and caressing, as if somehow promising a lot of things: "Red, that old man there knows that I know he murdered my father! He'll kill me because I can have him hanged!"

Red simply backed off without a word. He had an almost scared feeling as if she were something strange and dangerously evil.

4

From inside the closet Buck yelled threats at the punchers who swung their axes. He shot again and again into the door. They yelled back at him, jeering; said for him to keep right on shooting and so choke himself to death on smoke. He tried to scare them by saying if they didn't stop he would come busting out with guns blazing when the door was chopped down. They told him to come a-whoopin' just any old time he took the notion.

The door was heavy and the hinges had been hammered out of iron. It was a job to cut the door down because it opened on the inside and the hinges were fastened on the inside; but the punchers swung joyfully as if doing something that was a lot of fun.

Buck suddenly changed his tune and called, "Fellers? Hey fellers, lis'en! "

The punchers paused to hear what he had to say. Grimes told them to keep at work. "We," said Grimes, "don't care what he says."

Buck got louder and louder with a kind of panic in his voice. His bad temper had cooled down into a plain realization of what he was up against.

"I ain't hurt her! I wouldn't hurt a woman! I was only bluffin' a while ago! But she has fainted! So don't think I hurt 'er! I'll give up an' come out if you won't—"

At the offer to surrender the punchers swung down their axes and stepped back; but Grimes said, "Keep a-cuttin'!" It wasn't Grimes' way to parley with Buck's kind nor to accept a surrender.

The punchers understood and gave a glad yelp because they sure had it in for Buck and didn't want him to get off alive. They spit on their hands and went to it. They had never in their lives used an ax for more than cutting wood for a camp fire; but they put their weight into their blows and hacked raggedly. The door was soon shaky. The top hinge broke loose, swayed away from the post. They hooked the ax blades through the opening and swung back, heaving. There was a grinding sound, then the snap of the lower hinge breaking. The door swayed, turned a little. They took hold of it with their hands and pulled, careless of Buck's chance to shoot at them.

The door came free. They jumped back and let it go. It fell flat with smashing bang; and there stood Buck with hat still on and his hands away up. He said, quick and eager:

"I ain't armed! I give up! Don't shoot!"

His guns lay on the floor at his feet.

Red was so mad that he said things and looked about to shoot anyhow.

Grimes pushed in before Red and kept his rifle waist high, the muzzle almost against Buck's belly. Grimes, soft and calm as if talking to a child about how to play mumblepegs, said:

" 'Tain't right, son, for to shoot a man with his hands up!"

Buck grinned a little at that. Red snarled, "When did you go an' get softhearted!"

"Don't get overhet," Grimes advised with gentle bubble-like sound in his throat. "Things has to be done right." To Buck, "Git out here where I can have a good look at you." Buck moved, suddenly wary and anxious as he watched Grimes' face.

Grimes pulled loose the chin strap, took off Buck's hat, had a look, slapped the hat back on and said to the punchers, "Tie his hands behind him, good." To Red, "Go fetch in some horses."

Red paid no attention but went into the closet and struck a match. The closet was nearly suffocating with powder smoke. He shook out the match, gathered up the limp unconscious Dora and carried her out.

Buck said earnest and quick while the punchers were tying his hands behind him, "I din't touch her!"

"You're a liar!" said one of the punchers. The other, "We seen you hit 'er!"

"I just was crazy mad for a minute," said Buck. He seemed honestly to feel that the justification was quite the same as a denial. "She ain't hurt. Just scairt a little!"

"Go fetch in some horses, Red," Grimes told him again.

306

"All right. In a minute," Red said indifferently and got down on his knees beside the stolid Mexican woman who was putting water on Dora's cold pale face.

"I reckon," Grimes was saying to Buck, "that woman over there has made quite some fool out of you, after all, hm? Them bankers never told you to raid the Dobbses like you done. They got more sense!"

Mrs. Hepple yelled, "I didn't! I never! I don't know a thing about him! Them Johnsons sent him out with a letter and—"

She might as well have been talking to the wind for all the notice Grimes took of her. Grimes turned, spoke sharp to Red:

"Go fetch in horses!"

5

An hour later, or nearly that, when Red came back riding The Ghost and leading Grimes' ewe-neck and a couple more horses, Buck was sitting in a chair, looking glum. Grimes rested on a corner of the big table and looked more like something carved out of dark wood than a man, with the rifle across his knee. The two Hepple punchers also looked pretty solemn; and Mrs. Hepple was crying. Something had been talked about that Red didn't know about.

As soon as Red came in, Grimes straightened, "All right. Be a movin', Buck!"

Buck snuggled down heavier in the chair. "Why don't you take me into the sheriff? You ain't got no right for to—"

"You been took to sheriffs before, I reckon. An' got away. As for the right—how about you ridin' down on the Dobbses, killin' them dogs, burnin' houses, stealin' hosses, shootin' men, carryin' off women? You damn outlaws talk loud about law an' rights when you get caught. So don't argy. Walk or be drug. All the same to me, but you're goin'!"

Buck took a deep breath, tightened his mouth, shrugged his broad shoulders. He looked across toward Dora. His lips worked a little before he spoke. He looked at Grimes, but Grimes' wrinkled face was set and impassive. Buck looked from one to the other of the punchers. "Fellers," he said, "I ain't proud of what I done— hidin' behind her. But I was cornered with all my men killed. They seemed no other way to—to run a bluff. God A'mighty, I liked that girl! I was goin' to be good to her, but—"

Red fidgeted, wanting to speak up, mad; but he didn't.

"Past time for talk," said Grimes, and jerked his head.

"How about a cigarette first?" Buck's mouth looked queer, like he was trying a little to grin and his lips didn't want to. Somehow he seemed trying to be brave.

Grimes said to one of the punchers: "Twist 'im a smoke."

"Shore, oh, shore," said the puncher, nervous-like, but willing. The paper trembled in the boy's fingers and he spilled much tobacco but got a lump-bellied cigarette shaped up, put it to Buck's lips, struck a match.

Buck didn't say "Thanks." He seemed forgetful from having so much else to think about. He inhaled as if sighing and blew smoke in sigh-like puffs. "Two hours more an' I'd been headed for The Border. That there is luck f'r you!"

"Border or not," Grimes told him, "we'd've follered. I've done it for men I didn't want near as bad as you." Grimes took him by the arm. "Come 'long."

Buck looked as if he were going to pull back, but changed his mind and stood up. His lips moved. He was trying mighty hard to grin. His eyes went about to see if fellows were noticing that he was smiling; and they stared at him, solemn and tense.

Red and the punchers followed slow and walking light-toed as Grimes, with a hand on Buck's arm, marched him down along the hall, out of the house and up to the ewe-neck. Red and the punchers stopped and stood back a little way. They looked as if they wanted to be so quiet they wouldn't be noticed. The stolid Mexican woman, still holding a wet cloth, blotted out the light in a window where she leaned, peering.

Grimes took his rope from the ewe-neck's saddle, gave it a toss and pulled it slowly through his fingers, recoiling it. He made a small loop, took off Buck's hat, spun it off to one side and fitted the loop snug to Buck's neck.

Buck said in a husky voice, "I never did like neckties." He was making a little joke but nobody paid any attention.

"Help 'im climb up," Grimes ordered.

The two punchers edged forward, not eager. Buck said, savage, "I was a damn fool not to shoot it out instead of—oh Christ!" Nobody answered. For a moment or two he seemed making up his mind whether or not to struggle. He didn't struggle but wasn't helpful. He was a big, broad fellow and not easy to heave up with hands tied behind him. Then, suddenly, Buck said, "Oh, hell, let's have it over with!" He poked his foot into the stirrup and reeled up into the saddle. He settled himself with a kind of resolute straightening of shoulders and put his boot toe into the other stirrup. "My last ride, huh?" It sounded as if his throat was tight.

Grimes held the rope and took up the reins. He led the ewe-neck over into the shadows of the cottonwoods and stopped below a limb not more than four or five feet above Buck's head. Grimes kept a grip on the reins as he gathered the coil and tossed it up over the limb. The rope fell with a smooth slithering sound. He picked it up, tied the end about the tree, being careful to fix a knot that would not slip. Then he walked out in front of the horse, tugged at the reins and clucked. The horse seemed to know what was being done and didn't want to move.

Buck said in a kind of loud-tempered voice, as if desperate but bragging, too, "By God, I ain't scairt to die!" and drove his spurred heels into the ewe-neck's flanks.

The horse jumped. Grimes checked it back with high reach of arm and yank of reins. A sudden hard jerk of so much weight would have snapped the rope.

Grimes then simply walked forward, leading the horse and did not look back. When he turned and came around the other side of the tree the saddle was empty.

6

Grimes sat on a corner of the table with his rifle leaning close by and reached across for some bread and a piece of meat. Grimes was hungry. He hadn't had a bite at Macaw's and nothing all day. He folded the bread over the meat and chewed. Between bites he told Red to fix up the sick people as best he could, "then we'll be ridin', son."

Red asked, "What of her?" and pointed at Mrs. Hepple. He had known for a long time that there was some mystery between her and Grimes, and tonight her fear showed almost hysterically; but Grimes screwed his leathery neck around, took a look as if he hadn't noticed her before, chewed and swallowed. "She's ridin' with us." He took another big bite.

Mrs. Hepple gasped as if hard hit with a fist and threw herself back against the rocker. Her dark face looked as gray as dirty wool.

The two punchers fidgeted a little, and one said haltingly, "Maybe we did misjudge her some an' 'sides, she is our boss an'—"

Grimes pointed a long arm at the swinging couch where Hal Mason lay. "Feller, thar is yore boss. That Hepple kid. An' she as shore as hell meant to have them outlaws drag 'im off some'eres an' be murdered. Like she done ol' Dingley. Go take a look."

Red and the punchers, one holding a lamp, tiptoed through the sprawling house as if respectful and quiet for fear of waking old Dingley Hepple.

He had been shot in his bed. One of the punchers in a hushed voice said that something was wrong with his legs so he couldn't move them; had been like that for a long time.

Red stared at the big bony face with protruding bony lumps over eyes that had been fiercely bright and piercing. Red pulled a blanket up across the body. The puncher set the lamp on a stand and turned the wick low. They took off their hats then went out on tiptoes.

Grimes laid hold on another slice of bread and some more meat, reached afar for the mustard and dabbed on a thick spread, folded the bread and wadded a big bite into his mouth. He chewed complacently, as if meditating on how good it tasted.

Dora had been carried into a room and put to bed with the Mexican woman sitting by. Dora was almost out of her head in terror. The Mexican woman came with a kind of stolid haste into the dining room and called Red. He went in and sat on the bed with Dora staring hard at his face and holding tight to his hand. He told her over and over that Buck and his men were wiped out. She believed him but she could not feel secure.

She asked Red if there had been a stage robbery and murder, and did he think Charley Hepple had been in it? Red hesitated a little, then with vast assurance said: "Oh, Buck he was a powerful liar, some ways. You get some sleep."

The Mexican woman gave her a big drink of whisky in water. That seemed to relax Dora and she lay quiet as if she were sleeping uneasily with her eyes open.

When Red went back, Grimes was smoking a

cigarette and looking toward Hal as he talked to the punchers. Grimes' voice was low and had a purr.

". . . you boys keep him quiet as you can with cold water packs. He is sufferin' but they is nothin' more you can do till a doctor gets here. He is from the East an' soft, a little. But he is old Dingley's boy an' bein' easy scairt wasn't among the faults Dingley had. This boy takes after him some. An' like I said, he is yore boss from now on. What is more, he is married to Miz Dobbs' gran'daughter. Miz Dobbs'll hate the ground he walks on but they will be no more rowin' 'tween you fellers an' us Dobbses. Matter of fact, few years more an' nesters'll have all us outfits fenced off the range."

Grimes picked up his rifle and told Red to turn "that woman" loose.

She rocked back and shrank as much as she could. Her face was stretched wide with fright and she said, almost screaming, "I won't go with you!"

Grimes told her a low cold tone, "You throw a fit like I know you can, an' I'll leave you danglin' on the same cottonwood limb with that Buck feller!"

Mrs. Hepple gave a wild look about and called to Red, "You wouldn't let him—" Red didn't look helpful and she turned to the punchers: "I always liked you boys and now—"

Grimes noticed that they stirred uneasily. He said, "You boys had better set calm." It was a friendly warning, but a warning. He eyed them to see if they were going to take his advice; and when it looked like they were, he nodded a little in approval, then explained:

"F'r one thing, she ain't Miz Hepple a-tall. I mean her former husband, 'r one of 'em—she's had most a dozen I reckon—ain't dead. She done her best to be rid of him. An' her best is purty bad. Hired a couple o' fellers to kill 'im. They got bad hurt out in the hills, tryin' it. One of 'em he talked some after the other died with a wad o' rifle lead right square through his heart. Then her husband he changed clothes with one of 'em and rode off. Later on when the bodies was found, it 'peared like the husband was one of the dead men. Howsomeever, she soon knowed he wasn't 'cause he sent in word as how he hoped they'd meet again, soon. He done that just so she'd do some worryin'. But 'pears like she didn't, much. Not enough to spile her looks. She changed her name an' lit out for whar she wasn't knowed. That was purt-near twenty-five year ago, so you all can see that she started in mighty young. Me, I know where her husband is an' I'm goin' to see as how she has a talk with him."

Red had untied the rope. Mrs. Hepple rubbed at her arms and looked down, not moving. She was so scared she was weak. Grimes dropped the cigarette, stepped on it, walked over and took her by the arm, firmly.

She pushed at his hand. "You're hurting. I'll come." Her tone and air were sad and hopeless as if she were just a poor lone woman being mistreated.

Grimes kept hold on her arm and walked her out of the house. She dragged her feet a little and had her head down. Out in the shadows he let go of her arm and told Red to help her into the saddle. She had on skirts and it was a man's saddle. It wasn't easy for her to mount. She put her arm close around Red's neck and as he was trying to give her a lift she whispered quickly, "Help me and I'll—"

There was a shot. The horse jumped. Red jumped, too, and Mrs. Hepple almost fell.

Grimes spoke coldly: "Purt-near twenty-five year ago she cooked up a tale by whisperin' quick an' soft thataway as made me kill a feller as didn't deserve it. Now, Bess, if you start whisperin' again I'll shoot some'eres else than at the ground!"

The two punchers came running to the door and called, "What's the matter?"

Grimes told them quietly, "Nothin'—yet."

After that she climbed up on the horse pretty quick without Red having to help much. Grimes swung into his saddle and rode up alongside of her. When their horses were a little way off from the house, Grimes said:

"Red, jog along toward town, sorta at a walk after you get on ahead apiece. Me an' my wife is goin' have some talk, private."

Red said, "Sure," and spurred ahead. He felt queer and uneasy because Grimes was a dangerous man; and to Red's range-bred way of thinking, no matter what all Mrs. Hepple had done she was a woman, with the look of a lady about her. What maybe ought to be done to women wasn't to Red, or the men like him, the right thing to do, somehow. He rode about a quarter of a mile ahead and pulled down, sneaking a look once in a while back across his shoulder. Sometimes he could see shadow-blotches plodding along far back on the dusty-white road and sometimes he couldn't.

He rode on and on, walking his horse and trying to think things over, but his head wasn't clear, and now that the excitement had passed he was dead tired and worn out.

There was the sound of a gallop behind him. Grimes, alone, rode up alongside and said as they had better get on a little faster. They trotted for a spell in silence with Red hoping any moment that Grimes would speak up. Grimes didn't. Red felt he oughtn't be meddlesome; but he felt, too, that he would bust if he didn't find out, so he asked, "What'd you do, Jeb?"

Grimes spoke wearily. "Not right, son. I've made more mistakes with that woman than purt-near with ever'body else in the world put together." His voice was soft and low, almost as if wanting Red's approval: "I said for her to get out of the country an' never come back. That if she did, I'd kill her. Would, too."

"You've knowed all along these years who she was?"

"An' nearly busted my galluses a time 'r two keepin' her from findin' out who I was. You see, Red, when she showed up, I heard about the widder lady as was makin' a fool o' old Ding Hepple. But it's a way widders has, so I never thought. When one day I seen her—well, I didn't have no such likin' for Ding Hepple as to want to save him from the trouble she was shore to make 'im, sooner or later.

"Me, I decided to keep away from her, least-wise f'r a while, and say nothin'. The which I done. Sorta settin' by, so to speak, all these years with my ace in the hole. Tonight I played it in the showdown for to keep her an' Pink from gettin' that ranch. Sure as hell's a foot deep, she'd have had them Buck fellers drag off young Hal some'eres an' kill him."

"Who is Pinky, Jeb? An' Joe Bush?"

"Don't ask me. I bet both of 'em had diff'rent dads."

"Where'd she come from?"

"She was a gambler's daughter when I first knowed her over in Colorado. So purty you jest couldn't believe yore eyes. An' a selfisher critter never was on two legs."

"But where'll she go now?"

"To hell, I hope. But I bet from now on they is wrinkles a-plenty in her face."

"Jeb, do you think maybe she put Buck an' them up to burnin' us Dobbses out?"

"Well, son, I don't know. Maybe she did. Maybe Buck just done it out of his own cussedness. 'Twasn't them Johnsons, you can bet. An' right now, you can bet too, they are plenty scairt. That mortgage business'll fix the blame on 'em anyhow. Them riggin' a hold-up an' Cramer and the messenger bein' killed is plumb mighty bad. That sheep deal'll rile all the cowmen. Bein' in with gamblers was purty stinkin', too. An' us ridin' along into town now for to argy with 'em a little won't be very soothin'."

Red thought a while and his thoughts worked around until he said, "Pore old Bill Nims!"

"Yes sir, son, Bill he is in a bad way. With Sally Nims all riled over Bill not bein' plumb honest, and her savage old dad oilin' up his buffalo gun— well, sir, I reckon Bill'll purt-near wish he'd died o' croup in the cradle. I allus sorta half way liked Bill. He's good hearted."

They rode on a while, then Grimes spoke up, calm and mild:

"Now 'bout my wife. From now on, son, jest suppose you an' me don't ever make no reference to her between ourselves even, an' so of course not to other parties, ever."

Mrs. Hepple's body was found two days later. After the horse on which she rode off had returned to the ranch, trailing the reins with far side-reach of head to keep them from under its feet, men rode out, searching. The following day a cowboy cut 'cross country to where vultures gathered. It was evident from the condition of clothes and body that she had fallen from the saddle with her foot through the stirrup and been dragged to death.

CHAPTER FOURTEEN

It was long about one o'clock in the morning and some ten miles from town when they heard a buckboard coming fast out ahead of them on the road, and they saw a wagon rocking behind horses that were galloping. The dust flew up like smoke from under hoofs and wheels.

Grimes and Red put their horses in the middle of the road and waited. The driver pulled down and called doubtful, "Hey, what you fellers want?" He was the livery stable man.

A woman was on the seat with him. As Grimes and Red rode up close, Catherine cried out eagerly: "Oh, it's Red! And Jeb!"

Red said, "Of all folks! What the devil you doin' out here this time o' night?"

"I am going to my husband!"

Red whistled low and soft, half laughed, swore, said admiringly, "Well, can you beat that, Jeb!"

Grimes pushed up his hat. A nice smile showed in the starlight on his grim old face. He spoke in his softest tone: "I don't know which of you two kids ort to be proudest of the other. He's proved a good feller. And you've got the sort of spunk as has made Miz George's men."

"What of that Buck?" Catherine asked.

"We kept our promise," said Grimes, mild and grave.

"And Hal?" From the way she asked they could tell she was holding her breath for the answer.

"He got into the fight like a good feller!" said Red.

"And was he hurt?"

" 'Pears like he got nipped in the shoulder a mite. Leg, too, a little, but—"

"Oh, Hal has been shot? Is it serious?"

"Oh, nothin' your bein' by him won't cure. But how you come to be comin'—"

"Oh, Red, Grandmother was so mad over Hal— it was terrible! Just as bad as you said it would be. I thought she was going to use that quirt on me! She said for me to get out of her sight and never let her see me again! She said she never wanted to hear my name again! She wouldn't listen when I—"

"I knowed about how it would be," Red admitted.

"I didn't know what to do. I tramped up and down in the room there at the hotel until I dropped. I must have been worn out and slept. When I woke up I knew I ought to go to Hal. And the Hepple ranch was the only place I knew to look. I felt I just couldn't sit in a saddle again. I went to the livery stable and had a hard time to get the man there to get this driver for me. But here I am! And Hal isn't badly hurt, honest?"

"We'll be sendin' Doc Barstow along out. Don't you fret."

Catherine shook the driver's arm. "We must hurry!" She threw up a hand and called, "Oh, Red, I hear that the doctor says Sara has a chance!"

The driver, making ready to send the horses on their way, spoke loud: "Folks has been ridin' out to Huskinses an' comin' back with their eyes poppin'! You boys 'pear to be mighty economic in your shootin'—one bullet, one hide!"

He shook the reins, yelled. The horses jumped. Catherine was rocked back against the seat and passed with hand a-flutter at Grimes and Red.

Red looked after the dust cloud that rolled along the road. "I hope I didn't lie too much about Hal not bein' bad hurt. But he 'pears to be a feller with grit enough to brace up and get well to please a girl like that. Here me, I been frettin' about a Hepple maybe gettin' our ranch, and from now on it is a Dobbs as will run theirn. Miss Kate is a Dobbs, hair, hide, and hoof! Nice folks, them Dobbses—though I am goin' to get my hide tanned, I bet, right soon by the nicest of 'em!"

2

Grimes and Red jogged into town a little before three o'clock. The town lay dark and quiet. Some of the all night places had their doors wide open and lights showed through, but nobody was making noise. Even the all-night girls had gone to bed. In passing the Best Bet Red leaned low in the saddle for a better look and saw a few figures huddled about a poker table and a bartender drowsing with head propped on hand and elbow.

When they were near the bank, Red reined up with an air of something being wrong.

"What is it, son?"

Red pointed toward the bank. Grimes stared a little. "I don't see nothin'."

"That's the jigger. It is dark as the inside of a pill box. And allus they is two lamps burnin' low at the back there."

"What you figger?"

"That something is wrong, somehow. My dad used to tell folks anytime they see no light burnin' in the back to come to him and say so; and if he was out of town to take a scatter gun and go look for 'emselves. Do we go round back and have a look?"

They rode to the corner, dismounted, and started down the alley. Grimes said in hushed approval, "I reckon as how you've got a good smeller!"

There were some horses in the alley back of the bank, five, saddled and bunched together.

A little thread's glimmer of light came through a crack out of a back window. Red put his nose near the crack, studied for a time, turned and whispered, "Folks is in there, talkin'. Blankets have been hung before the windows."

"I heard voices."

"I can't see good, Jeb. They are along up to about the middle of the room, where the safe is. We will just have a look in."

Red slowly took a firm hold on the door knob. He pulled the door tight against the jamb and turned the knob. There was a slight scrape of moving latch. He pushed on the door a very little. Even then the angle was such that he could not see very well, but he could hear. He and Grimes crouched low, listening.

Bill Nims was saying in a deep slow voice, stubborn and angry, "I done wrong to be takin' money thataway from gamblers. I sorta wanted my wife to think I was a good business man. I told her it was money for cows—"

Old Johnson spoke up, throaty and irritable. "We ain't carin' what you told her. I'm tellin' you, you are a damn fool if you think you are goin' to stop us all from leavin' town an'—"

Nims interrupted, patient and deep of voice. "I've told you it was over that stage robb'ry an' killin' the messenger an' Cramer, the which I can't overlook—"

"How about you overlookin' what all Red Clark has done?" said young Milt Johnson, sarcastic and angry. "He killed Joe Bush and some other fellows! Him an' Grimes murdered them sheepherders, then look last night what happened at Huskinses'! Besides all that he shot my dad there from the dark—"

"Milt," Nims cut in, deep of voice and now a little impatient, "I told you I had a letter from old Timton sayin' he shot your dad. He said that Red was a good feller an' as how he wouldn't have him blamed for—"

"I don't b'lieve 'im!" said Milt.

"Nor me!" said old Johnson.

" 'Twas just a put up job to take the blame off Red!" That was a smooth, mean, sneering voice, and Red recognized it as Pinky's.

"I ain't goin' to let you all cut and run!" said Nims, firm and stubborn.

"Aw the hell you ain't!" Pinky squawked. A shot followed.

Old Johnson bellowed, "Now you have played hell!" but Milt was saying, "You done right, Pinky!" just as Red went through the door with an almost gleeful yell:

"Get 'em up! Or don't! Suits me!"

Bill Nims had been shot through the head with his hands down and his gun in its holster. He was bulky and filled the chair so tight that he sat upright with head rolling off to one side as if in a drunken sleep.

There were four other men in the room, one of them young Windy Jones. At the sight of Red, and Grimes following with rifle leveled waist-high, Windy jumped back and sent his hands a-kiting. Old Johnson, with his right arm in a sling, was standing by a table. His hand rested on some small tightly filled canvas sacks. He looked like a great big fat frog that had learned to stand on its hind legs and was now badly scared. He and Milt were dressed in old clothes with boots and spurs, ready to ride.

Milt Johnson had a gun strapped on him but he jumped back for the bank's shotgun that was leaning against the wall.

Pinky had his smoking gun in his hand as Red came through and spoke. Pinky blurted, "Ow, God Almighty!" and ducked down under the table, firing across the top. His aim was pretty good for a man so bad scairt. The bullet snagged Red's right arm and the jerk knocked him off balance. The rifle went off and Pinky settled down on the floor as if his legs had melted. There was about two ticks of a watch, then Red shot with his left hand just as the rifle went off again and Milt Johnson spilled out from behind the shelter of the safe and lay on top of the cocked shotgun with two holes right through his head.

Old Johnson had his hand high up, but bellowed, "You've killed my boy!"

Red snapped, "Yes, and I'd like to kill you, you—"

Grimes cut in, spoke cool, eying old Johnson:

327

"And if you know what is good for you, you'll make some move so we can. 'Twill beat prison at yore age!"

But old Johnson got right up on tip-toes so he could put his one good arm up higher and he begged, "Ow, don't, boys! Please—I—"

Windy was back to the wall with his hands high in the air and his face looked woeful. Windy was just a good easy-going kid who had got mixed up with a bad lot. His mouth twitched a little before the words came.

"Red, I'm a goner!"

"I reckon you are, Windy. A toss-up between prison an' the rope."

"But Red, honest to God, I didn't have no part in killin' Cramer an' the messenger!"

" 'Cept you throwed-in with them as did, Windy."

"But 'twas Buck an' 'Gene. Buck he said he'd show us all how to hold up a stage, an' Red! Red, you give me a chanct an' I'll help you get that feller Buck 'cause he's swore to kill you an'—"

"He's danglin' by the neck on a cottonwood, Windy, over to Hepple's Ranch!"

Windy said, "Oh, God!" and leaned back against the wall as his knees suddenly went weak.

Grimes fingered one of the canvas bags. It was full of money, gold by the weight. "Hm, they was ready to ride—and pack!"

3

Fellows came running from late poker games and a bartender or two with white aprons tucked inside waistbands. Word got about through the town and many folks were awakened to hear the news, dressed, and came.

It was easy to guess that the Johnsons had planned to rob their bank, clear out of the country, taking along Pinky and Windy as a sort of guard.

Mrs. George came from the Golden Palace. She hadn't been asleep, not even undressed, but sat smoking and thinking. She looked pretty tired and much thinner, with deepened wrinkles in her tanned old face.

Men fell back to make way for Mrs. George. She came in walking slow and looked all about. Her gray eyes were bright and keen, but for once she didn't appear to know how to say something that was on her mind.

Red noticed with a sinking heart that she gave him merely a glance, sort of like he was a stranger, and that was all.

She stopped before the dead sheriff, put her hand to her mouth, looked down at him a long time and said, "Poor old Bill." Then she added with a kind of catch in her voice, "Poor Sally!" She turned around and looked hard at old Johnson, but didn't say anything. Didn't need to. She just looked everything she felt and old Johnson seemed to sag and shrivel a little.

Her hand rested on a canvas sack and she leaned there a while before she realized what it was and fingered the coin through the canvas. Then she sort of absently brushed her fingertips together as if brushing away some dirt.

All of a sudden she stiffened, turned on Grimes: "Jeb, I won't stand for no damn foolishness out of you. You've quit my ranch. So I'm going to see that you're put where you'll do this country some good. You've got to be sheriff! You hear me? I don't think any folks will object. They'd better not!"

Grimes said, "Shucks, Miz George!" but he was pleased.

Mrs. George turned around and looked at Windy. For a moment he stared back, hopeful and pleading, then his eyes fell. Windy had been a boy she liked onct, and she felt some hurt that he had turned out bad.

She asked for papers and tobacco. Red made a jump to offer his, but she appeared not to notice and took them from a bald bartender. As she rolled the cigarette her eyes sort of sneaked slantwise toward Red. A man struck a match and she lit the cigarette, then as if not able to hold herself in any longer, snapped:

"Red!"

"Yes'm, Miz George."

"I ain't never going to forgive you! Not to

330

my dying day I won't! Helping Kate fool me thataway a—a *Hepple!*"

Red said nothing. She sure sounded mad, but somehow a little as if not quite so mad as she sounded.

"Well, ain't you got anything to say for yourself?"

"No'm, Miz George. 'Cept he showed hisself to be a good feller an'—"

"I don't want to hear! I don't want to hear even his name mentioned, ever! Nor hers!"

Red spoke humbly. "I reckon you won't from me, then."

Mrs. George looked him up and down, saw that there was blood on the arm that Red had been holding behind him. Her eyes brightened anxiously and she came up, took hold of him. "It ain't nothin'," he said.

"Red?" Her tone changed to a friendly sound and her face softened into a vague smile. "Red, I won't ever forgive you, but I owe you a mighty big apology. When I came back to town from the Nims ranch, I had a talk with Deputy Marr and he was so positive and earnest about it being you that shot Johnson—well, Jeb there was right! I ought've had more sense."

Red, all warm and pleased, said, "Aw, shucks."

"And Red?"

"Yes, mom!"

"They's no use, I reckon, hoping you'll ever

change, much. A body has to put up with you the way you are. You know cows and you know men. Poor old Robertson is dead. Jeb here is to be sheriff. Harry Paloo and Slim Hawks are both too lazy for any earthly use except when there is some trouble. So I guess I'll have to put you in as foreman!"

4

It was about seven months later that Mrs. George and Red rode up on lathered horses one afternoon and swung off under the cottonwoods before the Hepple ranch house. She went hurrying right along in without knocking and Red tagged after her.

Mrs. George had never in her life been near the house before and she looked about, turning this way and that, until, guided by a thin wail, she set off down the hall, flung open a door and walked in.

Hal was there, looking helpless and anxious. The fat stolid Mexican woman bent over the bed where Catherine lay, pale and tired and worried. The squalling baby waved both clenched fists as if in anger at high heaven, its face distorted and red.

Mrs. George stripped her gloves, flung them at the floor, pushed the speechless Hal out of her way, shouldered off the Mexican woman, and said, "Give me that young un!"

She grabbed up the boy-baby like a kidnaper and struck aside Catherine's feeble protesting hands. Catherine seemed to think that a baby was something like brittle spun glass and as easily broken.

Mrs. George sat down brusquely, put the baby face down on a knee, joggled her foot, patted its back. The baby belched a little two or three times and stopped yelling. Then Mrs. George cuddled it close up to her breast, swayed slightly as if rocking and began crooning low.

The name of the baby was Clark Grimes Hepple, and it straightened up, stared with vague eyes at Mrs. George's sharp wrinkled face, then began to gurgle and wave its fists, gleefully.

Red took a furtive tug at Hal's arm, led him out of the room, closed the door softly.

"Ever'thing it is all right now, Hal. You kids are forgiven. She can't resist babies. That's how I get on so well with her. She remembers when I wore diapers."